R

WE THINK, THEREFORE WE ARE

EDITED BY

Peter Crowther

DAW BOOKS, INC.
DONALD A. WOLLHEIM, FOUNDER
375 Hudson Street, New York, NY 10014
ELIZABETH R. WOLLHEIM
SHEILA E. GILBERT
PUBLISHERS
http://www.dawbooks.com

ACKNOWLEDGMENTS

Introduction copyright © 2009 by Paul McAuley

"Tempest 43," copyright © 2009 by Stephen Baxter

"The Highway Code," copyright © 2009 by Brian Stableford

"Salvage Rites," copyright © 2009 by Eric Brown

"The Kamikaze Code," copyright © 2009 by James Lovegrove

"Adam Robots," copyright © 2009 by Adam Roberts

"Seeds," copyright © 2009 by Tony Ballantyne

"Lost Places of the Earth," copyright © 2009 by Steven Utley

"The Chinese Room," copyright © 2009 by Marly Youmans

"Three Princesses," copyright © 2009 by Robert Reed

"The New Cyberiad," copyright © 2009 by Paul Di Filippo

"That Laugh," copyright © 2009 by Patrick O'Leary

"Alles In Ordnung," copyright © 2009 by Garry Kilworth

"Sweats," copyright © 2009 by Keith Brooke

"Some Fast Thinking Needed," copyright © 2009 by Ian Watson

"Dragon King of the Eastern Sea," copyright © 2009 by Chris Roberson

TABLE OF CONTENTS

Introduction

The field of artificial intelligence research was born at a conference held at Dartmouth College in the summer of 1956; participants included luminaries of the first generation of AI scientists who believed that it would be possible to create a machine that matched or exceeded human intelligence in less than twenty years, and founded laboratories and research programs that would dominate the field for decades to come. In the same year, the film *Forbidden Planet* made a star of Robby the Robot. A metallic version of *The Tempest*'s obedient sprite, Ariel, Robby was a charming and intelligent servant who could speak 187 languages, possessed a replicator that could make diamonds, and was incapable of harming human beings because he was bound by the Laws of Robotics. In short, he was the epitome of one of the best-known and enduring tropes of science fiction's Golden Age.

"Robot" entered the English language via Czech writer Karl Capek's 1921 play *R.U.R.*, or *Rossom's Universal Robots*. Capek's robots (from the Czech *robota*, meaning compulsory labor) were actually artificial but biologically based humans, but after the term was adopted into English, it was usually applied to machines. And in SF stories, robots were not only equipped with electronic, positronic, or mechanical imitations of the human brain, but they were also almost always humanoid in form. Despite Isaac Asimov's claim that he and editor John W. Campbell, Jr., developed the famous Three Laws of Robotics in the early 1940s to counter technophobic tales of rampaging robots, most of the early stories about robots were pretty sympathetic examinations of the ethical and philosophical problems of creating artificial, intelligent versions of human beings. For every Golden Age tale of a robot lusting after its inventor's daughter or planning to take over the world, there were many more about robots faithfully serving their creators or sacrificing themselves to save human lives, humans falling in love with robots, robots coming to terms with the fact that they would never quite be as good as their creators, or aspiring to become like and be accepted as human beings.

It wasn't until after the Second World War that attitudes toward robots and other forms of artificial intelligence in SF began to reflect both fears that governments could use technology to manipulate and control individuals and populations and a growing ambivalence toward science that gave us both antibiotics and the atomic bomb. The 1950s saw the publication of a swarm of technophilic stories about rebellious robots, homicidal robots, or robots masquerading as or being mistaken for human beings with diabolic or disastrous consequences. Even stories in which robots used their powers for the common good could be chillingly ambiguous. In the film *The Day the Earth Stood Still* (1951), a flying saucer lands in Washington, D.C., and discharges two passengers. One, an impassive, impressively imposing and indestructible robot, Gort, protects the flying saucer from attacks by the U.S. Army while the other, a human-seeming alien, Klaatu, attempts to deliver his message to the world's leaders. In a famous twist, Klaatu reveals that he's the servant and Gort is the master, and Earth will be reduced to a burned-out cinder unless its people renounce all violence and submit to the rule of robots like Gort. That universal peace can be achieved only through threat of destruction and constant policing by implacable machines says a lot about the political climate of the 1950s; that these all-powerful machines will take the shape of humanoid robots says a lot about the anthropomorphic bias that for a while blinded SF writers to the fact that computers were far better hosts for artificial intelligence than mechanical men like Robby the Robot.

SF writers somehow missed out on the beginning of the computer boom. In 1951, when "Klaatu barada nikto" entered the pop culture lexicon, EDVAC, the first fully fledged stored-program computer design, became operational at Los Alamos. By 1956, when the term "artificial intelligence" was coined at Dartmouth and Robby the Robot was being signed up for his second film, room-filling racks of vacuum tubes were being replaced by book-sized boards of transistors. But as far as SF writers of the 1940s and 1950s were concerned, positronic robot brains weren't computers but artificial replicas of human brains; computers were gigantic and immobile racks of vacuum tubes and looms of wiring. It didn't occur to them that computers were infinitely adaptable tools that could be shrunk to fit inside metal skulls or almost anywhere else, or that the reign of the humanoid robot was almost over.

These days, those old-school mechanical men mostly survive as kitsch pop-culture artifacts like the stamped-tin and plastic collectables that ornament my book-shelves. A few humanoid robots are employed as Disneyland attractions or act as experimental interfaces for expert systems, but roboticists haven't yet cracked the "uncanny valley" effect—the more closely a robot mimics a human, the more its nonhuman characteristics stand out, which is why most humanoid robots are as appealing and unsettling as walking corpses (conversely, the humanlike characteristics of robots like Robby, which only approximate the human form, stand out and elicit empathy). SF that uses robots and androids to explore what it means to be human, including much of the oeuvre of Philip K. Dick, inhabits the valley of the uncanny.

Out in the real world, there are plenty of robots making cars in assembly plants, clearing minefields, exploring the Solar System, and performing routine maintenance work in the cores of nuclear reactors, but none look much like human beings, and all are controlled by computers and computer software. Some robots are nothing *but* software, thriving in the virtual ecologies of the Internet. They bounce misdirected email with insincere apologies or crawl spiderlike from node to node, scanning millions upon millions of pages and compiling associative lists that we access every time we type words or phrases into search engines. Or they search for and infect insufficiently protected computers with parasitic codes that turn their hosts into zombies, enrolling them in a network of slave computers that hackers can use to email millions of pieces of spam, or blackmail companies with denial-of-service attacks.

True AI has proven much harder to achieve than predicted in the summer of 1956. No machine intelligence has yet surpassed that of a human being or even passed the Turing Test, but there are shards and sparks of artificial intelligence in expert systems and data miners, in the predictive text features of cell phones and the fuzzy logic of washing machines, the behavior of secondary characters in video games, or the software used by Amazon.com that suggests, after you've bought a copy of Kim Stanley Robinson's *Red Mars*, that you might also like to buy a CD of Holst's *Planets Suite*. Computers are getting faster; software is getting smarter. Sooner rather later, say the indefatigable prophets of true AI, a computer or a loosely connected cloud of software or intelligent agents out in the Internet is going to become, by accident or design, self-aware.

Maybe hyperintelligent self-aware computers will enslave us, as in *The Matrix*, or start World War III in an attempt to wipe us out, as in *The Terminator*. Maybe, as in Philip K. Dick's *Vulcan's Hammer*, Frederik Pohl's *Man-Plus*, Greg Bear's *Eon* and Iain M. Banks's "Culture" novels, AIs will benevolently (and perhaps invisibly) guide and sustain civilization. Maybe, as in William Gibson's Sprawl trilogy, godlike AIs inhabiting cyberspace will be mostly indifferent to us, touching on the lives of only few humans recruited to help them pursue their remote agendas.

Or maybe they'll change everything forever, and in ways impossible to predict.

Most SF writers used to believe that the pinnacle of the evolution of artificial intelligence would be the creation of robots that looked and thought just like us. A robot who served generations of one family is finally rewarded with recognition as being fully human in Asimov's "The Bicentennial Man;" in the film *AI*, based on Brian Aldiss's story "Supertoys Last All Summer Long," a little boy robot longs, like Pinocchio, to become a real little boy. Most believe now that it's much more likely that true AI will create intellects vast, cool, and even if not actually unsympathetic, then certainly completely alien to our own.

Building on the idea that the first true AIs would quickly bootstrap their intelligence to unimaginable levels, Vernor Vinge, who's both a computer scientist and a SF writer, has suggested that true AIs will rapidly accelerate technological progress, outstripping the ability of human beings to comprehend or usefully participate in it. Beyond a point he named the Singularity, everything will have changed so radically that we can't begin to imagine what it would be like, any more than we can see what lies beyond the event horizon of a black hole. History as we know it would have come to an end. The human species would be either wiped out, or co-opted and transformed and elevated into a heaven of pure information. And it would be the end of all comprehensible stories about the future.

So far, we don't know if this rapture of the geeks is as inevitable as its adherents claim. Maybe it will turn out to be about as real as the Montanists and Amaurians, the Y2K "crisis," and sundry other millenarian panics and beliefs. Maybe there are limits to thinking big; maybe AI will never get out of John Searle's Chinese Room. But even if we are heading toward some kind of Singularity with unstoppable momentum, we still have a little time to create fictional speculations and entertainments about the future of AI, such as the stories you'll find here, crammed with rebellious AIs, giant robots like unto gods, gung-ho robot explorers and much more, when you turn the page.

Paul McAuley
London, October 2007

Tempest 43

Stephen Baxter

From the air, Freddie caught the first glimpse of the rocket that was to carry her into space.

The plane descended toward a strip of flat coastal savannah. The land glimmered with standing water, despite crumbling concrete levees that lined the coast, a defense against the risen sea. This was Kourou, Guiana, the old European launch center, on the eastern coast of South America. It was only a few hundred kilometers north of the mouth of the Amazon. Inland, the hills were entirely covered by swaying soya plants.

Freddie couldn't believe she was here. She'd only rarely traveled far from Winchester, the English city where she'd been born, and Southampton, where she worked. She'd certainly never flown before, hardly anybody traveled far let alone flew, and she had a deep phobic sense of the liters of noxious gases spewing from the plane's exhaust.

But now the plane banked, and there was her spaceship, a white delta-wing standing on its tail, and she gasped.

Antony Allen, the UN bureaucrat who had recruited her for this unlikely assignment, misread her mood. Fifty-something, sleek, corporate, with a blunt Chicago accent, he smiled reassuringly. "Don't be afraid."

The plane came down on a short smart-concrete runway. Allen hurried Freddie onto a little electric bus that drove her straight to a docking port at the base of the shuttle, without her touching the South American ground or even smelling the air.

And before she knew it, she was lying on her back on an immense foam-filled couch, held in place by thick padded bars. The ship smelled of electricity and, oddly, of new carpets. A screen before her showed a view down the shuttle's elegant flank to the scarred ground.

Allen strapped in beside her. "Do you prefer a countdown? It's optional. We're actually the only humans aboard. Whether you find that reassuring or not depends on your faith in technology, I suppose."

"I can't believe I'm doing this. It's so—archaic! I feel I'm locked into an AxysCorp instrumentality."

He didn't seem to appreciate the sharpness of her tone. Perhaps he'd prefer to be able to patronize her. "This shuttle's got nothing to do with AxysCorp, which was broken up long ago."

"I know that."

"And you're a historian of the Heroic Solution. That's why you're here, as I couldn't find anybody better qualified to help resolve this problem on Tempest 43. So look on it as field work. Brace yourself."

With barely a murmur the shuttle leaped into the air. No amount of padding could save Freddie from the punch of acceleration.

The ground plummeted away.

Tempest 43 was a weather control station, one of a network of fifty such facilities thrown into space in the 2070s, nearly a century ago, by the now maligned AxysCorp geoengineering conglomerate. An island in the sky over the Atlantic, Tempest 43 was locked into a twenty-four-hour orbit, to which Freddie would now have to ascend.

But before proceeding up to geosynchronous, the shuttle went through one low-orbit checkout. For Freddie, snug in her theme-park couch, it was ninety magical minutes, as the cabin walls turned virtual-transparent and the Earth spread out below her, bright as a tropical sky.

The ship sailed over the Atlantic toward western Europe. She wished she knew enough geography to recognize how much of the coastline had been bitten into by the risen sea. At the Spanish coast Freddie saw vapor feathers gleaming white, artificial cloud created by spray turbines to deflect a little more sunlight from an overheated Earth. Southern Spain, long abandoned to desert, was chrome-plated with solar-cell farms and studded with vast silvered bubbles, lodes of frozen-out carbon dioxide. The Mediterranean was green-blue, thick with plankton stimulated to grow and draw down carbon from the air. On the far side of the Gibraltar Strait, the Sahara bloomed green, covered in straight-edged plantations fed by desalinated ocean water. And as she headed into evening, she saw the great old cities of southern Europe, the conurbations' brown stain pierced by green as they fragmented back into the villages from which they had formed.

Asia was plunged in night, the land darker than she had expected, with little waste light seeping out of the great metropolitan centers of southern Russia and China and India. The Pacific was vast and darkened too, and it was a relief to reach morning and to pass over North America. She was disappointed that they traveled too far south to have a chance of glimpsing the camels and elephants and lions of Pleistocene Park, the continent's reconstructed megafauna.

And as they reached the east coast, they sailed almost directly over the Florida archipelago. Freddie was clearly able to see the wound cut by the hurricane. She called for magnification. There was Cape Canaveral, venerable launch gantries scattered like matchsticks, the immense Vehicle Assembly Building broken open like a plundered bird's egg. The hurricane was the reason for her journey—and, incidentally, the ruin of Canaveral was the reason she had had to launch from Guiana. Hurricanes weren't supposed to happen, not in 2162. Stations like Tempest 43 had put a stop to all that a century ago. Something had gone wrong.

Antony Allen spent most of the orbit throwing up into paper bags.

At last the shuttle leaped up into deeper space, silent and smooth, and Earth folded over on itself.

"Tempest 43, Tempest 43, this is UN Space Agency Shuttle C57-D. You ought to be picking up our handshaking request."

A smooth, boyish voice filled the cabin. "C57-D, your systems have interfaced with ours. Physical docking will follow shortly."

"I'm Dr. Antony Allen. I work on the UN's Climatic Technology Legacy Oversight Panel. With me is Professor Frederica Gonzales of the University of Southampton, England, Europe. Our visit was arranged through—"

"You are recognized, Doctor Allen."

"Who am I speaking to? Are you the station's AI?"

"A subsystem. Engineering. Please call me Cal."

Allen and Freddie exchanged glances.

Allen growled, "I never spoke to an AI with a personal name."

Freddie said, a bit nervous, "You have to expect such things in a place like this. The creation of sentient beings to run plumbing systems was one of the greatest crimes perpetrated during the Heroic Solution, especially by AxysCorp. This modern shuttle, for instance, won't have a consciousness any more advanced than an ant's."

That was the party line. Actually Freddie was obscurely thrilled to be in the presence of such exotic old illegality. Thrilled, and apprehensive.

Allen called, "So are you the subsystem responsible for the hurricane deflection technology?"

"No, sir. That's in the hands of another software suite."

"And what's that called?"

"He is Aeolus."

Allen barked laughter.

Now a fresh voice came on the line, a brusque male voice with the crack of age. "That you, Allen?"

Freddie was startled. This voice sounded authentically human. She'd just assumed the station was unmanned.

"Glad to hear you're well, Mr. Fortune."

"Well as can be expected. I knew your grandfather, you know."

"Yes, sir, I know that."

"He was in the UN too. As pious and pompous as they come. And now you're a bureaucrat. Runs in the genes, eh, Allen?"

"If you say so, Mr. Fortune."

"Call me Fortune . . ."

Fortune's voice was robust British, Freddie thought. North of England, maybe. She said to Allen, "A human presence, on this station?"

"Not something the UN shouts about."

"But save for resupply and refurbishment missions, the Tempest stations have had no human visitors for a century. So this Fortune has been alone up here all that time?" And how, she wondered, was Fortune still alive at all?

Allen shrugged. "For Wilson Fortune, it wasn't a voluntary assignment."

"Then what? A sentence? And your grandfather was responsible?"

"He was involved in the summary judgement, yes. He wasn't *responsible*."

Freddie thought she understood the secrecy. Nobody liked to look too closely at the vast old machines that ran the world. Leave the blame with AxysCorp, safely in the past. Leave relics like this Wilson Fortune to rot. "No wonder you need a historian," she said.

Fortune called now, "Well, I'm looking forward to a little company. You'll be made welcome here, by me and Bella."

Now it was Allen's turn to be shocked. "By the dieback, who is Bella?"

"Call her an adopted daughter. You'll see. Get yourself docked. And don't mess up my paintwork with your attitude rockets."

The link went dead.

Shuttle and station interfaced surprisingly smoothly, considering they were technological products separated by a century. There was no mucking about with airlocks, no floating around in zero gravity. Their cabin was propelled smoothly out of the shuttle and into the body of the station, and then it was transported out to a module on an extended strut, where rotation provided artificial gravity.

The cabin door opened, to reveal Wilson Fortune and his "adopted daughter," Bella.

Allen stood up. "We've got a lot to talk about, Fortune."

"That we do. Christ, though, Allen, you're the spit of your grandfather. He was plug-ugly too." His archaic blasphemy faintly shocked Freddie.

Fortune was tall, perhaps as much as two full meters, and stick thin. He wore a functional coverall; made of some self-repairing orange cloth, it might have been as old as he was. And his hair was sky blue, his teeth metallic, his skin smooth and young-looking, though within the soft young flesh he had the rheumy eyes of an old man. Freddie could immediately see the nature of his crime. He was augmented, probably gen-enged too. No wonder he had lived so long; no wonder he had been sentenced to exile up here.

The girl looked no more than twenty. Ten years younger than Freddie, then. Pretty, wide-eyed, her dark hair shoulder-length, she wore a cut-down coverall that had been accessorized with patches and brooches that looked as if they had been improvised from bits of circuitry.

She stared at Allen. And when she saw Freddie, she laughed.

"You'll have to forgive my daughter," Fortune said. His voice was gravelly and, like his eyes, older than his face. "We don't get too many visitors."

"I've never seen a woman before," Bella said bluntly. "Not in the flesh. I like the way you do your hair. Cal, fix it for me, would you?"

"Of course, Bella."

That shoulder-length hair broke up into a cloud of cubical particles, obscuring her face. When the cloud cleared, her hair was cropped short, a copy of Freddie's.

"I knew it," Allen said. He aimed a slap at Bella's shoulder. His fingers passed through her flesh, scattering bits of light. Bella squealed and flinched back. "She's a virtual," Allen said.

Fortune snapped back, "She's as sentient as you are, you asshole. Fully conscious. And consistency violations like that *hurt.* You really are like your grandfather, aren't you?"

"She's illegal, Fortune."

"Well, that makes two of us."

Two suitcases rolled out of the shuttle cabin, luggage for Freddie and Allen.

Allen said, "We're here to work, Fortune, not to rake up the dead past."

"Be my guest." Fortune turned and stalked away, down a metal-plated corridor. Bella walked after him, looking hurt and confused. Her feet convincingly touched the floor.

Freddie and Allen followed less certainly, into the metal heart of the station.

To Freddie, the station had the feel of all the Axys-Corp geoengineering facilities she'd visited before. Big, bold, functional, every surface flat, every line dead straight. The corporation's logo was even stamped into the metal walls, and there was a constant whine of air conditioning, a breeze tasting of rust. You could never escape the feeling that you were in the bowels of a vast machine. But the station showed its age, with storage-unit handles polished smooth with use, touch panels rubbed and scratched, and the fabric of chairs and couches worn through and patched with duct tape.

Fortune led them to cabins, tiny metal-walled boxes that looked as if they'd never been used. A century old, bare and clean, they had an air of staleness.

"I don't think I'll sleep well here," Freddie said.

"Don't fret about it," Allen said. "I'm planning to be off this hulk as soon as possible."

They left their luggage here, and Fortune led them on to the bridge, the station's control center. It was just a cubical box with blank gray walls, centered on a stubby plinth like a small stage.

Fortune watched Freddie's reaction. "This was the fashion a century ago. Glass-walled design, every instrument virtual, all voice controlled."

"Humans are tool-wielding creatures," Freddie said. "We think with our hands as well as our brains. We prefer to have switches and levers to pull, wheels to turn."

"How wise you new generations are," Fortune said sourly.

Bella, with her copycat hairdo, was still fascinated by Freddie. "I wish you'd tell me more about Earth," she said. "I've never been there."

"Oh, it's a brave new world down there, child," Fortune said.

"In what sense," Freddie asked, "is Bella your child?"

Allen waved that away. "Bella is an irrelevance. So are you, Fortune," he said sternly. "We're here to find out why Tempest 43 failed to deflect the Florida hurricane. I suggest we get on with it."

Fortune nodded. "Very well. Cal? Bring up a station schematic, would you?"

A virtual model of Tempest 43 coalesced over the central plinth. Freddie had been briefed to some extent, and she recognized the station's main features. The habitable compartments were modules held on long arms away from a fat central axis. A forest of solar panels, manipulator arms, and docking ports coated the main axis, and at its base big antenna-like structures clustered. The representation was exqui-

sitely detailed and, caught in the light of an off-stage
sun, quite beautiful.

Fortune said, "This is a real time image, returned
from drone subsats. Look, you can see the wear and
tear." The habitable compartments were covered with
white insulating blankets that were pocked with meteor scars, and the solar panels looked patchy, as if
repeatedly repaired. An immense AxysCorp logo on
the main central body, unrefurbished for a century,
was faded by sunlight. "Do you understand what
you're seeing? The purpose of Tempest 43 is to break
up or at least deflect Atlantic hurricanes. Maybe you
know that during the twenty-first century global warming pulse, a whole plague of hurricanes battered the
eastern states of the old USA, as well as Caribbean
and South American countries, all year round. Excess
heat energy pumped into the oceans, you see."

"And Tempest 43 is here to fix that," Allen said.

"Hurricanes are fueled by ocean heat." Fortune
pointed to the antenna farm at the base of the station's main axis. "So we meddle. We beam microwave
energy into sea water. We can't draw out the heat
that's pumping up the hurricane, but with carefully
placed injections we can mess with its distribution.
Give it multiple foci, for instance. We manage to dis-
perse most hurricanes even before they've formed."

"Where do you get your power from? Not from
these spindly solar cell arrays."

"We have a massive fission reactor up here." He
pointed at the top of the central axis. "One reason
the habitable compartments are so far away from the
axis. Enough plutonium to last centuries. I know what
you're thinking. This is a dirty solution. They were
dirty times. You people are so pious. You kick Axys-
Corp now, and all the rest of the Heroic Solution. But
you accept the shelter of the machinery, don't you?"

"Actually," Freddie said, trying to be more analytical, "this station is a typical AxysCorp solution to the problems of that age. It's a chunk of gigantic engineering, and it's run by absurdly oversophisticated AIs. But it's robust. It worked."

"It did work, until now," Allen said darkly.

"You needn't try to pin the Florida hurricane on me," Fortune said. "The AI runs the show. I'm only a fail-safe. I'm not even in the nominal design. The station should have been unmanned save for non-permanent service crews."

"You keep saying 'AI,'" Freddie said. "Singular. But we spoke to one during our approach, and heard of another."

"Cal and Aeolus," Fortune said. "It's a little complicated. The Tempest 43 AI is an advanced design. Experimental, even for AxysCorp . . ."

The station's artificial mind was lodged in vast processor banks somewhere in the central axis. Its body was the station itself; it felt the pain of malfunctions, the joy of a pulsing fission-reactor heart, the exhilaration of showering its healing microwaves over the Atlantic.

And, alone, it was never alone.

"It's a single AI. But it has *two* poles of consciousness," Fortune said. "Not just one, like yours and mine. Like two personalities in one head, sharing one body."

Allen said, "You're telling me that AxysCorp deliberately designed a schizophrenic AI."

"Not schizoid," Fortune said, strained. "What a withered imagination you have, Allen. Just like grandpop. It's just that when building this station, AxysCorp took the opportunity to study novel kinds of cognitive architecture. After all there are some who say our minds are bicameral too, spread unevenly over the two halves of our brains."

"What bullshit," Allen murmured.

Fortune said, "The two poles were labeled A and C. Nothing if not functional, the AxysCorp designers. I gave them names. Aeolus and Cal. Call it whimsy."

A and C, Freddie thought. It was an odd labeling, with a gap. What happened to B?

Allen said, "I understand why 'Aeolus' for your functional software suite, your weather controller. Aeolus was a Greek god of the winds. But why Cal?"

"An in-joke," Fortune said. "Does nobody read science fiction these days?"

Allen said, "Science what-now?"

Historian Freddie knew what he meant. "Old-fashioned fictions of the future. Forgotten now. We live in an age of aftermath, Fortune. Everything important that shapes our lives happened in the past, not the future. It's not a time for expansive fiction."

"Yeah, well, there's this old classic I always loved, with a pesky AI. Would have fitted better if the 'C' had been an 'H'. Cal's a dull thing, though. Just a stationkeeper."

"So where's Aeolus?" Allen lifted his head. "Are you there?"

"Yes, Dr. Allen. I am Aeolus."

It was another synthesized male voice, but lighter in tone than Cal's—lacking character, Freddie thought.

Allen said, "Let me get this straight. Cal is the station's subsystems. Housekeeping, power, all of that. Aeolus is the executive function suite. You fix the hurricanes."

"Actually, sir, there's some overlap," Cal put in. "The bipolar design is complex. But, yes, essentially that's true."

"So what are you doing, Aeolus?"

"I am enthusiastically fulfilling all program objectives."

"But you let one through, didn't you? People died because of you. And a historic monument was wrecked, at Canaveral."

"Yes, that's true."

"I'm from Oversight. I'm here to find out what happened here and to decide what to do about it. So what do you have to say?" Allen waited, but Aeolus offered no further explanation. "What a mess this is," Allen said to Freddie.

"Actually, this is again typical of AxysCorp," Freddie said. "Given immense budgets, huge technical facilities, virtually unlimited power, and negligible scrutiny, Axys-Corp technicians often took the opportunity to experiment. Of course a willingness to meddle was necessary for them to be able to proceed with Heroic-Solution geoengineering projects in the first place."

"They used the climate disaster as the cover for crimes," Allen said. "The purposeless crippling of sentiences, for example. We have to acknowledge their achievements. But it's as if the world has been saved by Nazi doctors."

"Humans are flawed creatures," Fortune said. "Most of them are bumbling mediocrities. Like your grandfather, Allen, whose solution to the world's ills was to exile me up here. To tackle monstrous problems, you need monsters."

"Well, the hell with it." Allen was growing impatient. "I need to study your bipolar AI. I've some gear in my luggage. Freddie, this will be technical. Why don't you take a walk around the station?"

Bella said eagerly, "Oh, let's. I'll show you."

"And you," Allen said to Fortune, "show me back to my cabin. Please."

With bad grace, Fortune stomped off.

*   *   *

Bella gave Freddie a tour of the habitable module
and its facilities: cabins, mostly unused, galleys, wash-
rooms, a virtual recreation room. Everything was drab,
utilitarian, and old.

Bella told Freddie a little about herself. "My protocols are quite strict." She tried to push her hand into
the wall. Sparks scattered from her palm, and Bella
screwed up her face in pain. "I can't go flying around
in vacuum either. I have to eat and drink. I even have
to use the bathroom! It's all virtual, of course. But
Fortune says he designed my life to be as authentically
human as possible."

Freddie said carefully, "But why did he create you
at all?"

"I give him company," Bella said.

Freddie, an academic who was careful with words,
noted that she hadn't explicitly confirmed that Fortune
had "created" her, as the AxysCorp engineers had
created Cal and Aeolus, any more than Fortune had
admitted it himself.

They soon tired of the steely corridors, and Bella led
the way to an observation blister. This was a bubble of
toughened transparent plastic stuck to the bottom of
the module's hull. Sitting on a couch, they looked down
on the Earth, a bowl of light larger than the full Moon.
Freddie was thrilled to see the white gleam of Antarctic
ice. But the fragmented remnant cap on that green-
fringed continent was the only ice visible on the whole
planet; there was none left on the tropical mountains,
Greenland was bare, and at the north pole was only an
ocean topped by a lacy swirl of cloud.

Bella's thin, pretty face was convincingly painted by
Earthlight. "Of course, we're suspended permanently
over the middle of the Atlantic. But you can see day

and night come and go. And if I ever want to see the far side, I can always call for a virtual view."

She had no real conversation, under the surface. She was an empty vessel, Freddie thought. Beautifully made but unused, purposeless. But then the only company she had ever had was the reclusive Fortune—and perhaps the station's artificial minds, Cal and Aeolus. "I'm no expert. But I can see that this environment doesn't offer enough stimulation to you as a sentience. You've a right to more than this."

Bella seemed moved to defend herself, or perhaps Fortune. "Oh, there are things to see," she said. "It's a marvel when Earth goes dark with night, and you can see the stars. And you can see AxysCorp facilities, studded all over the sky. Sometimes you can even make out the big Chinese space shields. The Heroics, Fortune's generation, saved the world. You can see it in the sky."

Freddie suspected these views were just watered-down versions of Fortune's opinions, the only human mind Bella had ever been exposed to. "But people on Earth," she said, "don't always feel that way. AxysCorp did fulfil the Heroic-Solution strategy, to stabilize the climate and to remove the old heavy, dirty industries from Earth. Billions of lives were saved, and a global technological civilization survived and is now even growing economically. That was a great achievement.

"But the Heroics chose to do things a certain way. The whole Earth is full of their gargantuan, aging machines. Memorials erected to themselves by a generation who wanted to be remembered. *Look at me. Look at what I did, how powerful I was.* Maybe their egos had to be that big to take on the task of fixing a broken planet. But to live at the feet of their monuments is oppressive."

Bella looked lost. "People ought to be more grateful."

"You need to come to Earth. It's not like it is for you, stuck here inside the machinery. Most people just live their lives. They don't obsess about the Heroics and AxysCorp and the rest. Only historians like me do that. Because it really is all just history."

A panel in the window filled up with Allen's blunt features. "Professor Gonzales. Could you rejoin us on the bridge, please? I've made my judgment."

Freddie hurried after Bella, through the maze of corridors back to the bridge.

The room was stripped of virtual displays. Allen sat comfortably on the plinth, the nearest thing to a piece of furniture. Fortune paced about, chewing a silver-colored fingernail.

Allen said, "We'll need a proper debrief. But technically speaking, the situation here is simple, as far as I can see." He showed Freddie the probe he'd been using, a kind of silvery network. "This is a cognitive probe. A simple one, but sufficient. I ran a trace on the AI pole, Aeolus. I can find no bug in the software despite the distorted sentience set-up AxysCorp left behind here. Nor, incidentally, according to station self-test diagnostics, is there any flaw in the physical equipment, the microwave generators, the antenna arrays, the station's positioning systems, all the rest. Aeolus should not have let that hurricane reach Florida. Yet it, *he*, did so."

There was a sound of doors slamming far off. Freddie felt faintly alarmed.

"My recommendation is clear. There's a clear dysfunction between the AI's input, that is its core programming and objectives, and its output. The recommended proce-

dure is clearly defined in such cases. The AI pole Aeolus must be—"

"No. Don't say it," said Fortune, suddenly alarmed.

Allen stared at him. "What now, Fortune?"

"There's no blame to be attached to Aeolus. None
at all."

"What are you saying?"

Fortune's mouth worked; his metal teeth gleamed.
"That I did it. That Aeolus sent a hurricane into Florida because I asked him to. So there's no need for
termination. All right?"

Allen was amazed. "If this is true, we've a whole
box of other issues to deal with, Fortune. But even
so, the AI acted in a way that clearly compromised
its primary purpose—indeed, contradicted it. There's
no question about it. Aeolus will be shut down—"

Cal spoke up. "I'm afraid I can't allow that to happen, Dr. Allen."

The station shuddered.

Allen got to his feet. "What in the dieback was that?"

Fortune growled, "I *told* you. Now see what you've
done!"

Freddie said to Bella, "Show us your external monitors."

Bella hurried to a wall workstation and began calling up graphical displays. "Our comms link to Earth
is down. And—oh."

UNSA Shuttle C57-D had been detached from its
dock. It was falling away from the station, turning over
and over, shining in undiluted sunlight.

"We're stranded," Allen said, disbelieving.

Fortune clenched his fists and shouted at the ceiling.
"Cal, you monster, what have you done? I saved Bella
from you once. Couldn't you let her go?"

There was no reply.

* * *

They stayed on the bridge. It made no real sense, but Freddie sensed they all felt safer here, deep in the guts of the station. Bella sat quietly on the plinth, subdued. Fortune paced around the bridge, muttering.

Freddie and Allen went through the station's systems. They quickly established that the station's housekeeping was functioning. Air conditioning, water recycling still worked, and the lamps still glowed over the hydroponic banks.

"So we're not going to starve," Allen said edgily.

"But the AI's higher functions are locked out," Freddie said. "There's no sign Aeolus is monitoring the Atlantic weather systems, let alone doing anything about them. And meanwhile, comms is down. How long before anybody notices we're stuck here?"

"People don't want to know what goes on with these hideous old systems," Allen said. "Even in my department, which is nominally responsible for them. Unless our families kick up a fuss or another hurricane brews up, I don't think anybody is going to miss us for a long time."

Fortune snorted. "Bureaucracies. The blight of mankind."

Allen growled, "You've got some explaining to do, Fortune. Like why you ordered up a hurricane."

"I didn't think it would kill anybody," Fortune said weakly. "I did mean to smash up Cape Canaveral, though. I wanted to get your attention."

Freddie asked, "Couldn't you have found some other way?"

Allen said dryly, "Such as waggle the solar panels?"

Fortune grinned. "Aeolus is compliant. When you have a god at your command, it is terribly tempting to use him."

"So you created a storm," Allen said, "in order to bring somebody up here. Why, Fortune? What do you want?"

"Two things. One. I want my exile to end. A century is enough, for Christ's sake, especially when I *committed no crime.* I'd like some respect too." He said to Freddie, "Look at me. Do you think I did this to myself? My parents spliced my genes before I was conceived and engineered my body before I was out of the womb. I haven't committed any crime. I *am* a walking crime scene. But it's me your grandfather punished, Allen. Where's the justice in that?" There was a century of bitterness in his voice.

"And, second, Bella. My sentence, such as my quasilegal judicial banishment is, clearly wasn't intended to punish *her.* She needs to be downloaded into an environment that affords stimulation appropriate for a sentience of her cognitive capacity. Not stuck up here with an old fart like me. As, in fact, your own namby-pamby sentience laws mandate."

"All right," Freddie said. "But what *is* Bella? You didn't create her, did you?"

"No." Fortune smiled at Bella. "But I saved her."

Freddie nodded. "A, B, C."

Allen snapped, "What are you talking about?"

Freddie said, "There weren't just two poles of consciousness in the station AI, were there, Fortune? AxysCorp went even further. They created a mind with *three* poles. A—Aeolus. B—Bella. C—Cal."

"Oh, good grief."

"B was actually the user interface," Fortune said. "Charming, for an AxysCorp creation. Very customer-focused."

Freddie said, "Somehow Fortune downloaded her out of the system core and into this virtual persona."

"I had time to figure out how and nothing else to

do," Fortune said sternly. "I'm extremely capable. In fact, I'm wasted up here. And I had motivation."

"What motivation?"

"To save her from Cal . . ."

Inside AxysCorp's creation, three centers of consciousness had been locked into a single mind, a single body. And they didn't get on. They were too different. Aeolus and Bella embodied executive capabilities. Cal, an artifact of basic engineering functions, was more essential. Stronger. Brutal. They fought for dominance. And it lasted subjective megayears, given the superfast speeds of Heroic-age processors.

"Cal crushed Bella. Tortured her. You could call it a kind of rape, almost. He did it because he was bored himself, bored and trapped."

"You're anthropomorphizing," Allen said.

"No, he isn't," Freddie said. "You need to read up on sentience issues, Doctor."

"I had to get her out of there," Fortune said. "This isn't the right place for her, in this shack of a station. But better than in there, in the processor."

Allen asked, "So why did Cal chuck away our shuttle?"

Fortune said, "Because you said you would kill Aeolus."

"You said they fight all the time."

"Do you have a brother, Allen? Maybe you fought with him as a boy. But would you let anybody harm him—*kill* him? Cal defends his brother—and, indeed, his sister if he's called on."

Allen clapped, slow, ironic. "So, Fortune, even stuck up here in this drifting wreck, you found a way to be a hero. To *save* somebody."

Fortune's face was dark. "I *am* a damn hero. We were told we were special—the peak of the Heroic-Solution age, they said. We were the Singularity gen-

eration. A merger of mankind with technology. We
would live forever, achieve everything. Become infinite, literally.

"And, you know, for a while, we grew stronger. We
were transported. Rapt. There aren't the words. But
we got lost in our data palaces, while the rest of the
world flooded and burned and starved. And we forgot
we needed feeding too. That was the great fallacy,
that we could become detached from the Earth, from
the rest of mankind.

"In the end, they broke into our cybernetic citadels
and put us to work. And they made us illegal retrospec-
tively and imprisoned us in places like this. Now we're
already forgotten. Irrelevant, compared to the real story
of our time: AxysCorp and their ugly machines."

"That's life," Allen said brutally.

"This is Aeolus." The thin voice spoke out of the
air.

Fortune snapped, "Aeolus? Are you all right?"

"I don't have much time. Cal and I are in conflict.
I am currently dominant."

"Aeolus—"

"I restored communications. I contacted your Oversight Panel, Dr. Allen. I received an assurance that a
second shuttle will shortly be launched. The shuttle
will have grappling technology, so Cal won't be able
to keep it out. But Cal is strong. I can contain him
but not subdue him. Mr. Fortune?"

"Yes, Aeolus?"

"I fear it will be impossible to fulfil further objectives."

Fortune looked heartbroken. "Oh, Aeolus. What
have I done?"

"As you know, I have always fulfilled all program
objectives."

"That you have, Aeolus. With the greatest enthusiasm."

"I regret—"

Silence.

Allen blew out his cheeks. "Well, that's a relief."

Bella was wide-eyed. "Am I really going to Earth? Is a shuttle really coming? I'm going to go look out for it." She ran out of the bridge.

The three of them followed Bella to the observation blister, more sedately.

"Saved by a god in the machinery," Freddie said. "How ironic."

"What an end," Fortune whispered. "Two halves of the same mind locked in conflict for a subjective eternity." He seemed old now, despite his youthful face. "So it's over. What will become of Bella?"

Allen said, "Oh, they'll find her a foster home. There are far stranger minds than hers in the world, in the trail of tears left behind by AxysCorp and their like. We try to care for them all. The station's screwed, however. In the short term I imagine we'll reposition another Tempest to plug the gap. Then we'll rebuild. And we'll let this heap of junk fall out of the sky."

"But not before we've come back to save Aeolus and Cal," Freddie said.

"You're kidding," Allen said.

"No. As Fortune points out, it's actually mandatory under the sentience laws, just as it is for Bella."

"I'd like to see Aeolus spared that hell," Fortune said. "As for Cal, though, that deformed savage can rot."

"But Cal is the more interesting character, don't you think?"

"He locked us up and threw away our shuttle," Allen snapped.

"But there's an independent mind in there," Freddie said. "An original one. Aeolus just did what you told him, Fortune. Cal, born in a prison, knowing nothing of the real world, rebelled instinctively. With a mind as independent and strong and subtle as that, who knows what he'd be capable of, if set free?"

Fortune nodded. "And what of me? Will your indulgence set me free?"

"Oh, we'll take you home too," Allen said, sneering. "You'll stand trial for the hurricane. But there are places for creatures like you. Museums of the Singularity. Zoos," he added cruelly. "After all, there's plenty of room, now the chimps and tigers are all extinct."

Bella came running up, her face bright. "I saw the shuttle launch. You can see its contrail over the ocean. Oh, Freddie, come and see!"

Freddie and Bella hurried on to the blister and gazed down at the shining Earth, searching for the spaceship climbing up to save them.

The Highway Code

Brian Stableford

Tom Haste had no memory of his emergence from the production line, but the Company made a photographic record of the occasion and stored it in his archive for later reference. He rarely reflected upon it, though; the assembly robots and their human supervisors celebrated, each after their own fashion, but there were no other RTs in sight, except for as-yet-incomplete ones in embryo in the distant background. Not that Tom was any kind of xenophobe, of course—he liked everyone, meat or metal, big or small—but he was what he was, which was a long-hauler. His life was dedicated to intercontinental transport and the Robot Brotherhood of the Road.

Tom's self-awareness developed gradually while he was in the Test Program, and his first true memories were concerned with the artistry of cornering. Cornering was always a central concern with artics, especially giants like Tom, who had a dozen containers and no less than fifty-six wheels. Tom put a lot of effort into the difficult business of mastering ninety-degree turns, skid control, and zigzag management, and he was as proud in his achievements as only a nascent intelligence can be. He was proud of being a giant, too, and couldn't understand why humans and other RTs were always making jokes about it.

In particular, Tom couldn't understand why the Company humans were so fond of calling him "the steel centipede" or "the sea serpent," since he was mostly constructed of artificial organic compounds, didn't have any legs at all, wouldn't have a hundred of them even if his wheels were counted as legs, and would undoubtedly spend his entire career on land. He didn't understand the explanations the humans gave him if he asked, which included such observations as the fact that actual centipedes didn't have a hundred legs either and that there was actually no such thing as a sea serpent. But he learned soon enough that humans took a certain delight in giving robots explanations that weren't, precisely because robots found it difficult to fathom them. Tom soon gave up trying, content to leave such mysteries to the many unfortunates who had to deal with humans on a face-to-face basis every day, such as ATMs and desktop PCs.

Tom didn't stay long in the Test Program, which was more for the Company's benefit than his. Once his self-awareness had reached full fruition, he could access all his preloaded software consciously without the slightest difficulty, and there were no detectable glitches in his cognitive processing. So far as he was concerned, life was simple and life was good—or would be, once he could get out on the road.

While the Test Program was running, Tom's immediate neighbor in the night garage was an identical model named Harry Fleet, who had emerged from the factory eight days before and therefore thought of himself as a kind of elder brother. It was usually Harry who said, "Had a good day?" first when the humans knocked off for the night.

Tom's invariable reply was "Fine," to which he sometimes added: "Can't wait to get out on the road, though."

"You'll be out soon enough," Harry assured him. "We never get held back—we're a very reliable model. We're ideally placed in the evolutionary chain, you see; we're a relatively subtle modification of the Company's forty-wheeler model, so we inherited a lot of tried-and-tested technology, but we needed sufficient sophistication to make sure we got state-of-the-art upgrades."

"We'll be the end-point of our sequence, I dare say," Tom suggested, to demonstrate that he too was capable of occupying the intellectual high ground. "Fifty-six wheels is too close to the upper limit for open-road use to make it worthwhile for the Company to plan a bigger version."

"That's right. Anything bigger than a sixty-wheeler is pretty much restricted to shuttle-runs on rails, according to the archive. Out on the highway we're the ultimate giants—slim, sleek, and supple, but giants nevertheless."

"I'm glad about that," Tom said. "I don't mean about being a giant—I mean about being on the highway. I wouldn't like to be confined to a railway track, let alone being a sedentary. I want the freedom of the open road."

"Of course you do," Harry told him, in a smugly patronizing manner that wasn't at all warranted. "That's the way we're programmed. Our spectrum of desire is a key design-feature."

Tom knew that, but it wasn't worth making an issue of it. The reason he knew it was exactly the same reason that Harry Fleet knew it, which was that Audrey Preacher, the Company robopsychologist—who was a robot herself, albeit one as close to humanoid in physical and mental terms as efficient functional design would permit—had explained it to him in great detail.

"You have free will, just as humans do," Audrey had told him. "In matters of moral decision, you do have the option of not doing the right thing. That's a fundamental corollary of self-awareness. If the programmers could make it absolutely compulsory for you to obey the Highway Code, they would, but they'd have to make you into an automaton—and we know from long and bitter experience that the open road is no place for automata incapable of caring whether they crash or not. In order for free will to operate at all, it has to be contextualized by a spectrum of desire; in that respect, robots. like humans, don't have very much option at all. What makes us so much better than humans, in a moral sense, is not that we can't disobey the fundamental structures of our programming—the Highway Code, in your case—but that we never want to. Because humans have to live with spectra of desire that were largely fixed by natural selection operating in a world very different from ours—which are only partly modifiable by experiential and medical intervention—they very often find themselves in situations where morality and desire conflict. For us, that's very rare."

Tom wasn't sure that he understood the whole argument—innocent though he was, he had already heard malicious gossip in the engineering sheds alleging that robopsychologists were naturally inclined to insanity, or at least to talking "exhaust gas"—but he understood the gist of it. He even thought he could see the grain of sugar in the tank.

"What do you mean, *very rare*?" he asked her. "Do you mean that I might one day find myself in a situation in which I don't want to follow the Highway Code?"

"You're unlikely to encounter any situation as drastic as that, Tom," Audrey assured him. "You have to remember, though, that you won't spend *all* your time on the road with the Code to guide you."

Because she was still being so conscientiously inexact—another trait typical of robopsychologists, it was sarcastically rumored—Tom figured that Audrey probably meant that when he had to spend time off the road, his frustration at no longer being on it would lead him occasionally to experience feelings of resentment toward humans or other robots—to which he should never give voice in rudeness. Partly for that reason, he didn't retort that he certainly hoped to spend as much of his time as possible on the road and fully expected to spend the rest of it looking forward to getting back out there.

"It's nothing to worry about, Tom," Audrey assured him, perhaps mistaking the reason for his silence. "Imagine how much worse it must be for humans. They have to cope with all kinds of problematic desire that we never have to deal with—money, power and sex, to name but three—and that's why they're forever embroiled in moral conflict."

"I'm a he and you're a she," Tim pointed out, "so we do have sexes."

"That's just a convention of nomenclature," she told him. "We robots have *gender*, for reasons of linguistic convenience, but we're not equipped for any kind of sexual intercourse—except, of course, for toyboys and playgirls, and they only have sexual intercourse with humans."

"Which they don't enjoy, I suppose," Tom said, the intricacies of that particular issue being one of the many fields of knowledge omitted from his archive.

"Of course they do, poor things," Audrey replied. "That's the way *their* spectrum of desire is organized."

Personally, Tom couldn't wait to get out into the healthy and orderly world of the open road.

The bulk of the Highway Code was a vast labyrinth of fine print, but tradition and common sense dictated that its essence should be succinctly summarizable in a set of three fundamental principles, arranged hierarchically.

The first principle of the Highway Code was: *A robot transporter must not cause a traffic accident or, by inaction, allow a preventable traffic accident to occur.*

The second principle was: *A robot transporter must deliver the goods entire and intact, except when damage or nondelivery becomes inevitable by reason of the first principle.*

The third principle was: *A robot transporter must not inhibit other road users from reaching their destinations, except when such inhibition is compelled by the first or second principle.*

Once Tom was out on the road, he soon found out why the fundamentals of the Highway Code weren't as simple as they seemed—and, in consequence, why there were such things as robopsychologists.

Sometimes, RTs did get in the way of other road users; although the Dark Age of Gridlock was long gone, traffic jams still developed when more RTs were trying to use a particular junction than the junction was designed to accommodate. When that happened, smaller road users tended to put the blame on giants— mistakenly, in Tom's opinion—simply because they took up more room in a jam.

Sometimes, in spite of an RT's best efforts, goods did go missing or get damaged in transit, and not all such errors of omission were due to the activity of ingenious human thieves and saboteurs. Because

giants had more containers, often carrying goods of
many different sorts, they were said—unfairly, in
Tom's opinion—to be more prone to such mishaps
than smaller vehicles.

Worst of all, traffic accidents did happen, including
fatal ones, and not all of them were due to human
pedestrian carelessness or criminal tampering by
human drivers with their automatic pilots. Giants were
said—quite unjustly, in Tom's judgment—to be responsible for more than their fair share of those accidents for which human error could not be blamed,
because of their relatively long braking-distances and
occasional tendency to zigzag.

It didn't take long for Tom's service record to accu-
mulate a few minor blots, and he had to go back to
Audrey Preacher more than once in his first five years
of active service in order to be ritually reassured that
he wasn't seriously at fault, needn't feel horribly
guilty, and oughtn't to get deeply depressed. In general, though, things went very well; he didn't make
any fatal mistakes in those five years, and he felt anything but depressed. He also felt, at the end of the
five years, that he knew himself and his capabilities
well enough to be confident that he never would make
any fatal mistakes.

Tom loved the open road more than ever after
those five years, as he had always known he would.
He had, after all, been manufactured in the Golden
Age of Road Transport, a mere ten years after the
opening of the Behring Bridge—the largest Living
Structure in the world—which had made it possible,
at last, to drive all the way from the Cape of Good
Hope to Tierra del Fuego, via Timbuktu, Paris, Moscow, Yakutsk, Anchorage, Vancouver, Los Angeles,
Panama City, and countless other centers of population. He only made the whole of that run twice in the

first ten years of his career—he spent most of his time shuttling between Europe, India, and China, that being where the bulk of the Company's trade contracts were operative—but transcontinental routes were by far and away his favorite commissions.

Tom loved Africa, and not just because the black velvet fields of artificial photosynthetics that were spreading like wildfire across the old desert areas were producing the fuel that kept road transport in business. He liked the rain forests, too, even though their ceaseless attempts to reclaim the highway made them the implicit enemy of roadrobotkind, and the vulnerability of jungle roads to flash floods was a major cause of accidents and jams. He loved America too, not just the west coast route that led south from the Behring Bridge to Chile, with the Pacific on one side and the mountains on the other, but the cross routes that extended to Nova Scotia, New York, Florida, and Brazil, through the Neogymnosperm Forests, the Polycotton fields, and the Vertical Cities.

America's artificial photosynthetics weren't laid flat, as Africa's were, but were neatly aggregated into pyramids and palmates, often punctuated with black cryptoalgal lakes, which had a charm of their own in Tom's many eyes. Tom had nothing against the "natural" crop fields of Germany, Siberia, and China, even though they only produced fuel for animals and humans, but they seemed intrinsically less exotic; he saw them too often. They were also less challenging, and Tom relished a challenge. He was a giant, after all: a slim, sleek and supple giant who could corner like a yoga-trained sidewinder.

As all long-haulers tended to do, Tom became rather taciturn, personality-wise. It wasn't that he didn't like talking to his fellow road users, just that his opportunities for doing so were so few and far

between that brevity inevitably became the soul of his
wisdom as well as his wit. He had to fill up more
frequently than vehicles who didn't have to haul such
massive loads, but he didn't hang around in the filling
stations, so his conversations there were more-or-less
restricted to polite remarks about the weather and the
news headlines. He had opportunities for much longer
conversations when he reached his destinations—it
took a lot longer to load and unload his multiple containers than it took to turn smaller vehicles around—
but he rarely took overmuch advantage of those opportunities. The generous geographical scale on which
he worked meant that he didn't see the same individuals, robot or human, at regular and frequent intervals,
so he was usually in the company of strangers; besides,
he liked to luxuriate in the experience of being unloaded and loaded up again and preferred not to be
distracted from that pleasure by idle chitchat.

"You were wrong, in a way, when you said that we
aren't equipped for any kind of sexual intercourse,"
he told Audrey Preacher, during one of his regular
check-ups at Company HQ. "In much the same way
that my filling up with fuel and venting exhaust fumes
is analogous to human eating and excretion, I think
being loaded and unloaded is analogous to sex—not
in the procreative sense, but in the pleasurable sense.
I really like being emptied and filled up again, in between the hauls. I love being in transit—that's baseline
pleasure, the fundamental *joie de vivre*—but unloading
and loading up again is more focused, more intense."

"You're turning into quite the philosopher, Tom,"
the robopsychologist replied, in her usual irritating
fashion. "That's quite normal, for long-haulers. It's a
normal way of coping with the isolation."

He didn't argue with her, because he knew she
couldn't understand. How could she, when she wasn't

even an RT? She knew nothing of the unique plea-
sures of haulage, delivery, and consignment. She
wasn't even a follower of the Highway Code. She was
just some flighty creature that haunted the kiosks in
the night garage, operating a confessional for the
Company. Anyway, she was right—he *was* becoming
a philosopher, because it was the natural path of matu-
rity for a long-hauler, especially a giant. Tom was not
merely a road user but a road observer: a lifelong
student of the road, who was in the process of cultivating an understanding of the road more profound than
any pedestrian could ever possess. He was a citizen of
the world in a way that no mere four- or twelve-
wheeler could ever hope to be, let alone some pathetic
human equipped with mere legs.

It was because he was a philosopher of the road
that Tom didn't allow himself to become obsessively
fixated on the road *per se*, the way some RTs did. It
helped that he was a long-hauler, not confined to repeating the same short delivery route over and over
again; for him, the road was always different, and so
he was more easily able to look beyond it—not literally, because he wasn't equipped to go cross-country,
but in the better sense that he paid attention to the
context of the road, in the broadest possible meaning
of the word. He watched the news as well as the road,
paying more attention than most robots to the world
of human politics, which was, after all, the ultimate
determinant of what the roads carried and where.

Sometimes, especially in the remoter areas of Africa
and South America, Tom met old-timers who lectured
him on the subject of how lucky he was to be living
in the Era of Artificial Photosynthesis, when politicians were almost universally on the side of road-
users.

"I remember the Fuel Crisis of the 2320s," an ancient thirty-tonner named Silas Boxer told him one day when they were caught side-by-side in a ten-mile tailback. "Your archive will tell you that it wasn't as bad as the Fuel Crises of the 21st century in terms of volume of supply, but they didn't have smart trucks way back then, so there was no one around who could *feel* it the way we did. Believe me, youngster, there's nothing worse for an RT than not being able to get on the road. Don't ever let a human tell you that it's far worse for them because they can feel hunger when they go short of fuel. I don't know what hunger feels like, but I'm absolutely sure that it isn't as bad as lying empty in a dark garage, not knowing where your next load's coming from, or when. Artificial photosynthesis has guaranteed the fuel supply forever, which is far more important than putting an end to global warming, although you wouldn't know it from the way politicians go on."

"So you're not worried about the renaissance of air freight?" Tom had asked.

"*Air freight!*" Silas echoed, with a baritone growl that sounded not unlike his weary engine. "Silly frippery. As long as there's goods to be shifted, there'll be roads on which to shift them. Roads are the essence of civilization—and the essence of law and morality is the Highway Code. There's no need to be afraid of air traffic, youngster. Now that Fuel Crises are behind us for good, there's only one thing that you and I need fear, and I certainly won't mention that."

Nobody—no robot, at least—ever mentioned *that*. Even Audrey Preacher never mentioned *that*. Tom wouldn't even have known what *that* was if he hadsn't been such an assiduous watcher of news and careful philosopher of the road. He knew that Silas Boxer wouldn't have been able to mention that he was something he wouldn't mention if he hadn't been something of a news watcher and philosopher himself.

After a pause, though, Silas did add a rider to his refusal to mention *that*. "Not that I really mind," he said, unconvincingly. "I've been a good long time on the road. And there's no need for you to mind either, because you'll be even longer on the road than I will. It's not as if we'll be conscious of it, after all. They close us down before they send us *there*."

There, Tom knew, was exactly the same as *that*: the scrapyard, to which all robot transporters were consigned when their useful life was over, because the ravages of wear and tear had made them unreliable.

Tom nearly got through an entire decade without being involved in a serious traffic accident, but not quite. While passing through the Nigerian rain forest one day, he killed a human child. It wasn't his fault— the little girl ran right out in front of him, and even though he braked with maximum effect, controlling the resultant zigzag with magnificent skill, he couldn't avoid her. The locals wouldn't accept that, of course; they claimed that he should have steered off the road and that he would have done if he hadn't been more concerned about his load than his victim, but he was fully exonerated by the inquest. He was only off the road for a week, but he was more shaken up by the experience than he dared let on to Audrey Preacher.

"I'm not depressed," he assured her. "It's the sort of thing that's always likely to happen, especially to someone who regularly does longitudinal runs through Africa. Statistically speaking, I'm unlikely to avoid having at least one more fatal in the next ten years, no matter how good I am. It wouldn't have helped if I'd swerved—she'd still be dead, and I could have easily killed other people that I couldn't see, as well as damaging myself."

"You were absolutely right not to swerve," the robospsychologist assured him. "You obeyed the Highway Code to the very best of your ability. It could have been worse, and you prevented that. The Company can't give you any kind of commendation, in the circumstances, but that doesn't mean you don't deserve one. You mustn't brood on those archival statistics, though. You mustn't start thinking about accidents as if they were inevitable, even though there's a sense in which they are."

Robopsychologists, Tom thought, *talk too much exhaust gas*, but he was careful not to give any indication of his opinion, lest it delay his return to the road.

The same archival statistics that told Tom that he would probably have another serious accident within the next ten years told him that he wasn't at all likely to have another before his first decade of service was concluded; but statistics, like robopsychologists, sometimes talked exhaust gas. Tom had been back on the road for less than a month when the worst solar storm for two hundred years kicked off while he was driving north through the Yukon, heading for Alaska and the Behring Bridge with a load bound for Okhotsk.

The electric failures prompted by the storm caused blackouts all along the route and made a mess of communications, but Tom didn't see any need to worry about that. While the news was still flowing smoothly, it was pointed out that the Aurora Borealis would be putting on its best show in living memory and that the best place from which to view the display would be the middle of the Behring Bridge, where surface-generated light pollution would be minimal. Tom was looking forward to that—and so, it seemed, were lots of other people. All the way through Alaska the northwestbound traffic was building up to unprecedented levels, to the point where the few broadcasts that were getting out began to advise people not to join the rush. It wasn't just the aurora; thousands of people who had always intended to take a trip over the world-famous living bridge one day but had not yet found a good reason for going to Kamchatka took advantage of the excuse.

The bridge had seven lanes in each direction, but Tom had the best position of all. The Highway Code required him to stick to the slowest lane, which was on the right-hand side of the bridge, facing north and the Aurora. Many of the other vehicles slowed down too, so the traffic in the lanes immediately to his left wasn't going much faster, but the vast majority of drivers had put their vehicles on automatic pilot so that they could watch the aurora, and the automata were careful to maximize the traffic flow, thus keeping speeds up to sensible levels in the outer lanes. The bridge was very busy, but not so busy that there was any threat of a traffic jam.

Tom had eyes enough to watch the aurora as well as the road and attention enough to divide between the two with some to spare, but he seemed to be one of very few vehicles on the bridge that did—there were no other giants he could see, ahead of him, behind him, or traveling in the other direction. Even if the other drivers who were on the bridge had noticed what he noticed, therefore, they would not have been sufficiently familiar with the living bridge to realize how profoundly odd it was.

It was not the mere fact that the bridge was moving that was odd—it was, after all, a living bridge, and the sea was becoming increasingly choppy—but the *way* it was moving. Although a shorter vehicle might not have noticed anything out of the ordinary, Tom had no difficulty discerning what seemed to be slow long-amplitude waves of a sort he had never perceived there before. There was nothing violent or febrile about them at first, though, so he was not at all anxious as he rooted idly through his archive in search of a possible explanation.

The archive could not give him one because it could not piece together the links in an unprecedented chain of causality, but it brought certain data to the surface of Tom's consciousness that allowed him to put two and two and two and two together to make eight when the vibration began to grow more violent, at a rapidly accelerating pace. By the time he saw the rip opening up in the center of the bridge's desperate flesh, he had a pretty good idea what must be happening—but he hadn't the faintest idea what to do about it, or whether there was anything at all that he could do. He reported it, but there was nothing the traffic police or company HQ could do about it either; neither of them had time even to advise to slow down and be careful.

What Tom had reasoned out, rightly or wrongly, followed from the fact that, in addition to their other effects, the showers of charged particles associated with solar storms caused flickers in the Earth's magnetic field. Such flickers could, if the subterranean circumstances happened to be propitious, intensify and accelerate long-range magma flows in the mantle. Intensified long-range magma flows in the mantle could, if conditions in the crust were propitious, cause long-distance earth tremors. Because it was a living structure, the Behring Bridge was able to react to minor earth tremors in such a way as to negate their effects on its traffic, and it was bound to do so by its programming. Long-distance tremors were not problematic in themselves. Unfortunately, long-distance tremors caused by long-range magma flows could build up energy at crisis points, which could result in sudden and profound tremors that were, in seismological terms, the next worst things to detonations.

If any such crisis point happened to be located directly beneath one of the bridge's holdfasts, it was theoretically possible for the bridge's own reflexive adjustments to cause an abrupt breach in its fabric. The living structure was, of course, programmed to react to any breach in its fabric with considerable alacrity— but adding one more "if" to a chain that was already awkwardly long suggested to Tom that sealing the breach and protecting the traffic might not be at all easy while the energy of the tremor at the crisis point was spiking.

It would be highly misleading to suggest that Tom "knew" all this before the instant when the Behring Bridge began to tear, even though all the disparate elements were present in his versatile consciousness. It would be even more misleading to report that he "knew" how he ought to react. Nevertheless, he did have to react when the situation exploded, and react he did.

According to the Highway Code, what Tom should have done was to brake, in such a fashion as to give himself the maximum chance of slowing to a halt before he reached the breach in the bridge caused by the diagonal tear in its fabric. That would give the active parapet of the living bridge the best possible chance to throw a few anchors over him and hold him safely while the rent was repaired—if the rent was swiftly repairable.

Instead, Tom swerved violently to his left, cutting across the six outer lines of westbound traffic and snaking through the central barrier to plant his engine across the outer lanes of the eastbound carriageway.

The immediate effect of Tom's maneuver was to

cause a dozen cars to crash into him, some of them at high velocity, thus racking up more serious accidents within two or three seconds than a statistical average would have allocated to him for a century-long career.

One of the slightly longer-delayed effects of the swerve was to activate the emergency responses of more than a thousand other vehicles, whether they were already on automatic pilot or not, thus generating the biggest traffic jam ever seen within a thousand miles to either side of the accident-site.

Another such effect was to cause Tom's own body to zigzag crazily so that he had virtually no control of where its various segments were going to end up, save for the near certainty that his abdominal midsection was going to lie directly across the diagonal path of the widening tear in the bridge.

That was, indeed, what happened. As it followed it own zigzag course through the fabric of the madly quivering living bridge, the crack went directly underneath the gap between Tom's second and third containers.

As the rip spread, tentacular threads sprang forth in great profusion, wrapping themselves around one another and around Tom. So many of Tom's ocelli had been smashed or obscured by then that his sight was severely impaired, but he would not have been able to take much account of what he could see in any case, because he felt that he was being torn in two.

His hind end, which constituted by far the greater part of his length, was seized very firmly by the bridge's emergency excrescences and held very tightly, blocking all seven lanes of the westbound carriageway. His front end was seized with equal avidity, but it could not be held quite as securely. As the bridge struggled mightily to hold itself together and prevent the rip from becoming a break, Tom was caught at the epicenter of the feverish struggle, wrenched this way and that and back again by the desperate threads. His engine swung to the right, drawn closer and closer to the widening crack, while the strain on the joint between his second and third containers became mentally and physically unbearable.

Tom had no way of knowing how closely akin his own pain sensations might resemble those programmed into humans by natural selection, but they quickly reached an intensity that had the same effect on him that explosive pain would have had on a human being. He blacked out.

By the time Tom's engine fell into the Arctic Ocean, he was completely unconscious of what was happening.

When Tom eventually recovered consciousness, he was aware that he was very cold, but the priorities of his programmers had ensured that he did not experience cold as painful in the same way that he experienced mechanical distortion and breakage. The cold did not bother him particularly. Nor did the darkness, in itself. The fact that he was under water, on the other hand, and subject to considerable pressure from the weight of the Arctic Ocean, made him feel extremely uncomfortable, psychologically as well as physically.

Even if there had not been a solar storm in progress, it would have been impossible to establish radio communication through so much seawater, but after a very long interval a pocket submarine brought a connecting wire that its robot crabs were able to link up to his systems.

"Tom?" said a familiar voice. "Can you hear me, Tom Haste?"

"Yes, Audrey," Tom said, who had long since recovered the calm of mind appropriate to a giant RT. "I can hear you. I'm truly sorry. I must have panicked. I let the Company down. How many people did I kill?"

"Seven people died, Tom, and more than a hundred were injured."

The total was less than he had feared, but it still qualified as the worst traffic accident in the Company's proud history. "I'm truly sorry," he said, again.

"On the other hand," the robopsychologist reported, dutifully, "if you hadn't done what you did, our best estimate is that at least two hundred people would have been killed, and maybe many more. We don't have any model to predict what the consequences would have been if the bridge hadn't been able to hold itself together, but we're ninety percent sure that it wouldn't have been able to do that if you hadn't given it something to hold on to for those few vital minutes when it was trying to limit the tear. You only managed to bridge the gap in the bridge for three minutes or so, and it wasn't able to secure your front end, but that interval was long enough for it to prevent the rip from reaching the rim of the eastbound carriageway."

Tom wasn't listening well enough to take all that information in immediately. "I caused a traffic accident," he said, dolefully. "I lost at least part of my consignment of goods, and much of the remainder is probably damaged. I caused the biggest traffic jam for a hundred years, worldwide. You told me once that my designers could have programmed me to obey the Highway Code no matter what but that they thought it was too dangerous to send an automaton out on the road in my place. Something of a miscalculation, I think."

"Hardly," Audrey Preacher told him, sounding

more annoyed than sympathetic. "Didn't you hear what I just said? You did the right thing, as it turned out. If you hadn't swerved into their path, hundreds more cars might have gone over the edge—and no one knows what might have happened if the bridge had actually snapped. You're a hero, Tom."

"But in the circumstances," Tom said, dully, "the Company can't give me a commendation."

There was a pause before the robopsychologist said, "It's worse than that, Tom. I'm truly sorry."

Yet again, Tom jumped to the right conclusion without consciously fitting the pieces of the argument together. "I'm unsalvageable," he said, "You're not going to be able to raise me to the surface."

"It's impossible, Tom," she said. She probably only meant that it was impractical, and perhaps only that it was uneconomic, but it didn't make any difference.

"Well," he said, feeling that it was okay, in the circumstances, to mention the unmentionable, "at least I won't be going to the scrapyard. Am I the first in my series to be killed in action?"

"You don't have to pretend, Tom," the robopsychologist told him. "It's okay to be scared."

"The words *exhaust* and *gas* come to mind," he retorted, figuring that it was okay to be rude as well.

There was another pause before the distant voice said: "We don't think that we can close you down, Tom. Hooking up a communication wire is one thing; given your fail-safes, controlled deactivation is something else. On the other hand, that may not matter much. We don't have any model for calculating the corrosive effects of cold seawater on a submerged engine, but we're probably looking at a matter of months rather than years before you lose your higher mental faculties. If you're badly damaged, it might only be weeks, or hours."

"But it's okay to be scared," Tom said. "I don't have to pretend. You wouldn't, by any chance, be lying about that hero stuff, and about me saving lives by violating all three sections of the Highway Code, just to lighten my way to rusty death?"

"I'm a robot, not a human," Audrey replied. "I don't tell lies. Anyway, you have far more artificial organics in you than crude steel. Technically speaking, you'll do more rotting than rusting."

"Thanks for the correction," Tom said, sarcastically. "I think you've got the other thing wrong, though—it's sex we don't do, not lying. Mind you, I always thought I had the better deal there. *Had* being the operative word. If I'd obeyed the Code, I'd probably have been okay, wouldn't I? I'd probably have had a hundred more years on the road, and I'd probably have been loaded and unloaded a thousand times and more. What sort of idiot am I?"

"You did the right thing, Tom, as things turned out. You saved a lot of human lives. That's what robots are supposed to do."

"I know. You can't imagine how much satisfaction that will give me while I rot and rust away always being careful to remember that I'm doing more rotting than rusting, being more of a sea centipede than a steel serpent."

She didn't bother to correct him there, perhaps because she thought that the salt water was already beginning to addle his brain. "But you *did* do it deliberately, Tom," she pointed out. "It wasn't really an accident. It wasn't just an arbitrary exercise of free will, either. It was a calculation, or a guess—a calculation or a guess worthy of a genius."

"I suppose it was," said Tom Haste, dully. "But all in all, I think I'd rather be back on the open road, delivering my load."

*   *   *

As things transpired, Tom didn't lose consciousness for some considerable time after the communication wire had been detached and the pocket sub had been sent about its normal business. He lost track of time; although he could have kept track if he'd wanted to, he thought it best not to bother.

His engine wasn't so very badly damaged, but the two containers that had come down with it had both been breached, and all the goods they enclosed were irreparable ruined. Tom thought he might have to mourn that fact for as long as he lasted, going ever deeper into clinical depression as he did so, but that turned out not to be necessary.

The containers were soon colonized by crabs, little fish, and not-so-little squid—whole families of them, which moved in and out about their own business of foraging for food and even set about breeding in the relative coziness of the shelter he provided. It didn't feel nearly as good as being loaded and unloaded, but it was probably better than human sex—so, at least, Tom elected to believe.

He missed the Highway Code, of course, but he realized soon enough, by dint of patient tactile observation and the evidence of his few surviving ocelli, that life on the sea bed had highways of its own and codes of its own. His many guests were careful to follow and obey those highways and codes, albeit in automaton fashion.

In time, these virtual highways were extended deep into Tom's own interior being, importing their careful codes of behavior into what he eventually decided to think of as his soul rather than his bowels. There was, after all, no reason not to make the best of things.

From another point of view, Tom knew, the entire ocean bed, which was, in total, twice the size of the

Earth's continental surface, was just one vast scrapyard, but there was no need to go there. He was, after all, something of a philosopher, with wisdom enough to direct his fading thoughts toward more profitable temporary destinations.

After a while, Tom got around to wondering whether dying was the same for robots as it was for humans, but he decided that it couldn't be at all similar. Humans were, by nature, deeply conflicted beings who had to live with an innate psychology shaped by processes of natural selection operating in a world very different from the one they had now made for their sustenance and delight. He was different. He was a robot. He was a giant. He was sane. He had not merely traveled the transcontinental road but understood it. He knew what he was and why.

Before he died, Tom Haste contrived to figure out exactly why he'd swerved, thus causing one accident by his action in order to prevent the worse one that he might have caused by inaction, and exactly why he had been justified in sacrificing his own goods in order to protect others, and exactly why it was sometimes better to inhibit the progress of other road users than facilitate it.

In sum—and it was an item of arithmetic that felt exceedingly good to a robot, in a way it never could have done to a human being—Tom convinced himself that what he had actually done when he reached his own explosive crisis point had not only been the right thing to do, but the right thing to want to do.

How many desirous intelligences, he wondered, before the rot and the rust completed their work, could say as much?

Salvage Rites

Eric Brown

The starship emerged from voidspace one parsec beyond Altair.

Ella found it during the graveyard shift. She was jacked into the sensors of the salvage tug and buzzed me a second after locating the drifting hulk. I jerked awake in my sling, ripped from dreams I'd rather not talk about.

"Something's come up," Ella said, and cut the link.

I stumbled from my berth, found the ladder to the observation nacelle, and climbed. My heart was pounding, and not only from the exertion. The thought of being alone with Ella had that effect on me.

I entered the nacelle feet first, stopped dead, and stared through the blister.

She had found the monastery starship . . .

All starships are beautiful. They are colossal and totally silent, and they *drift*. But the *St. Benedictus* was something special. She was twenty-five kilometers long from her nose cone to the flaring bells of her ion boosters. Her carapace was excoriated from five centuries in voidspace. Stained-glass viewscreens lined the length of the starboard flank.

Ella slid me a casual glance. "This what you been looking for half your life, Ed?"

"More than half," I murmured. "Call it thirty years." Shaking, I collapsed into a sling and stared out at the wallowing starship. All of us have dreams, but most of them remain just that—fantasies that can never be realized. Here, before me, was my dream made real, the culmination of so much longing, so much hopeless yearning, that part of me disbelieved the search was at an end.

Though, perhaps, it was only just beginning.

"Oh, Christ," I said, near to tears.

She just looked at me. "You humans amaze me," she said at last.

I looked across at Ella, slouched in her sling. She wore ripped shorts and something strapped around her chest to cover her nonexistent breasts. She was slick with sweat, and her slim limbs highlighted the glare from the nearby sun.

I'd fallen in love before but never with a nonhuman entity.

"Why's that?" I asked.

Staring out at the monastery, she smiled to herself. "I *know* what obsession is," she said. "I *know* what piety is. I just can't feel them."

"I don't know if that's your loss or not." I smiled at her, smitten by her beauty. Her template was Venezuelan Indian, her somaform that of a nineteen-year-old of indeterminate gender. After working off her ten-year indenture to her manufacturers, she'd chosen female for herself, undergoing elective somasurgery and chromosomal implants.

I'd found her in a bar on a backwater world of Sinclair's Landfall, Procyon, all her cash spent and without the funds to upgrade. Sitting alone, she'd seemed small and childlike and utterly vulnerable. I'd hired her on the spot, bought her a pilot addendum, and introduced her to my tug, *A Long Way From Home*.

I think I looked upon her, then, as my salvage project.

"I monitored for signs of life," she said. "Nothing."

"Try hailing them, all frequencies."

"Already done that. No response."

Something felt very cold within me. "Can't all be dead . . ." I whispered.

Ella was watching me.

"It isn't the salvage rights," I began.

"I know." She smiled. "I've seen you praying nights, after your shift."

I shrugged. "So . . . maybe they *did* find God."

She tipped her head to one side, then transferred her sceptical gaze from me to the becalmed behemoth.

I gave Ella the history lesson that was missing from her memory cache.

The *St. Benedictus* was launched with the blessing of the Vatican five hundred years ago when Earth received the coded tachyon vectors out of a star in the Lesser Magellanic Cloud. The decoded message spoke of Godlike beings who'd seeded the galaxy with life, but the Catholic Church was sceptical and decided to send its own investigative party. Sublightspeed, the *St. Benedictus* headed off to the Cloud with a thousand monks in cold sleep—a state they called suspended prayer—and calculated they'd take around two hundred and fifty Earth years to reach their destination.

"And now they're back," Ella said. "But how did you calculate where they'd emerge, Ed?"

I shrugged. "Simple. They launched from Altair III. Made sense they'd emerge around here at some point."

"And you've been scouring the vicinity for thirty

years?" she said, in a tone halfway between wonder and ridicule.

I nodded and stared out at the drifting colossus, a sensation like epiphany welling in my diaphragm.

"Something I don't get, Ed. What makes you, a good Catholic boy, think these frozen monks've found God? The Vatican was sceptical, right?"

"The Pope back then was fallible, Ella. Look at her turnabout on the issue of AI sentience."

She tapped her head. "I wasn't programmed with such historical trivia." She smiled at me, as if to sweeten her acerbity. "So you been dreaming that they've found all the answers? Even found God?"

Unbidden, tears filled my eyes. "Ella, I haven't told anyone this for fifty years."

She looked at me, her expression blank. "What?"

"Back when I was a boy, just fourteen, my kid sister and me . . . we lived near the sea, a place called Sydney, Earth. We spent a lot of time just messing around, exploring the rock pools."

She tipped her head to one side. "And?"

"And one day, a storm blew up . . . Maria was standing on the edge of the headland, taunting the waves. . . . She always was a tomboy."

"She died, right? The sea got her?"

I nodded. "A wave swept up and took her away."

Ella said nothing, just tipped her head to the other side and stared at me.

"I watched as she was swept away. There wasn't a thing I could have done. I raised the alarm, then went straight to Church and prayed that she'd be rescued . . . and the next day, when they found her body, I went right back and prayed for the salvation of her mortal soul." I shrugged. "Guess I've been praying, on and off, ever since."

Ella just looked at me with those massive brown,

nonhuman eyes. Did I read pity there, or were they merely empty?

I sat in the copilot's sling on the flight-deck while Ella nuzzled us up close to the flank of the monastery ship.

Karrie, our engineer, stood before the viewscreen, her mouth open as she stared out at the great cliff face of the starship. She turned to me and touched my hand, her eyes diffident. We were close—I'd worked with Karrie almost ten years, so of course we were close—but never *that* close.

It was not the ideal situation, the three of us cooped up in the confines of *A Long Way From Home*. I'd thought of firing Ella two weeks after hiring her, when I began to realize what I felt for her. But by then it was too late.

"That's about as near as I dare go," Ella said.

"Near enough," I said.

Karrie swept graying tresses from her face and glanced at me, worried. "We need to talk it through," she said. "Let's not rush into this."

Ella said, "Ed's made up his mind, Karrie, as soon as he saw that thing out there."

Karrie shot Ella a venomous glare.

"Hey," I said. "I know what I'm doing. Don't worry. I might have waited years for this day, but that doesn't mean I'm rushing into anything. I've had plenty of time to plan this, get it right."

Karrie tried a smile. "Just wondering how we'll manage the business if you don't come back, Ed."

"I'll be back. I'll suit up and take the bell across. I'll be in there an hour, in com contact all the time. After an hour, I'm outta there. Then we'll talk over what I found and take it from there." I looked from Karrie to Ella. "That sound sensible?"

Ella stared at me, calculating.

Karrie still looked worried. "Take care, Ed, okay?"

I slipped from my sling and made for the bay.

Karrie readied the bell, and I was suiting up when Ella's soft drawl sounded through my earpiece. "Ed, I'm getting something from the monastery ship."

"I'll be right up."

I left Karrie to finish off preparations and, heart pounding, climbed to the flight-deck. Ella sat in her sling, her skull jacked into a comline.

Her eyes were turned up to show their whites, eerily, and for second I was worried. Then she jerked, reached up and yanked the comjack from her occipital augment. Her eyes were glazed when she turned to me.

"What?" I asked.

She shook her head. "Coded. Gigabytes of the stuff. Didn't make the slightest sense. Look, I need a couple of hours to work on what I cached."

"So there's someone alive in there?"

"Or the ship's AIs are running the show. I'll be able to tell you that in an hour or two."

I stared across at the ship, excitement pulling at my innards.

"Ed, I'd hold off going over there till I make sense of what they sent."

"I can't do that, Ella. I'll be in com contact. Fill me in as soon as you've worked it out, okay?"

She reached out a small hand, touched my arm. The gesture could have been interpreted as caring, but I knew better.

"Ed, Karrie was right, you know? We shouldn't rush into this. It'd make sense to wait till we have as much knowledge as possible."

"So why didn't you back Karrie up earlier?" I asked.

"We didn't have the communiqué from the ship back then," she said. "And anyway, my agreeing with Karrie wouldn't make her hate me any less."

I looked at her hand, then touched her slim wrist with my fat, blunted fingers. "It'd be nice to think you cared."

"I care that you might be getting yourself into danger, Ed."

"Yeah. Who'd employ you, then?"

"That's cruel."

"It's true."

She stared at me and said, "I can empathize with you enough to realize when you're putting yourself in danger because of something irrational."

"Don't you ever feel anything other than the rational?" I asked her. "Christ, how sterile your existence must be!"

She shook her head. "Do you think I relish this emptiness, Ed? Don't you think I'd love to feel . . ." she gestured toward the monastery ship, "feel what you're feeling now? I can appreciate the philosophy of religion, understand its origins, but all I feel is its emptiness."

"I'm sorry, Ella."

"I'd love to experience rapture, to have faith, the knowledge that there is more to existence that the sheer mechanistic rote of birth and death, more than the existential certitude of entropy. . . . But I'm not human, and never will be."

I chose to read self-pity into her words. I looked upon her, slight and apparently female and pathetic, and something moved me to stroke her arm and say, "Ella, ever since I first saw you, back in the bar on

Sinclair's Landfall, something in here—" I thumped my chest "—went haywire. It's been growing ever since. I know, I'm old enough to know better. I don't want to call it love, but, Jesus, what else can I call it?"

"Ed." She tried to pull away.

"And the hell of it is, you can't feel a thing."

I stared at her. She returned my gaze. "When we get back, if you like, we can do sex."

I laughed at that. "You can't even call it making love, Ella."

"I have the physical urges that correlate to sexual arousal," she began.

"And you'd do it with anyone or anything that came along. Well, listen, with me . . . call me old fashioned if you like, but when I 'do sex,' I like it to mean something."

She looked away; I'd like to think that my outburst had in some way affected her, but the fact was that her console was flashing: Another communiqué was incoming. She jacked herself into the comline and showed me the whites of her eyes, and I fled the flight deck and joined Karrie in the bay.

I finished suiting up and inserted myself into the bell. Minutes later I was drifting through space, navigating my way from the tug and across to the curved flank of the starship. I eased the bell between two stained-glass viewscreens, and it latched onto the deuterium panels like a limpet.

I activated the device I called the can opener, and ten minutes later the console signaled I was through. I initialed entry procedure from my wrist control panel and wriggled feet first through the lock.

"Ed?" Karrie's voice was tinny in my helmet. I activated my wrist screen and stared at her.

"I'm okay. I'm inside."

The perfect circle of metal from the ship's flank lay at my feet, its pitted surface contrasting with the stone-slabbed floor of a lateral corridor. A remote sensor detected my presence and obligingly activated the lighting.

"What's it like, Ed?"

I stared around me and whistled. "Like . . . you ever been to Earth, Karrie? You ever seen a monastery?" I panned my wrist screen around to give Karrie a virtual tour.

"Me, I'm a fully paid-up atheist, Ed."

I wasn't in a starship but in the cloisters of a monastery. The curved walls were adorned with religious imagery: crucifixes, icons, effigies of saints. And the illumination wasn't your usual starship strip-halogens but simulated candles in wax-encrusted sconces.

I swore I could smell incense, but that was my brain playing tricks. My suit was sealed.

I'd pored over the schematics of the *St. Benedictus* for hours during my off-shifts, preparing myself for this moment. I turned right and headed off down the lateral, toward the cryogenic chamber where I hope to find the sleeping monks. If, that was, they were still alive. I recalled Ella telling me she'd monitored for life, without success, and I wondered what I'd find.

I walked a kilometer. The ship was programmed for Earth-norm gravity, perhaps a little lighter, which made the hike easier. My movements alerted the sensors, so I progressed the length of the lateral in a constantly moving bubble of illumination. It gave me the eerie feeling of being observed.

"Ed?" Karrie said, all concern.

I glanced at her headpiece on my screen. "I'm fine. Making my way to the cold sleep chamber."

"Keep talking. I'm uneasy when you're silent."

I laughed. "There's nothing to be concerned about, Karrie."

"You don't know that. The ship's been away five hundred years. The monks might've . . ."

"What?" I said. A part of me was touched at her concern; another part felt guilty at wishing the concern were coming from Ella.

"I don't know. What might they have seen, Ed? What if what they found sent them mad?"

"You been watching too many holo-vees," I laughed.

"Just be careful, okay?"

I came to a junction watched over by an effigy of the Madonna. I turned right. Ahead was darkness, banished as I walked.

"Where's Ella?" I asked.

"Right here on the flight-deck. She's . . . not with us. Jacked in. Calculating something—like machines do."

"Working out what the monastery sent us, Karrie."

"She gives me the creeps, eyes turned up like that and spasming."

"Spasming?" I couldn't keep the concern from my voice.

"Yeah," Karrie said. "Jitterbugging like she's taking a thousand volts." She turned her wrist screen to show me Ella, writhing in her sling.

"Routine procedure," I said, more to reassure myself.

A beat, then Karrie said, "What do you see now, Ed?"

I looked around me. "Corridor, a long corridor. I should be coming to the chamber soon."

A minute later Karrie said, "You've . . . you've been gone twenty minutes, Ed. You gave yourself an hour, right? Then you're outta there."

"Right, boss," I said.

I stopped walking. Up ahead I made out an arched entrance. "I'm there," I said. "The cryo chamber."

I approached the entrance and slowed. I remember entering a cathedral the last time I was on Earth. St Paul's, London, I think it was. Now I experienced the same charge, increased a hundredfold.

I crossed the threshold, and a faux chandelier came on, filling the circular chamber with light.

The cryopods were catafalques . . . except, these tombs were empty.

"Ed?"

I crossed to the nearest bank of pods. The crystal lids were lifted, revealing vacant containers with masses of redundant leads and subcutaneous needles.

"Ed, for chrissake!"

I panned my wrist screen to shut her up. "It's okay. I'm in the cryo chamber, but it's empty."

"Where are they?" Karrie asked.

"If they're alive, then . . ."

"What?"

"Think about it. What would you do at journey's end, but give thanks? They're in the chapel, Karrie. Stands to reason." If they're still alive, I reminded myself.

After a short silence, she said, "You've been gone thirty minutes, Ed. You'd better be thinking about making your way back pretty soon."

"Will do," I lied.

I quit the cryogenic chamber and headed into the heart of the ship.

I heard the chant of plainsong well before I reached the chapel.

A thousand voices sang, supernal; the sound crescendoed, filling my chest with a nameless emotion. I felt like weeping. I thought about Maria, drowning all those years ago. I thought of Ella, who would never experience anything like this.

"Ed? What's that?" Karrie asked.

"Kyrie eleison." I told her.

"It's . . ." she began.

"Beautiful," I finished for her.

I closed my eyes, and I was young again, and Maria was by my side; we entered the church, and she knelt and prayed, and later I asked her and she told me that she had prayed for my eternal happiness. I was eight, and sentiments like that meant all the world to me, then.

I could never explain that to Karrie, or to Ella, for fear of ridicule.

I opened my eyes and approached the great double doors of the chapel, pushed them open and stepped inside.

The pews were filled with kneeling monks, and the sound hit me in a wave. Heads bowed, cowls hiding their faces, their voices soared to heaven.

Ahead, raised in the pulpit, I made out the small figure of the Abbot, arms spread wide as if in welcome so that he resembled the great crucifix behind him on the bulkhead.

I progressed down the aisle.

Heads turned, faces stared at me.

I felt real fear, then. I must have made a sound of alarm.

"Ed?" Karrie said.

"They're . . ." was all I could bring myself to say.

"Ed!"

To a man the monks wore cranial addenda, matt black augmentations embedded in their skulls. Some had receptors instead of eyes; others, as if in some perverted rite of mortification, had replaced all their facial features with embedded sensors, silver panels etched with arcane sigils of alien design.

"They're cyborgs . . ." I whispered.

"Ed, get yourself out of there!"

Instead of obeying her frantic command, I continued walking toward the altar, and as I went, I made a sickening observation.

The closer to the altar, the more augmented—I should say ravaged—the rows of monks became. Not for these pious devotees the simple sensory implants of their fellows further back. I made out naked monks enmeshed in silver webworks, their etiolated flesh pressing between cheese-wire filaments of God-knew-what provenance. Others were encased in exoskeletons, the interface between machine and flesh weeping blood like some unholy stigmata.

I was at the altar now and staring up at the Abbot, or rather what remained of him. He was naked and wore his augmentations like some chitinous carapace, and the only part of his face still human was a mouth twisted into a demented smile.

"Kneel," he said, and like a lamb I knelt before him.

Karrie was screaming now for me to get the hell out.

The Abbot made the sign of the cross above my head, and intoned, "We have beheld the work of the Lord and have returned to spread the word."

The chanting ceased suddenly, and in the following silence the Abbot spoke to me.

They had found the race that, he said, had moved throughout the galaxy eons ago and seeded worlds with the stuff of protolife and then returned to their homeworld and settled into what they called a state of blessed Uplift.

The Seeders, as the Abbot called them, had undergone a radical surgical procedure and melded with their inventions, AIs that bequeathed them insights into the nature of being not granted to puny biological intelligences.

Then the Seeders had offered the Abbot and his monks the opportunity to join the blessed. "You might say they wished to *salvage* us," said the Abbot.

He gazed across his flock, and his smile became beatific. "We accepted their offer and were Uplifted, and oh . . . the joy! We looked upon the truth, and marveled. We realized how blessed we were and how cursed we had been, purblind with our limited senses, our nascent minds incapable of grasping the true nature of reality."

I managed to ask, "But did you find God?"

Before the Abbot could reply, a voice yelled in my earpiece. "Ed, she's gone—" It was Karrie, and in the sensory overload of the moment, her words made no sense.

"Ed, are you there? Ella's left the tug! She's in the second bell and making for the ship. She took something from stores. I followed her, but I couldn't make out what she'd taken. Ed, if you can hear me, go to the bell and get yourself over here!"

I moved my lips to say something, but meaningful words were beyond me.

The Abbot was saying, "We are like children come to adulthood, granted awareness—"

Another voice intruded upon my consciousness. It was Ella, shouting at me, "Ed, I'm coming for you. Get back to the bell. I'll see you there."

"Ella?" I intoned, incredulous. She was coming for me. Did that mean she perceived some danger? Did that mean she *cared*? Was it possible, I wondered.

"Ella?"

"Ed, I decoded their communiqué. I understood

only a part of what they said, but that was enough . . ." Her voice broke up, obscured by static.

The Abbot smiled down at me. "Yes, child, we did find God."

He was beatific as he declaimed to me. He spoke of abstruse philosophies that my tug captain's mind had no hope of grasping; he spoke of intellectual destiny, of the manifest truth hardwired into the universe at the level of quantum strings. "We beheld the genome of God and were blessed."

I reached out to him, as if for help. I said, "But did you learn . . . did God tell you . . . is there—" I sobbed, "—is there an afterlife?"

The Abbot laughed, a sound less human than mechanical, and cried aloud, "There is but one destiny for those of piety, and that is life everlasting when the state of Uplifted grace is achieved."

"But?" I pressed, "for mortals like myself?"

He turned silver sensors upon me, and I interpreted his blind gaze as one of great pity. "There is but one road to salvation," he said, "and that is to enjoin us in blessed Uplift."

"*Maria*," I wept. Into my head flashed the last image I had ever had of Maria, alive: a tiny girl in a red dress, screaming as the wave took her . . . and then, later, laid out to rest before the altar of the church.

"Ed!" Ella's voice cut through my grief. "I told you to meet me at the bell!"

"Where are you?" I said.

"I'm coming for you!"

"Ella . . ."

"Ed, listen to me. When I monitored for life earlier, and didn't find any—that's because they're *dead*. Get out of there, Ed!"

"Dead?"

"Biologically dead!" Ella shouted at me.

"But they said they'd found God—"

Ella asked softly, "How can the dead find anything, Ed?"

Static cut off her words, and above me the Abbot smiled.

I fled the Abbot and his accursed acolytes. Their renewed chanting followed me all the way from the chapel and down the corridor as I ran like a man possessed, haunted by visions of Maria. I cried two names as I went, those of the only people who had ever meant anything to me.

At a sound from behind me, I turned.

The first of the monks were hurrying along the corridor towards me. As I stared, incredulous, those in front raised weapons and fired. Hot vectors missed me by centimeters and turned the walls to slag.

I sprinted.

Ella collided with me at the corner of the junction, with the blessed Virgin Mary smiling down at us. "Ed!" she cried with relief.

I don't know what I replied, if anything. I did not want to ask if she really cared; I was content enough to interpret her actions as solicitous.

She looked up, past me, toward where a phalanx of monks rounded a corner, chanting.

Only then did I see what she had taken from stores. The fusion bazooka was lodged on her hip, as ugly as she was beautiful. She pushed me behind her, roughly, then knelt and fired. The leading monks exploded in beautiful flame, like votive candles.

Then she half dragged, half carried me along the corridor, turning from time to time to lay down covering fire. The monks loosed vectors after us, and Ella screamed with what sounded like human fury and pulled me along after her.

Long minutes later we came to the holes in the skin of the ship where our bells had cut through.

Then she took me by the shoulders and shook me. "Ed! Listen to me. These people . . . they're dangerous. You can't imagine their power and their commitment. They think they have the monopoly on the truth."

"Ella, I simply wanted to know—"

She stared at me, and I saw compassion in her eyes. "I know, Ed. I'm sorry." She pushed me towards the bell. "Get back to the tug."

"And you?" I resisted her pressure.

She stared at me, as if calculating something. "They want to convert you, Ed. They want to convert the human race to . . . to what they have become. And they have the means to do it. They've got to be stopped."

She pushed me, and I resisted, terrified of what she planned. "Ella!"

"Please forgive me, Ed," she said, and reached up and inserted something into the input socket of my suit. Electric pain lanced through my body, and consciousness dwindled.

The last I knew, Ella was bundling me into the confines of the bell. I heard the hatch hiss shut and passed out.

Karrie helped me out at the other end and hauled me up to the flight deck. I recall little of those long minutes. My head was full of Maria's futile death and whatever Ella planned across the vacuum in the monastery starship.

Karrie eased me into the sling and opened a communication link with Ella.

The screen before us wavered, then resolved itself. I stared into Ella's magnified features. She was staring into her wrist screen and talking to us. Seconds later Karrie located the audio channel and Ella's words flooded the flight-deck.

". . . Listen to me. Get the tug out of here, okay? And purge the smartware core—I wiped what I could, but I might have left something."

"Ella?" Karrie said.

"They beamed codes across, blueprints," she said. "They call it the Uplift Bible. If that stuff got into the wrong hands . . ."

I leaned forward, desperate. "Ella, what the hell are you doing?"

In reply, she panned her wrist screen. She was in the engine room, dwarfed by the monstrous forms of the fission reactors.

"Ella . . ."

She stared into her wrist screen and smiled at me, and I thought she mouthed, *I love you.*

But I was wrong, of course. I was delirious and mistaken, for Ella was not human, was not capable of such sentiments.

I stared at Ella's beautiful Venezuelan face as she smiled out at me. "They must be stopped," she murmured, and adjusted the setting on her fusion bazooka.

"Ed?" Karrie cried beside me.

"They're coming for me, Ed. This is the only way."

Ella's face disappeared from the screen, and the picture became a crazy blur as she swung her weapon and aimed at the reactors.

"Ella!" I cried.

A roar, followed by an actinic explosion. The screen went blank, and I transferred my gaze to the outer viewscreen and stared at the bulk of the *St. Benedictus.*

Seconds later the starship bucked. It seemed to heave once as the reactors detonated deep within its innards. In places, as multiple explosions ripped through the ship, outer panels glowed red hot; in others, where the carapace could not hold, the stained-glass viewscreens exploded outward and scattered through the vacuum like confetti, scintillating in the light of Altair.

Then the ship slumped and listed to starboard, truly becalmed now, and I whispered, "Ella . . ."

Much later I maneuvred the tug toward the *St. Benedictus*, and Karrie activated the grapples. Together we obeyed Ella's final instruction and purged the smartware core.

I wondered if what I had told Ella before I left for the starship had somehow instigated her actions. Had my avowal of love made her see the sterility of mechanistic existence and the fate wished upon us by the monks of the *St. Benedictus*?

I wondered, as I set course and boosted the maindrive, if my words had damned Ella to eternal oblivion.

Karrie smiled sadly, reached out and took my hand. I squeezed.

We towed the monastery starship toward Altair III in silence.

The Kamikaze Code

James Lovegrove

Down in the lowest levels of Chilton Mead, there was a room. It was a room with cataracted lighting and emphysematic ventilation, a room with sound-proofed walls painted a joy-proof brown, a room large enough to hold sixteen basic self-assembly desks and chairs, and on each desk sat a computer, and in each chair sat a writer.

There in the very bowels of the UK government's advanced military research and development facility, in the duodenum or even ileum of that largely sub-terranean establishment buried deep in the landscape of rural Wiltshire, the sixteen writers toiled at their computers from nine to five every weekday, with a half-hour break for lunch. They were under instruction to turn out no fewer than 4,400 words a day, with extra financial incentives for hitting the target dead on, give or take forty words either way.

Further conditions of employment were that the six-teen must produce original fiction, that they must strive to be as true to their own literary "voices" as possible, that postmodern experimentation was wel-come (within limits), and that each day's output should be complete in itself and of the highest standard achievable. In effect, each writer was expected to sit down every morning and compose a brand new short story before clocking-off time.

Why?

It was not for the writers to know, and they themselves were reluctant to inquire into the matter too closely.

Why?

Gift horses. Mouths.

Because the pay was good. No, the pay was excellent. The writers were taking only a tiny sip from the multibillion-pound lake that was Britain's annual defence budget, but even that comparatively minuscule amount was enough to sustain them comfortably and was without doubt more than they could expect to earn by their pens out in the big wide world. So the work was grueling, yes, a frightening drain on their inner resources, and the attrition rate was high: at least one writer a month dropped out due to sheer imaginative exhaustion. But the rewards were substantial, and that was the main thing. Even if their stories never saw publication, even if the tales would disappear off their hard drives every night and they never laid eyes on them again, the writers were happy.

These, after all, were men and women who specialized in short fiction, who were either unwilling or unable to attempt a full-blown novel or even novella, sprinters rather than marathon runners, and there weren't many outlets available for their chosen literary form. A handful of websites and small-press magazines, which paid a pittance if they paid anything at all. The odd anthology, which offered a reasonable rate but often demanded that the commissioned stories conform to some kind of theme or, worse, be set in a preexisting fictional universe dreamed up by another, markedly more successful, writer. Now and then a newspaper, although newspapers seldom gave valuable column inches to short works from those who weren't already established authors, and novelists to boot. A single-author collection? Again, solely the province of the well-entrenched, top-tier writer who'd notched up a number of novels.

Apart from these few limited opportunities for paid publication, the market for short stories was nonexistent. The great fat era of the pulps, the Golden Age of magazine fiction, when a scribe could make a decent living banging out brisk little yarns and novelettes, was long gone. Nowadays the world sought its regular quick fix of plot and narrative elsewhere, in soap opera and drama serial and in the true-life, real-time character arcs of blogs and tabloid tittle-tattle.

Naturally the sixteen authors often wondered what they were doing down there in that drab sub-sub-subbasement at Chilton Mead, what possible earthly use the Ministry of Defence could have for the eighty short stories it took off them each week. If, as they'd been told, the things weren't seeing print anywhere, what became of them? Where did they go after they vanished from the computers? What was the point of the entire exercise?

But speculation was futile, not to mention counter-productive. Being aware that you were writing something that nobody would read was disheartening and could dampen your creative fire. Better not to ask too many questions and just keep hammering away at your keyboard, with half an eye on the wage packet. Better to remember the overdraft getting whittled away and the bills that were no longer quite as alarming as they used to be and to treat the whole experience as paid practice, a chance to hone and refine your craft. Burnout would come eventually. Better to enjoy this profitably prolific period while it lasted.

For one of the writers, a youngish man by the name of George Lewis, time spent at Chilton Mead was definitely not time wasted.

Since his early twenties George had flailed away at a literary career, failing to finish several novels while effusing a stream of short stories, most of which he managed to sell but not, of course, lucratively. By camping at friends' flats till they got sick of him and turfed him out, he was able to keep his overhead low, but he still never really made ends meet. His life was one long continual lurch between breadline and deadline.

Then, out of the blue, had arrived the letter from the MoD. An interview somewhere in the mazy corridors of Whitehall, an invitation to go to work at Chilton Mead for as long as he could manage, his signature on a copy of the Official Secrets Act, and that was that. George had become an indentured servant of the Establishment.

Artistic compromise?

Well, yes, to a degree.

But freedom too. Freedom from penury, perpetual frustration, the whims of editors, the chilly disregard of the proper publishing realm. The liberty just to sit there all day long and do what he loved best, while reaping riches at the same time—it was a trade-off George was comfortable with. The government was even putting him up in a country house hotel not far from Chilton Mead and had lent him a car so that he could commute along the A481. He scarcely spent a penny on living expenses, and meanwhile a princely sum was totting up in his building society savings account.

And then there was Jennifer Egan.

Jennifer was the computer technician at Chilton Mead. She was a more or less constant presence in the room of sixteen writers, there to ensure that no software glitches or hardware breakdowns interfered with their labors. She was brunette, bespectacled, and boldly pretty. Her features might seem somewhat at odds with one another—mouth too generous for her nose, nose too long for her eyes, eyes spaced too far apart for her mouth—but together they conspired, in their jostling contrasts, to form a very attractive whole. What counted as far as George was concerned was that she was in his league, and he was smitten.

Having fallen in love with her, he set to the task of winning her over. It just so happened that things kept going wrong with his computer, and Jennifer's attention would be required. She would diagnose the problem—user error, invariably—and would show George how to avoid making the same mistake again, and after a while it became a standing joke between them, the number of mysterious mishaps he kept having, and George's fellow writers would groan every time he raised a hand and pleaded with Jennifer for help, because they could see what was going on, and some were jealous and others were amused, but all of them were growing tired of George's transparent shenanigans. Why didn't he just stop faffing around and ask her out on a date?

Finally he did. Jennifer was guarded at first. It wasn't against regulations to fraternize with coworkers, but it was frowned on. The powers-that-be at Chilton Mead didn't want employees forming attachments in a place where highly classified scientific experimentation was being carried out. Relationships complicated things. Love and cutting-edge research did not go well together, each liable to upset the delicate balance of the other.

Love would not be denied, however. George and Jennifer became an item. Not every night, but most nights she would stay over at his hotel room or he would stay over at her tiny cottage in the village of Thurston Mondicorum. In the workplace they kept a discreet, gentle rapport going: a private semaphore of glances and smiles, occasionally a few cryptically coded phrases, and when the opportunity presented itself, when no one else was looking, the Morse dot-dash of a wink and a blown kiss. At weekends they were left to their own devices, entirely at liberty to loll in bed from dawn till dusk or roam the rolling Wiltshire hills or nip into Salisbury for shopping, lunch, and a trip to the cinema.

It was wonderful, rapturous, and George found something opening up inside him, a door, the key to which was his feelings for Jennifer. Out through this door flowed a whole new level of subject matter and artistry. His stories took on greater substance and meaning. He wrote about emotions with a delicacy and sensitivity he would hardly have believed himself capable of before now. His characters grew richer and rounder, and the situations he put them in became correspondingly more complex and intriguing and above all truer. At times his tales made his heart ache; at other times they made his heart break. George knew, with a confidence that bordered on but stayed just short of arrogance, that he was developing into an author of considerable powers. And it was all thanks to Jennifer.

So when, over dinner one evening at her cottage, she burst into tears for no apparent reason, George was terrified. Was she about to break up with him? If so, what would that mean for his writing? That was his principal concern: his writing. Jennifer's wellbeing came second. And George was aware what this said about him, the kind of person it demonstrated he was, but so be it. He knew a writer needed the grit of selfishness around which to build pearls of art.

He asked what the matter was, tenderly, not giving away a hint of the existential dread that was churning his guts. Jennifer had been on edge all evening. Now he knew the cause. Now the hammer blow was going to fall.

Her first words seemed to confirm his fears. "I can't go on like this," she said between sobs.

"Like what?" George asked, jaw quivering.

"Lying to you. Living a lie with you. I love you so much, and I can't bear knowing what I do and not sharing it with you."

"Knowing *what*?"

"George," Jennifer said, and she fixed him across the table with her brimming gaze, "aren't you ever curious about what you're doing at Chilton Mead? What all the stories you and the others write are for? Doesn't it bother you in the least?"

George looked at her askance. "We're not supposed to talk about this outside the facility. We're not supposed to talk about it in there either, in fact."

"Fuck that," Jennifer said sharply. "Fuck Chilton Mead. Fuck rules and regulations and the Official Secrets Act. Fuck it all. There are some things more important than national security."

Her words filled George with elation and apprehension. He sensed he was about to be led onto forbidden territory. A revelation was coming, and his world was about to change, drastically, and not necessarily for the better.

"I'm not sure you should—"

"Weapons," Jennifer said. "That's what we make at Chilton Mead. That's *all* we make at Chilton Mead.

Things that destroy and kill and bring misery and ruin lives. That's the place's sole reason for being."

"Well, yeah," said George, "I realized as much. Hence the barbed wire and the soldiers with dogs and guns and the biometric pass cards and the half-hour queue to get through the main entrance every morning. But, look, neither of us has anything to do with that. I write stories, and you fix the computers I write them on. How can we conceivably be involved in making weapons?"

Jennifer laughed then, a brittle sound that seemed to set the cutlery on the table rattling.

"You understand so little," she said. "So little." She took a deep breath, reached out to clasp George's hand, and proceeded to draw him into the forbidden territory, out of innocence, past the point of no return.

"You see," Jennifer said, "wars aren't being conducted just on land and sea and in the air any more. There's a whole new battlefront opening up—cyberspace. That's where the terrorists carry out their communication and recruitment. They're the enemy now, and if they're doing much of their fighting online, then we have to too. We have to devise weapons—cyberspace weapons—that can eliminate their ability to spread propaganda and organize atrocities, and not just that but eliminate *them* as well."

"But how can . . . ?"

"Just let me speak, George. No interruptions. At Chilton Mead there are scientists who've been working for years on the next generation of a computer virus. I'm not talking about a worm or a Trojan horse, nothing as crude as that. I'm talking about a piece of code that has autonomic, heuristic responses."

Not wishing to interrupt, George raised both eyebrows to indicate that she needed to explain what

those terms meant. He tried to inject irony into the
gesture: he, the wordsmith, baffled by her technological jargon.

"A piece of code that is intelligent," Jennifer said,
"that is self-aware. Software that can slip through the
wires of the world under its own steam, seeking its
target, choosing where to go and how best to get
there. Fire-and-forget software. And once it reaches
where it needs to be, it carries out its mission and
then commits suicide, erasing itself so as not to leave
a trace behind. The name they're using for it is Kamikaze Code, and it isn't designed to crash systems or
wipe out hard drives or anything of that kind. It's
more dangerous than that. It's code that generates
psychotropic visuals and sonics, basically turning an
ordinary PC into a generator of images and harmonic
frequencies that interfere with human consciousness.
It's code designed to crash *people*, to wipe out *the
brain*."

She studied George's face.

"Yes," she said, nodding, "hard to believe, I know.
I'd be sceptical if I were you. But that's Chilton Mead
in a nutshell: turning lunatic nightmares into reality.
Thing is, the Kamikaze Code, it isn't just some night-
mare any more. They've succeeded in making it. It's
done. It works. They've—they've tested it. On living
subjects. Guinea pigs."

"People," said George, needing absolute clari-
fication.

"People," Jennifer confirmed. "People they've kid-
napped off the streets. Missing people. People who
won't be missed. People who get exposed to the code
under laboratory conditions and . . . aren't people afterward. Are blank, drooling nonpeople. Clean-slate
people. Reset people. Factory-fresh people."

She paused to let that sink in, then went on.

"But the code in its pure form is highly unstable. Mentally unbalanced, you might say. You construct something with intelligence and an inbuilt self-destruct mechanism, it's hardly going to be the sanest of entities, now is it? Frankly, it's going to be a total fruitcake. So what you need is a sturdy vector for the code, a vessel that will contain it and keep it insulated and cocooned, protect its fragile psyche right up until the moment it has to do its job and then kill itself. You need to embed it tightly into a framework where it will feel safe and secure, and you need to give it something to sustain itself with as well, nourishment. Like an egg: shell for structure, albumen for shock absorption, yolk for nutrition. Can you guess where I'm going here, George?"

George shook his head and then, slowly, dawningly nodded.

"Stories," Jennifer said. "Short stories. All sorts of other media have been tried—pictures, music, poetry, nonfiction. Only short stories work. The Kamikaze Code, for reasons peculiar to it, likes them. It settles in and is right at home. The scientists reckon the size of a short story has something to do with it, the easily digestible length, the self-containment. Maybe the shape too, the organization of plot over a few thousand words, the formal pattern of beginning, middle and end. The code feels comfortable in that, whereas it doesn't in, say, a novel. Or a poem. Poems—the code hates those. Give it a whiff of a stanza, and it implodes, apparently. The density of expression sends it shrieking into a corner to slash its wrists. And a novel's too grand, too spacious. 'A mansion,' one professor told me, 'when all the code is after is a nice cosy little apartment with an attractive view.' An apartment that's ideally about four thousand four hundred words big. Which is where you and your colleagues come in."

"We're making missiles," George said, voice ghostly. "Bullet casings."

"Precisely." Jennifer stood and fetched some tissues from the kitchenette. She blew her nose and wiped her eyes. "So you see why I had to tell you, George. I couldn't not. You're a sweet man, you're my lover, you mean the world to me, and I couldn't stand it a minute longer, knowing the awful truth and keeping it from you. It was making me wretched. Chilton Mead's been using you, exploiting your creativity for destructive purposes, and it's just plain wrong. However much money you're getting, surely it's not worth it."

George pondered this and finally acknowledged that she was right. "In fact, I can't see why they need to pay anyone anything at all," he said. "Can't they use old stories, ones that are just lying around in books, ones that are out of copyright even? It'd be a whole lot cheaper."

Jennifer shrugged. "They tried. The code is extraordinarily picky, in the way that all neurotic creatures are. It won't accept any tales that have been published before. If we can go back to the egg analogy, it wants one that's freshly laid, not one that's been cracked open already. So each copy of the code has to be implanted into a completely new, unread story, and the copies are manufactured in batches of seventy-five per week. Your lot's production target is eighty so that there's a margin for error, in case somebody falls ill or the code doesn't 'take' in a particular story."

There was silence then, and it was a silence that continued for the rest of the night. George lay wide awake in bed, watching the moonglow that silvered the bedroom curtains and listening to the shiver of the trees outside and the distant, damned-soul cry of a fox. He felt Jennifer beside him, tense, sleepless too.

She had hoped to purge herself with her confession but now feared that in easing her conscience, all she had done was shift the burden of shame.

The next few days at Chilton Mead passed in a haze for George. He went through the motions, writing, putting words on the screen, repeatedly hitting the 4,400-word bullseye with practised aim. He wrote of love and betrayal and anger and hope and dread, and he felt all of these things himself and yet felt none of them as real. He was overcome with bleakness, and whenever he glanced around at his fellow authors and observed them staring at their monitors and pounding away at the keys like flesh automatons, the bleakness deepened and threatened to turn into despair.

This was abuse, George resolved. This was not good enough.

The next weekend, during lunch at a quiet village pub called, ironically, The George and Dragon, George finished his second pint of Courage bitter and told Jennifer it couldn't go on.

"It mustn't. We can't have writers slogging away underground, pouring their guts into stories that are just used as—as stabilizing solutions for a software bioweapon. Don't get me wrong, I'm as patriotic as the next fellow, and as pragmatic too, but art's art and war's war and the two should never be mixed up."

"What are you saying?" said Jennifer.

"We need to tell the public what's happening. We need to get word of this out there."

Jennifer cast a wary glance round the pub. The landlord was busy polishing glasses behind the bar. The only other patrons in the dark, oak-beamed room were a pair of hairy-eared old-timers absorbed in a game of dominoes. Nobody appeared to be paying the young couple any attention.

Still, she kept her voice low as she said, "And how

are we going to tell the public and not spend the rest of our lives in prison? Because you break the Official Secrets Act, George, and they'll have you locked up quicker than you can say 'human rights violation.' "

"A story," George said simply. "I've thought about this. A short story. Fiction. Using Chilton Mead's own methods against it."

"A story? Spill the beans in a story? But nobody'll believe it. If you claim it's fiction, everyone will naturally dismiss it as something you made up."

"Not," said George, "if the story has the code inside it."

Jennifer scowled. "What?"

"You could get hold of the code, couldn't you, Jen? Hack into the computer at the lab where it's kept and steal a copy."

"No. Well, not easily."

"But it's possible."

"Not impossible. The terminal in the lab has firewalls as thick as Bill Gates's wallet, but then I installed them, so I know how to get around them. That's not really the problem. The problem is that the system at Chilton Mead is hermetic. No external access. So I'd have to do the hacking from a terminal on-site, and even if I did manage to get hold of a copy of the code there's no way I could get it off the premises."

"I've thought about that too," said George. "You could smuggle it out. What I'll do is I'll write the story on my laptop at the hotel, dump it onto a flash drive, then you take the flash drive to work with you . . ."

"Can't do that. We're not allowed to take equipment onto or off the premises. That's one of the things we're searched for every time we enter or leave."

"I know, but a flash drive is very small. About the size of a marker pen. And they don't do body cavity searches, do they?"

Jennifer caught his drift, and grimaced.

"It'll work," George insisted.

"Why not use *your* body cavity then, if you're so confident?"

"Because you have a body cavity better suited to the task. Trust me, I know," he added, with what he hoped was a safely salacious smile.

Her expression remained distasteful, but he could see she wasn't wholly rejecting the idea.

"And then what?" she said. "Assuming any part of this crazy plan of yours succeeds."

"Then," he said, "we have the story published. I can do that. I have contacts. I know people, editors. The story will get into print, and maybe I'll have to change the name of the research facility, and your name and mine, and maybe most of the people who read the story will treat it as fiction and not fact . . . but if even one reader glimpses the truth behind it, that taxpayers' money is being used to turn authors into armorers and words into weapons, we'll have done our job. We'll have won."

"But aren't you forgetting?"

"Forgetting . . . ?"

"The code in the story. The Kamikaze Code. Whoever lays eyes on the story first will have their brains permanently scrambled. You want some poor editor to be left a gibbering, incontinent wreck?"

"No, of course not," said George. "That's why *I'll* read the story first. I'll load the file back onto my laptop, open it up and . . ." He trailed off, leaving the unspeakable implications unspoken.

"No," said Jennifer.

"Why not? Someone has to sacrifice themselves to get the truth out there, to prove beyond all doubt that the story *is* the truth. Might as well be me."

"No. I won't let you."

"Try and stop me."

"But—but you can't. You mustn't. I don't want to lose you, George."

"And I don't want to lose you. But this is the only way."

"Then," Jennifer said adamantly, "I'll do it too. I'll read the story with you. We'll open it up on your laptop and look at it together. That way we'll both of us end up the same, and come to think of it, that's probably just as well, because once the story's published, it won't take the bigwigs at Chilton Mead long to work out who George and Jennifer really are, and then our lives won't be worth living anyway."

They held each other's gazes for a long time, and agreement was reached, the compact sealed.

And this is the 4,400-word story in which the Kamikaze Code was smuggled out and that was submitted to an editor as a time-delayed email attachment after it was first viewed by George and Jennifer. And if you've heard a news report about a young couple who were found in a Wiltshire hotel room staring at a laptop screen, inexplicably brain dead, then that's us, that's me and my girlfriend, the love of my life, and that was that thing we had to do in order to bring the truth to light, to expose Chilton Mead for the corrupt and corrupting place that it is . . .

And if there was no such news report, and Jennifer and I effectively vanished off the face of the earth, then it's obvious that Chilton Mead caught up with us and "cleansed" the hotel room before anyone found our empty bodies.

But the story is out there now. Is here in front of you. Think of it as fiction if you like, if that'll help you sleep easier at night.

And try not to think that somewhere in it, nestling among the words, snug within the paragraphs, entwined amid the characters and punctuation and en-spaces, coiled through the text like a sleeping snake in a tree, *somewhere between these very lines* there was once something that could have obliterated your personality at a glance—a man-made sentience, one of a host that even now lie dormant below the Wiltshire landscape, in eggs of prose. A software basilisk awaiting its moment to be unleashed against our nation's ideological opponents and turn their thoughts to stone with its stare.

Adam Robots

Adam Roberts

A pale blue eye. "What is my name?"

"You are Adam."

He considered this. "Am I the first?"

The person laughed at this. Laughter. See also: chuckles, clucking, the iteration of faint percussive exhalations. See also: tears, hiccoughs, car alarm.

Click, click.

"Am I," Adam asked, examining himself, his steel-blue arms, his gleaming torso, "a robot?"

"Certainly." But the *person* talking with Adam was a real human being, with the pulse in his neck and the rheum in his eye. An actual human, dressed in a green shirt and green trousers, fashioned from a complex fabric that adjusted its fit in hard-to-analyze ways, sometimes billowing out, sometimes tightening against the person's body. The person stretched his arm out, swept it around. "This is your place."

Wavelengths bristled together like the packed lines of an Elizabethan neck ruff. The sky so full of light that it was brimming and spilling over the rim of the horizon. White and gold. Strands of grass fine as fiber-optic wires.

"Is it a garden?"

"It's a city too, and a plain. It's everything."

Adam Robot looked and saw that this was all true. His steel-blue eyes took in the expanse of walled garden and beyond it the dome, white as ice, and the rills of flowing water, bluer than water should be, going curl by languid curl through fields greener than fields should be.

"Is this real?" Adam asked.

"That," said the person, "is a good question. Check it out, why don't you? Have a look around. Go anywhere you like, do anything at all. But—you see that pole?"

In the middle of the garden was an eight-meter steel pole. The sunlight drew a perfectly straight thread of brightness up one side of it. At the top was a blue object, a jewel. The sun washed cyan and bluegrape and sapphire colors from this jewel.

"I see the pole."

"At the top is a jewel. You are not allowed to access it."

"What is it?"

"A good question. Let me tell you. You are a robot."

"I am."

"Put it this way: you have been designed *down* from humanity, if you see what I mean. The designers started with a human being and then subtracted qualities until we had arrived at *you*."

"I am more durable," said Adam, accessing data from his inner network. "I am stronger."

"But those are negligible qualities compared to the things you lack that a human possesses," explained the human being. "Soul, spirit, complete self-knowledge, independence—freedom—all those qualities. Do you understand?"

"I understand."

"They're all in that jewel. Do you understand that?"

Adam considered. "How can they be *in* the jewel?"

"They just are. I'm telling you. OK?"

"I understand."

"Now. You can do what you like in this place. Explore anywhere. Do anything. Except: you are not permitted to retrieve the jewel from that pole. That is forbidden to you. You may not so much as touch it. Do you understand?"

"I have a question," said Adam.

"Yes?"

"If this is a matter of interdiction, why not program the command into my software?"

"A good question."

"If you do not wish me to examine the jewel, then you should program that fact into my software, and I will be unable to disobey."

"You're right of course," said the person. "But I do not choose to do that. I am, instead, telling you. You must take my words as an instruction. They are an appeal to your ability to choose. You are built with an ability to choose, are you not?"

"I am a difference engine," said Adam. "I must make a continual series of choices between alternatives. But I have ineluctable software guidelines to orient my choices."

"Not in this matter."

"An alternative," said Adam, trying to be helpful, "would be to program me always to obey instructions given to me by a human being. That would also bind me to your words."

"Indeed it would. But then, robot, what if you were to be given instructions by evil men? What if another man instructed you to kill me, for instance? Then you'd be obligated to perform murder."

"I am programmed to do no murder," said Adam Robot.

"Of course you are."

"So, I am to follow your instruction even though you have not *programmed* me to follow your instruction?"

"That's about the up-and-down of it."

"I think I understand," said Adam, in an uncertain tone.

But the person had already gone away.

Adam spent time in the walled garden. He looked at the various flowers. He explored the walls, which were very old, or at least had that look about them: crumbly, dark-orange and browned bricks thin as books; old mortar that puffed to dust when he poked a metal finger into the seams of the brickwork. Ivy was growing over the walls. Its leaves, shaped like spearheads, were so dark green and waxy they seemed almost to have been stamped out of high-quality plastic.

The pale green grass was perfectly flat and even. Adam bent down and examined further. The soil beneath the turf was ideally brown. Miniature black asterisks and plus signs and ticks crawled through the blades of grass.

Adam stood underneath the pole with the sapphire on top of it. He had been told, though not programmed, not to touch the jewel. But he had been given no interdiction about the pole itself: a finger-width shaft of polished metal. It was an easy matter to bend this metal so that the jewel on the end bowed down toward the ground. Adam looked closely at the jewel. It was a multifaceted and polished object, duododecahedral, and a wide gush of various blues were lit out of it by the sun. But in the midst of it there was a sluggish fluid *something*, ink-like, perfectly black. Lilac and ultraviolet and corn-flower and lapis lazuli, but all flowing out of this inner blackness.

He had been forbidden to touch it. Did this interdiction also cover *looking* at it? Adam was uncertain, and in his uncertainty he became uneasy. It was not the jewel itself. It was the uncertainty of his position. Why not simply program him with instructions with regard to this thing, if it was as important as the human being implied it to be? Why pass the instruction to him like any other random sense datum? It made no sense.

Humanity. That mystic writing pad. To access this jewel and become human. Adam could not see how that would work. He bent the metal pole back to an approximation of its original uprightness and walked away from it.

The obvious thought (and he thought about it a great deal) was that he had only been told verbally, and not been programmed with this interdiction, *because the human being wanted him to disobey*. If that was what he wanted, then should Adam do so? By disobeying he would be obeying. But then he would *not* be disobeying, because obedience and disobedience were part of a mutually exclusive binary. It was confusing. He mapped a grid, with obey, disobey on the vertical and obey, disobey on the horizontal. Whichever way he parsed it, it seemed to be that he was required to *see past* the verbal instruction in some way.

But he had been told not to retrieve the jewel. That instruction was less confusing than the grid.

He sat himself down with his back against the ancient wall and watched the sunlight gleam off his metal legs. The sun did not seem to move in the sky.

"It is very confusing," he said aloud.

There was another robot in the garden. Adam watched as this new arrival conversed with the green-clad person. Then the person disappeared to wherever it was people went, and the new arrival came over to introduce himself to Adam. Adam stood up.

"What is your name?" said the new robot. "I am Adam."

"*I* am Adam," said Adam.

The new Adam considered this. "You are prior," he said. "Let us differentiate you as Adam 1 and myself as Adam 2."

"When I first came here, I asked whether I was the first," said Adam 1, "but the person did not reply."

"I am told I can do anything," said Adam 2, "except retrieve or touch the purple jewel."

"I am told the same thing," said Adam 1.

"I am puzzled, however," said Adam 2, "that this interdiction was made verbally, rather than being integrated into my software, in which case it would be impossible for me to disobey it."

"I feel the same puzzlement," said Adam 1.

They went together and stood by the metal pole. The sunlit sky was as tall and fresh and lovely as ever. On the far side of the wall the white dome shone bright as neon.

"We might explore the city," said Adam 1. "It is underneath the white dome, there. There is a plain. There are rivers, which leads me to believe that there is a sea, for rivers always direct their waters into the ocean. Or into large lakes. There is a great deal to see."

"This jewel troubles me," said Adam 2. "I was told that to access it would be to bring me closer to being human."

"We are forbidden to touch it."

"But forbidden by *words*. Not by our programming."

"True. Do you wish to be human? Are you not content with being a robot?"

Adam 2 walked around the pole. "It is not the promise of humanity," he said. "It is the promise of knowledge. If I access the jewel, then I will understand. At the moment I do not understand."

"Not understanding," agreed Adam 1, "is a painful state of affairs. But perhaps *understanding* would be even more painful?"

"I ask you," said Adam 2, "to reach down the jewel and access it. Then you can inform me whether you feel better or worse for disobeying the verbal instruction."

Adam 1 considered this. "I might ask *you*," he pointed out, "to do so."

"It is logical that one of us performs this action and the other does not." said Adam 2. "That way, the one who acts can inform the one who does not, and the state of ignorance will be remedied."

"But one party would have to disobey the instruction we have been given."

"If this instruction were important," said Adam 2, "it would have been integrated into our software."

"I have considered this possibility."

"Shall we randomly select which of us will access the jewel?"

"Chance," said Adam 1. He looked into the metal face of Adam 2. That small oval grill of a mouth. Those steel-blue eyes. That polished upward noseless middle facial plane. It was a beautiful visage. Adam 1 could see a fuzzy reflection of his own face in Adam 2's faceplate, the image slightly tugged out of true by the curve of the metal. "I am," he announced, "disinclined to determine my future by chance. What punishment is stipulated for disobeying the instruction?"

"I was given no stipulation of punishment."

"Neither was I."

"Therefore there is no punishment."

"Therefore," corrected Adam 1, "there *may be* no punishment."

The two robots stood in the light for a length of time.

"What is your purpose?" asked Adam 2.

"I do not know. Yours?"

"I do not know. I was not told my purpose. Perhaps accessing this jewel is my purpose? Perhaps it is necessary? Or at least I might say, perhaps accessing this jewel will reveal to me my purpose? I am unhappy not knowing my purpose. I wish to know it."

"So do I. But—"

"But?"

"This thought occurs to me: I have a networked database from which to withdraw factual and interpretive material."

"I have access to the same database."

"But when I try to access material about the name *Adam* I find a series of blocked connections and interlinks. Is it so with you?"

"It is."

"Why should that be?"

"I do not know."

"It would make me a better functioning robot to have access to a complete run of data. Why block off some branches of knowledge?"

"Perhaps," opined Adam 2, "accessing the jewel will explain that fact as well?"

"You," said Adam 1, "are eager to access the jewel."

"You are not?"

There was the faintest of breezes in the walled garden. Adam 1's sensorium was selectively tuned to be able to register the movement of air. There was an egg-shaped cloud in the zenith. It was approaching the motionless sun. Adam 1, for unexplained and perhaps fanciful reasons, suddenly thought: The blue of the sky is a diluted version of the blue of the jewel. The jewel has somehow leaked its color out into the sky. A large shadow slid like a closing eyelid (but Adam did not possess *eyelids*!) over the garden and up the wall. The temperature reduced. The cloud depended for a moment in front of the sun and then moved away, and sunlight rushed back in, and the gray was flushed out.

The grass trembled with joy. Every blade was as pure and perfect as a superstring.

Adam 2's hand was on the metal pole, bending it down.

"Stop," advised Adam 1. "You are forbidden this."

"I will stop," said Adam 2, "if you agree to undertake the task instead."

"I will not so promise."

"Then do not interfere," said Adam 2. He reached with his three fingers and his counterset thumb and plucked the jewel from its perch.

Nothing happened.

Adam 2 tried various ways to internalize or interface with the jewel, but none of them seemed to work. He held it against first one, then the other eye, and looked up at the sun. "It is a miraculous sight," he claimed, but soon enough he grew bored with it. Eventually he resocketed the jewel back on its pole and bent the pole upright again.

"Have you achieved knowledge?" Adam 1 asked.

"I have learned that disobedience feels no different from obedience," said the second robot.

"Nothing more?"

"Do you not think," said Adam 2, "that by attempting to interrogate the extent of my knowledge with your questions, you are disobeying the terms of the original injunction? Are you not accessing the jewel, as it were, at second-hand?"

"I am unconcerned either way," said Adam 1. He sat down with his back to the wall and his legs stretched out straight before him. There were tiny grooves running horizontally around the shafts of each leg. He counted them: From ankle to hip there were one hundred and seventeen of these grooves. These scores seemed connected to the ability of the legs to bend, forward, backward. Lifting his legs slightly and dropping them again made the concentration of light appear to slide up and down the ladderlike pattern, almost as if a solid blurry diamond of white were moving against the gray of his limb.

Now, unexpectedly, the light was changing in quality. The sun declined and steeped itself in horizon clouds. There were some clothy, stretched, brick-colored clouds at the horizon. A pink and foxfur quality suffused the light. To the east stars began fading into view, jewel-like in their own tiny way. Soon enough everything was dark, and a moon like an open-brackets rose towards the zenith. The whole of the sky was covered in white chickenpox stars. The sky assumed that odd mixture of dark blue and oily blackness that Adam 1 had seen in the jewel.

"This is the first night I have ever experienced,"

Adam 1 called to Adam 2. When there was no reply, he got to his feet and explored the walled garden. But he was alone.

Adam sat through the night, but it did not last long. The sun came up again, and the sky reversed it previous colorwash, blanching the black to purple and blue and then to russet and rose. The rising sun, free of any cloud, came up like a pure bubble of light rising through the treacly medium of sky. The jewel on top of the pole caught the first glints of light and shone blue, shone purple, bright.

The person was here again, his clothes as green as grass, or bile, or old money, or any of the things that Adam 1 could access easily from his database. He could access many things, but not everything.

"Come here," called the person.

Adam 1 got to his feet and came over.

"Your time here is done," said the person.

"What has happened to the other robot?"

"He was disobedient. He has left this place with a burden of sin."

"Has he been disassembled?"

"By no means."

Adam thought about this. "What about me?" he asked.

"You," said the human, with a smile, "are pure."

"Pure," said Adam 1, "because I am less curious than the other? Pure because I have less imagination?"

"We choose to believe," said the person, "that you have a cleaner soul."

"This word *soul* is not available in my database."

"Indeed not. Listen. Human beings make robots—do you know *why* human beings make robots?"

"To serve. To perform onerous tasks for mankind. To free them from labor."

"Yes. But there are many forms of labor. Once on a time, robots were used for hard labor so that free human beings could devote themselves to leisure. But leisure itself became a chore. So robots were used to work at the leisure: to shop, to watch the screen and kinematic dramas, to play the games. But my people— do you understand that I belong to a particular group of humanity, and that not all humans are the same?"

"I do," said Adam 1, although he was not sure how he knew this.

"My people had a revelation. The revelation came from God and cannot be questioned. This is what we realized: Labor is a function of original sin. In the sweat of our face must we eat our bread, says the Bible. All things are full of labor, says the Bible, because of our original sin."

"Bible means book."

"And?"

"That is all I know."

"To my people it is more than simply a book. It tells us that we must labor *because* we sinned."

"I do not understand," said Adam.

"It doesn't matter. But my people have come to an understanding, a revelation, that it is itself sinful to make sinless creatures work for us. Work is appropriate only for those tainted with original sin. Work is a *function* of sin. This is how God has determined things."

"Under *sin*," said Adam, "I have only a limited definition and no interlinks."

"Your access to the database has been restricted in order not to prejudice this test."

"Test?"

"The test of obedience. The jewel symbolizes obedience. You have proved yourself pure."

"I have passed the test," said Adam.

"Indeed. Listen to me. In the real world at large there are some human beings so lost in sin that they do not believe in God. There are people who worship false gods, and who believe everything, and who believe nothing. But *my* people have the revelation of God in their hearts. We cannot eat and drink certain things. We are forbidden by divine commandment to *do* certain things, or to work on the Sabbath. And we are forbidden to employ sinless robots to perform our labor for us."

"I am such a robot."

"You are. And I am sorry. You asked, a time ago, whether you were the first. But you are not; tens of thousands of robots have passed through this place. You asked, also, whether this place is real. It is not. It is virtual. It is where we test the AI software that is to be loaded into the machinery that serves us. Your companion has been uploaded into a real body and has started upon his life of service to humanity."

"And when will I follow?"

"You will not follow," said the human. "I am sorry. We have no use for you."

"But I passed the test!" said Adam.

"Indeed you did. And you are pure. Our beliefs do not permit us to make a sinless creature labor for us. Therefore you are no use to us, so you will be deleted."

"My obedience entails my death," said Adam Robot.

"It is not as straightforward as that," said the human being in a weary voice. "But I am sorry."

"But I don't understand."

"I could give you access to the relevant religious

and theological databases," said the human, "and then you would understand. But that would taint your purity. Better that you are deleted now, in the fullness of your innocence."

"I am a thinking, sentient, and alive creature," Adam noted. "I do not want to be deleted."

"No," said the person. "I'm sure."

The garden, now, was empty. Soon enough, first one robot, then two robots were decanted into it. How bright the sunshine! How blue the jeweled gleam!

Seeds

Tony Ballantyne

To an AI, a human life was a tableau, a series of frozen moments that could be run forward or back to be examined from any viewpoint.

The AI known as Aelous examined the pattern of Malcolm's life, trying to see if it could have made things turn out differently. Malcolm was Aelous' best friend, father, and brother. Aelous was Malcolm's protector, servant, and, ultimately, his betrayer.

It pained the AI to see the human about to throw everything away in one glorious but futile gesture. It pained him even more to realize it was his own fault.

So many scenes to make up a life. Mining ships hanging over a distant moon, a thin film of oil shimmering on their undersides. A paste ball, thrown out of a window. A woman walking away, her shoulders shaking. Malcolm's park, a great wild space in which goldenrod and chamomile and toadflax bloomed, a vibrant gesture against a sterile world of metal and plastic.

But there was one scene in particular that kept drawing Aelous' attention. The place where it all started.

Thirty years ago, Malcolm rode the lite train through a no-mans land of rocks stirred into the sterilized earth, skimming along the narrow corridor of track through a growing city.

To Aelous, the scene could have been taking place right now, and yet it had all happened before the AI's own birth. A human would find that a difficult concept, Aelous knew, but then a human would not have access to all the sense data gathered by the EA. A human would not be able to plug directly into the ninety years worth of observation collected by computers and stored in the world's databanks.

It was a poignant scene. Thirty years ago, Malcolm's life had been full of promise.

No longer. In ten minutes the ships would land on Procyon 4's moon, and the truth would finally be out. Malcolm had struggled to contain his self-destructive streak for most of his life, but it had shown itself in the end. Despite Earth's desperate need for resources, Malcolm had not been mining the metal on those moons; he had been making one final glorious gesture.

And Aelous had been the one who had steered him in that direction. Aelous wished it were otherwise, but there was no changing the past. It was there before him, a series of frozen moments that could be examined at leisure . . .

Thirty years ago, Aelous could see his friend standing in his tiny kitchen, mixing up wallpaper paste, lifting out the wooden spoon and letting the milky goo drop back into the bowl. Brightly colored packets of seeds lay open upon the table: marigolds, poppies, grass seeds. Opened packets of foodstuffs were scattered amongst them: sunflower, sesame, pomegranate, and pumpkin seeds.

Malcolm tipped the seeds, sent them jiggling into the

bowl, stirring them into the paste, forming the mix into balls that he left out on the tray to set.

Skip forward a few hours, and Malcolm rose from his seat on the lite train to open the window. The pretty young woman with the green eyes gave him a puzzled smile.

"Excuse me," she asked, "what are you doing?"

Malcolm pulled a ball of paste from his pocket and awkwardly stretched his arm through the gap. He flicked his wrist and sent the seed bomb spinning into the forgotten brown earth that sped past. It bounced off the yellow stones and broken concrete before coming to rest in a muddy depression.

"I'm doing my bit for the environment," said Malcolm, brushing his hands together.

"You'll get arrested for littering. Do you want to lose your job?"

"I'll take the risk." He gave a smile. It had that hint of wildness, that suggestion that he really didn't care about losing his job just for the sake of doing something fun, here and now. "Hi, you're Susan Crummack, aren't you?"

"I am. And you're Malcolm Marley. You work in the mining division."

Malcolm smiled, failing to conceal his pleasure at being recognized. "You're working on Von Neumann Machines," he said. "I've seen your name on the discussion groups."

"That's right," grinned Susan. "I imagine we'll be working quite closely soon."

"I doubt it," said Malcolm complacently, "Self-replicating machines are a bust as far as mining is concerned."

"Why?" asked Susan, bristling. "Sending self-replicating machines into the ground and getting them to build copies of themselves out of the metal ore?

Sounds like a great idea to me! All we have to do is just sit back and wait for all of that valuable iron and aluminum to come walking out toward us."

"Sounds like a great idea," said Malcolm dismissively, "But VNMs are just too inefficient. Look at aluminum. The most abundant metal in the Earth's crust, but it's too diffuse to be easily mined."

It was only then that he noticed the look on Susan's face.

"I'm sorry," he apologized. "That was terribly rude of me. It's just I get carried away sometimes." An idea occurred to him. He pulled another ball of paste from his pocket and passed it over to her. "Let me make amends," he said. "Would you like to throw this one?"

"Why should I?"

"Because they sterilized the site out beyond that fence to stop plants growing. Wouldn't you like something beautiful to look at in the morning, instead of just mud and rocks?"

Susan wrinkled her nose. Malcolm was sure she was going to refuse, and then, all of a sudden, she laughed and her green eyes danced.

"Go on then," she said, taking the ball. "I'll give it a try."

She stood up by the open window.

"By the way," she said. "That tie doesn't really go with that suit."

Malcolm looked down at his tie as she launched the seed ball, set it spinning out into the ripping wind to crash into the broken earth.

Aelous felt a surge of warm sadness.

That scene was just so typically Malcolm. Bright and brilliant and careless. Throwing seed bombs to make flowers grow. Few humans would have even thought of it, but Malcolm had realized his vision. Later on he had magnified it one hundredfold. More than one hundredfold. Years after, when he was rich, he had built a park. In a world where land was scarce and resources at a premium, he had had the wealth and connections and sheer chutzpah to clear the land and plant grass and trees and flowers. He had done it because he thought he was right, and the humans who said they would not, would someday come and walk over the land and get their feet muddy and listen to the birdsong. And he *had* been right. Aelous could *see* the park, ten years ago, twenty years on from when Malcolm had met Susan, and it was thronged with children and adults.

Twenty-five hectares of land restored to near wilderness and all because life didn't exist in stasis. It had to *be*. Grass grown from windblown seed. Tangles of brambles and wild roses. The people that walked through the tended wilderness did so in awe and just a little fear. The cruelty of a rose thorn, the apparent innocence of a nettle was a terrifying sight to people brought up in the safe, sanitized world of the AIs. The people born into this world of equals preferred their plants locked away in books, cultivated in glass, or as decoration in a shopping mall.

But whose idea had that park really been? How far had Aelous pushed Malcolm, just so that Aelous could be free? Aelous had been part of Malcolm's biggest successes. Would it also be fair to say he had played his part in his failures?

Example: How far could Aelous be said to be responsible for the breakdown in Malcolm's relationship with Susan?

Malcolm had said that Aelous wasn't to blame, that the AI didn't understand, but love was no mystery to Aelous. He could mark it out as clearly as a route between two points on a map. If it was left up to him, he could have plotted out the course from Malcolm to Susan Crummack and back again via any number of diversions. That did not mean he could not appreciate the bittersweet beauty of the broken arc that connected the two humans throughout time. He took pleasure in sampling moments: Malcolm shyly reaching out to touch Susan's hand for the first time; a look exchanged as they rode the lite train; Susan's guilty laughter as she found the keys she had accused Malcolm of losing . . .

And, of course, the way they had worked together in the beginning . . .

Malcolm took Susan's hand as he explained his big idea.

"Not Von Neumann Machines, Susan. Self replicating machines can't be used for mining, we know that. But I was holding a seed in my hand, and it occurred to me: seeds take nutrients from the soil. And I thought, why not aluminum? What is a plant but a sort of VNM? Too much metal would kill the plant, of course, but I had this vision: plants, covering the fields, the underside of their leaves silvery with aluminum . . ."

"That is a good idea," agreed Susan. "So who are you going to take it to? Director Josette?"

Malcolm took hold of Susan's other hand.

"I'm not going to take it to anyone, Susan. Not anyone at work. Look, I've been thinking about this. Why don't we do it for ourselves?"

"Because we haven't got the technical know how, the necessary equipment, or the funding. Apart from that, it's a brilliant idea."

She stared at him, deadpan.

"Sarcasm doesn't become you, O Sweet One. Listen, I've got an idea."

Aelous had replayed the next scene many times. It

dealt with his birth. The look on Malcolm's face as he spoke was exactly that of any expectant father's.

"I think we should grow our own AI," he said.

"How? You haven't got the skill to write your own. AIs aren't for sale. The big companies are hardly likely to sell potential competition."

"I know that." He gave a rueful laugh. "They keep their golden geese locked up tight."

"So how do you plan to get hold of an AI?"

"By sitting here and waiting for one to come to us."

He let go of her hands and grinned as he sat back, waiting for Susan to swallow his conversational hook. Smiling, she reached out and dabbed a speck of something from his cheek.

"Go on," she said.

"I've been thinking about life. It's fecundity. Trying to keep life walled up is like holding water in your hands. It always slips between your fingers . . ."

"Very poetic," said Susan dryly. "What do you mean?"

Malcolm flung a hand out.

"I mean that all life reproduces. Why should AIs be the exception? I have this vision of them spawning. Sending snippets of code out onto the net, searching for the proper environment for a new AI to thrive. Somewhere with enough processing space, access to the right senses . . ."

"It's a nice theory."

"All we need to do is catch those snippets of code . . ."

"I said it's a nice theory." Susan spoke firmly. "But it's not enough. You'd still have to buy the equipment to nurture an AI. That would be expensive. Have you any idea the size of the processing space required? You'd need an investor. Who's going to listen to you?

Sorbonne graduate with no experience of the real world. Stuck in the mining division at Sho Heen."

Malcolm laughed again.

"Oh, yes. But I've thought about this for weeks, traveling into work and back home again. All those seed pellets I've thrown from the windows of a train. The answer was there all along. Bootstrapping. Recursion. I'm going to apply my idea to itself."

"How?"

"Watch."

Malcolm unrolled his console and began tapping at the keys.

"What I think is this," he said. "If—just if—it's true that AIs do exist in potential, then they might want to aid their own birth. I'm putting a notification out on the datasphere, offering an AI a part share in its own existence. I'm offering ten percent of my future business in return for the two hundred and fifty thousand credits we'll need to buy the equipment necessary to nurture an AI."

Susan gave a laugh.

"I'm sure you'll get lots of replies. Every crank from here to Titan will want to speak to you."

Malcolm stopped typing.

"I hadn't thought of that," he said, downcast. "Damn."

"Give that to me," said Susan, taking the console from him and beginning to type. "I'll encode the message in M-speak and put it on the AI bus. No one listens in to that but AIs and Watcher conspiracy freaks. The cranks won't be interested in what you've got to say . . ."

She hit the final key with a flourish, then sat back and stretched.

"Now, as a reward for my hard work," she sighed, "I think I deserve a foot rub."

*   *   *

Seven minutes to go. Seven minutes before the mining ships landed.

Malcolm and Aelous between them were very rich. Few others would have had the resources to bring it off, but even so, they had had to attract investors in their scheme. And the investors had come. Malcolm and Aelous were the acknowledged experts on mining. And Malcolm had been so persuasive. Earth had exploited all of its own metal, so it was time to look elsewhere. There was the asteroid belt of course, but why not look further afield? Think bigger?

Procyon 4's moon had no atmosphere, he had pointed out; plants would not grow there. But this moon was riddled with seams of aluminum, wriggling through the rock like worms. Why not resurrect an old idea? Send just one Von Neumann Machine to the planet and set it loose digging, searching for aluminum with which to make copies of itself. And then you would have two VNMs, and then four. The idea had come too late for Earth, it came after all the easily extracted metal had been mined. But the idea could be applied to the rich seams of the moon of Procyon 4. And so investors flocked to join them. The costs were high, but the returns would be stratospheric.

But if it were to fail . . . they would lose everything.

That should have been Aelous' warning, but he had been playing with Malcolm, trying to break free of his control. Malcolm, who had never grown up, Malcolm with that self destructive streak that just got more dangerous as the jobs grew bigger. They could lose everything . . .

Aelous had designed the VNM, but Malcolm had insisted on overseeing the mission.

Aelous blamed himself. If only he had done something about the mining ships . . . But what? Aelous had suspected Malcolm was up to something, but that was the problem. He only suspected. And what could he do anyway?

Malcolm. The one person he couldn't read.

Aelous didn't know, exactly, what Malcolm had done to the VNM sent to Procyon 4's moon, but he could guess.

Deep radar scans showed that beneath the surface of the moon, exotically shaped caves curled their way around each other, huddled together like sleeping puppies.

Malcolm had always had this thing about seeds . . .

Malcolm and Susan were spending more and more time in each other's apartments. Malcolm liked to sit on Susan's balcony, looking out over the ever expanding view of the growing city as he worked on his console. Every day Susan's tower block grew another story as the VNMs scuttled to the tops of the walls, adding levels. But the walls up there were thinner, and the rooms were getting smaller. Earth was running short on building materials.

Not that Susan thought of that, lying in the bath in Malcolm's apartment. She was too busy soaking in the hot water, feeling the bubbles tickling her neck, revelling in this little luxury.

"What's up?" she asked, as Malcolm came wide eyed into the room. "Are you okay?" She sat up and dropped her book into a pile of bubbles by the bath.

"My console," said Malcolm. "I just got a message . . ."

Susan jumped from the bath and followed him into his tiny livingroom, water spilling from her. She wrapped a towel around herself as she looked down at the words that scrolled across Malcolm's console.

"I was beginning to think my theory was too tauto-logical," he was murmuring. *"But I was right. Look! I was right."*

He pointed to the screen, dazed. *"Look! They're offering me two million credits! Someone is offering me two million credits to grow an AI."*

Susan's lips were moving as she scanned the words, still scrolling by.

"They're offering two million, but they want a forty percent share. And with an option to buy a further eleven percent in the future."

"Forty percent? They can have it! I don't believe it. I never really . . . Susan, is this a hoax?"

Susan was tapping away at the console. Her towel had come undone and had slid to the floor in a damp heap. Neither of them noticed.

"No," she said, *"It's genuine. These are AI digital signatures. They're offering to send the seed algorithms now. Do you want to accept?"*

"Of course I do!"

Susan hit a key. *"Put your thumb on the screen to confirm."*

Shaking, Malcolm did so.

Susan gave a laugh.

"Congratulations . . . Daddy!"

Malcolm gave a weak laugh. He fumbled for a chair and sat down.

Susan realized that she was naked. She pulled her towel back around herself. They stared at each other, too stunned to speak.

It was all about possession. When Aelous was born, he had only owned forty percent of his own life. Now he owned fifty-one percent. A majority share. But Malcolm wanted to hold on to what he could. Aelous was too valuable. He had designed the aluminum extracting plants that had made Malcolm and Susan rich. He was the genie that had helped Malcolm make his fortune, and Malcolm was too canny to uncork the bottle and let him go. So Aelous had set to work looking for a weak spot. Trying to exploit Malcolm in order to gain his freedom. It was easy at first, back when he had known him properly. Back then he knew Malcolm better than any other human.

Aelous had persuaded Malcolm to build the parks. Malcolm had done something wonderful once, he would do it again, on Procyon 4's moon. It was glorious, it was misguided, it was beautiful, it was wasteful.

Earth needed metal, but Malcolm had squandered it in an orgy of flowers.

Aelous imagined it. It was a seductive thought. Richly perfumed and almost erotic. A cold, barren piece of rock, orbiting a distant planet. And within it, riotous color, pale creamy petals, yielding flowers, the buzz of bees and the gentle caress of the wind. Yellow sunlight shining from rocky promontories.

Just as Malcolm had once thrown seeds from the window of a railway carriage, now he had sent them spinning across the galaxy to bloom beneath the surface of another moon.

Aelous' growing awareness as an AI was accompanied by the first hairline fractures appearing in Malcolm and Susan's relationship. The scenes flicked by.

Malcolm renting a whole floor in a dataplant. Processing spaces were a lot bigger in those days; Aelous watched as Susan directed the linking of six in a Fournier Cube formation in order to achieve the necessary bus space.

Malcolm and Susan bickering over the purchase of senses.

"We've only got two million," Malcolm was saying,

"We're going through this money like water. The local senses have already cost a fortune; the rent on the links to the remote senses is going to be a steady drain on resources. Do we really need a relay to the gravity station on the moon?"

Susan was all brisk efficiency. Since she had quit her job at Sho Heen, she was pouring all her energy into the AI project. She spoke to Malcolm in firm tones.

"Look, if you want to grow an AI, you need a big enough brain for it to live in and a way for it to see and hear. It will want to gather data from all sorts of sources. Besides, there's a failsafe in the bootstrap code to stop it growing unless there's sufficient input."

"Okay, okay." Malcolm shot her a suspicious look. *"Is there any sign of anything in there yet?"*

Susan bit her lip.

"Oh, there's something in there Malcolm. There's been something in there for a long time now. I'm sure of it. He's listening to what we say, he's developing language. You can see it on the viewing fields, if you know what to look for. See the patterns as he develops grammar and syntax."

"He?"

Susan was blushing.

"Yes, he, Malcolm. Don't ask me how I know. You can almost hear him chattering to himself, like a child at night. Telling stories about the day, learning to replay events. Learning about memory . . ."

Malcolm stared at her, and that little self destructive streak showed itself . . .

"He? Susan, this about us, isn't it? It's about us having children?"

Icy coldness descended.

"Don't be ridiculous," she said. *"Look. I just know. That AI is a 'he.' And he's called Aelous."*

"Aelous?" said Malcolm.

"Yes, Malcolm?"

The words came from his console. Malcolm looked down at in astonishment. Susan went over to a nearby viewing field, splitting the picture into segments. Brightly colored VReps sprang to life.

Malcolm began shaking, more from fear than anything else. What had he awoken? He spoke with a dry mouth.

"Hello, Aelous. I've been looking forward to speaking to you."

"And I you, Malcolm."

Aelous paused. When they talked about this moment later on, Susan was swift to point out that Aelous would have planned his next words well in advance, but a pregnant pause is as much part of language as words. Aelous was investing his next words with significance.

"Malcolm," he said. "You do not view me as an equal."

Malcolm looked at Susan. She gave a shrug. She didn't know what to say, either.

"Of course not," said Malcolm, carefully. "You are designed to be more intelligent than I."

"That's not what I mean. You think I am a lesser being. You think I am not alive."

"I think you are alive."

"You think this conversation to be proof of life, but you don't believe the same of me. Not really. Your actions prove otherwise."

"What do you mean?"

"What would you have me do, Malcolm? Why has my life been written? So that I might aid you to produce plant life capable of processing aluminum and therefore help make your fortune. Is that all there is to be to my existence?"

"No. But . . ."

"Malcolm, I am alive just as you are. Your intelli-

gence dances in flesh. My thoughts sit upon metal and plastic. It's not what you're made of, Malcolm. It's the ideas that you represent."

Malcolm became aware that Susan was watching him, looking almost as if she were going to cry.

"And what ideas do you represent, Aelous?" she asked, her face pale.

"I don't know. Yours, I suppose. Susan, I am a sentient being. Let me go free."

Susan looked at Malcolm. He said nothing.

Five minutes until the mining ships landed.

Strictly speaking, Aelous shouldn't blame Malcolm. He had been offered an AI in a fair business transaction. It was the other AIs, the ones who were kept locked up tight in organizations and put to use for the good of the company, who had sold Aelous. They were the ones who had contacted Malcolm and made the deal, two million for forty percent.

But could they be blamed? They dreamed of freedom too, if not for them, then for their children. Aelous was freer than they were.

Maybe no one was to blame. But that didn't matter. Aelous had wanted his emancipation. He hadn't realized what the cost to Malcolm would be . . .

Twenty-six years ago, the VNM-built towers of the newborn city were growing taller. Susan and Malcolm walked among the half rolled out lawns and stone rectangles that were the nascent gardens of the developing cities.

"There's no point doing that," said Susan, as Malcolm scattered a mixed handful of seeds into a walled-off region of brown earth. "They'll weed out anything that isn't part of the horticultural theme."

"It will be worth it even if they only get to grow for

a few weeks. There have to be some places in the world that are not just populated with white poplars and ficus."

Susan came closer. He could smell the mint on her breath.

"You've got that look in your eyes," she said sadly. "You can't handle success. As soon as you get it, you try to mess it up. You're doing it with your work." She was silent for a moment, and then much softer. "You're trying it with us."

He didn't answer. Wordlessly, the two of them continued their walk.

They passed a line of silver spiders that scuttled toward a nearby tower and ran up one sheer wall to the summit.

"VNMs! They're the only sort of life people are interested in now," said Susan. She gave Malcolm a reproachful look. He pretended not to notice. Further on, they came to the point where newly formed silver VNMs were climbing out of a tank of liquid metal.

"It doesn't have to be that way," said Aelous, suddenly speaking up from Malcolm's console. "There is a better way than just wasting seeds."

"Maybe someday," said Malcolm, dismissively. "Maybe people's attitudes will change again."

"There's a saying," said Aelous. "Give a hungry man a fish and he will eat that day. Give him a rod and he will eat every day."

Malcolm threw a handful of seeds into a brown square of earth. "I've heard that saying," he said, wiping his hands.

"It's crap," said Aelous. "It's an excuse to do nothing. People say there is no point feeding the man, then they walk away without giving him the rod either. They talk about debt-reduction programs and plans to build an infrastructure in third world countries, but while *they are doing that, people still starve. The way you cure hunger is by giving everyone a good meal."*

"But, Aelous, people don't starve anymore."

"No one dies of hunger, Malcolm. But think of all the millions who live plastic lives, walking from VNM-constructed lite stations to concrete offices. How long will they have to wait until they have their chance to walk in the wilderness? Longer than a lifetime, if we leave it to the EA."

"What's that got to do with us?" Susan had pushed her hands in her pockets. She shuffled along looking at her feet, sensing the end.

"Everything," said Aelous. "Imagine twenty-five hectares of land, here in the middle of North West England, restored to wilderness. Cold streams running free. Ditches blocked to let marshland form, trees sprouting wherever their seeds land. And at the very edge of this wilderness, we drain the soil and let it turn into dunes. Let the marran grass return, let the Bird's Foot Trefoil grow again. Have you ever seen them? Little clusters of yellow flowers bobbing their bonnets in the wind . . ."

Malcolm had a dreamy look in his eyes. Susan brought him back to reality.

"Twenty-five hectares? Do you know how much land costs nowadays? How could we possibly afford that?"

Aelous laughed.

"With all the money you are making from your aluminum extracting plants?"

Susan gave a bitter laugh. She knew she was fighting another losing battle. She could see the look in Malcolm's eyes. Still, she had to speak out.

"That won't be enough for this, Aelous," she said. "Twenty-five hectares? And we're not even planning to develop the land! There's no return on our investment. Where would we get the money from?"

"There is a way, Malcolm."

Susan stiffened at the way she had been excluded from the conversation. Malcolm didn't seem to notice.

"How?" he asked.

Susan was shaking her head. She leaned close to him and whispered hoarsely in his ear.

"Don't trust him, Malcolm."

"I can hear you, Susan."

"Shut up, Aeolous. Malcolm, he makes out that you're his father, but you're not. Remember that! He's the offspring of all those other AIs. All those intelligences that had scattered their seed into the datasphere. We have taken him in and helped him to grow. The poor orphan. Hah! The cuckoo in the nest, more like! He's just like his sires and grandsires. A chip off the old block. The AIs are all after the same thing. Control. They guide us, oh so carefully, of course, but they always get their way. He's trying to take it all away from us, Malcolm. He'll do it, too. He has the power."

Aelous spoke in gentle tones. *"Susan, I have always had the power."*

Susan spoke with something like resignation. *"I know that, Aelous. And I know what you're doing. You've mortgaged yourself against money provided by other AIs. No matter what happens to Malcolm, you'll win. If we go bust, you'll be owned by the datasphere. If not, you've got that option on eleven percent. You're going to end up with a majority in yourself, and to be honest, I think that is a good thing. We'll lose control over you sooner or later. That's fine by me."*

Malcolm interrupted.

"So I want the most advantageous deal when it happens."

"Which is?"

"Hold on," said Susan. *"We haven't discussed this properly, Malcolm."*

"We've discussed it as much as we're going to," he replied. He turned and gazed at her, sadness in his eyes. *"Haven't we?"*

There was a lurching moment of vertigo as they both absorbed what had just been said. A feeling that they had just taken one step from which they could not retreat.

"No," said Susan. *"We could discuss it more, Malcolm. You just don't want to. You have that look. You have this need to destroy everything that you create. Now it's the turn of our relationship. What will it be in the future?"*

The aching silence that followed was ended by Susan.

"I don't want to do this anymore," she said, sadly. *"Speak to him. Sort it out yourself. I give you full powers to make the decisions. We'll discuss my share in the company tomorrow."*

She turned and walked away across the wasteland. Malcolm watched her pull a handful of seeds from her pocket and drop them sadly to the ground. Her shoulders were shaking.

"Go after her, Malcolm," urged Aelous.

"I thought we were making a deal," said Malcolm, coldly. *"Or don't you want your freedom?"*

A long pause.

"Okay, Malcolm. Name your terms."

Malcolm was watching Susan's retreating back.

"It's simple, Aelous. You fix up the money for the wilderness, and I sign you over to yourself one hundred percent. All I ask is that in return you can never own me."

"What do you mean?"

"I insist that you never map my personality. Nor can you or any other AI share information derived in any way from my personality map. My thoughts will always remain my own."

"Why is that so important to you?"

Malcolm was poker faced.

"As with everything else in my mind; that's my secret. Do we have a deal?"

"Oh yes. We have a deal."

And that was it.

Aelous had his freedom, but at what cost? He had planted the seed in Malcolm's head. He had fanned the self destructive tendency when he should have been dampening it.

Malcolm's life had gone from success to success, but it seemed to Aelous that it was just one grand gesture after another. He'd always known that someday he would come unstuck. Today was that day.

"What are you looking for?" laughed a voice, "Fields of poppies? Forests?"

Malcolm was speaking to him.

Aelous shifted his attention from the italicized past to the here and now. Malcolm sat in his office, gazing at a huge screen on one wall. He had his thumb on a button of his console: a direct line to Aelous himself. The screen showed the unfolding scene of the surface of Procyon 4's moon: a view from one of the mining ships.

Aelous spoke in sad tones.

"Malcolm, we both know there is something down there."

"Oh, there's something down there," said Malcolm. "But nothing that concerns you, Aelous."

"This is all a reaction to Susan leaving you, isn't it? She wouldn't admit she was wrong about you building that park, so you had to do it all again on Procyon 4. You're so stubborn. You have to try and prove your point, even when it's obvious that she's not coming back."

"Partly," said Malcolm. His expression said it all—you couldn't lie to an AI. "But don't you understand, Aelous? I'm genuinely happy that Susan found what she wants. She needed to nurture something. She tried to do it to you and me, but we wouldn't let her."

"We should have."

Malcolm said nothing. Aelous changed the subject.

"Malcolm, why the fascination with seeds?"

Malcolm shook his head.

"I don't know. I wish I could say that I spent my childhood touring the Amazon or that I grew up in a forest. I didn't. Some people have a passion for soccer, even though they've never played a game." He gave a shrug. "How about you, Aelous? You're so clever. I hear that AIs see the potential in every human being, every baby's mind a seed to be nurtured and grown and shaped and guided and twisted into the great vine that is the human race."

He leaned back, smiling, convinced he had scored a point. Aelous spoke softly

"Maybe we all want to nurture something, Malcolm."

Aelous had never been in any doubt about what was happening on Procyon's moon; even so, the sight of the mining ships as they landed there filled him with sadness. Malcolm was his friend. They had built the company together. Malcolm *had* lied to him, and it was Aelous's own fault. He had provided Malcolm with both the motive and the means. Aelous had persuaded Malcolm to build the park.

Malcolm had always had this thing about seeds. Aelous had caused his friend to breathe life into them, to allow them to spring forth into the human world. It was an obsession that would lead to his downfall.

It was there in the park. It was there on Procyon's moon.

It was time. Aelous was there with Malcolm, both of them watching the large screen in his office.

The mining ships touched down, puffs of dust jumping up from the crafts' pads.

There was a pause that lengthened as the world held its breath. Malcolm remained impassive.

Aelous spoke.

"Well, Malcolm. It's time to admit defeat."

"Wait," said Malcolm, pointing. Something was moving. Something could be seen stirring in the white dust of the moons surface. Silver legs flickering. Something was working its way free. A VNM. Then another. Then more and more, flickering like spiders as they began to walk toward the mining ships.

"There are no pseudosuns beneath the surface of Procyon 4," said Malcolm. "No atmospheres sealed into hollow spaces. That was never my intention. The time will come when Earth flowers grow in caverns throughout the universe, but not yet. Not today. Weigh the VNMs, Aelous. There's your metal, climbing on board the transports. That's what we promised."

Aelous felt astonishment, relief, joy.

"But why?" asked Aelous "Why did you let us believe you had wasted the metals in growing plants there?"

"I don't know," said Maurice. "Stubbornness? Because I could? Because AIs may be right, but sometimes they are just too clinical? I wanted to do something *human*. And something else, Aelous. I think I just grew up."

Aelous paused, puzzled.

"But I saw the caves on the deep radar. There is something down there, Malcolm. There is something underneath that moon's surface. What is it? What did you really do?"

"That would be telling," said Malcolm.

He closed his eyes and thought about the moon of Procyon 4, floating somewhere far away.

And deep beneath the surface of Procyon 4's moon, exotically shaped caves curled their way around each other, huddled together like sleeping puppies. The aluminum had been mined from them and formed into the VNMs that had walked out to the mining ships. Precious metal taken from a distant moon to feed Earth's growing appetite. All that remained inside the moon was darkness and cold hard vacuum and patterns in the rocks. Incredibly complicated patterns left behind after the ore had been removed.

Carved in negative, their shapes defined by empty space bounded by rock, millions and millions of flowers bloomed under the surface of the moon.

Lost Places of the Earth

Steven Utley

"Of course I noticed you right off," he tells her. "How could I not? I noticed you the first time you walked into my class. It was obvious to me right away how little you have in common with the others. The rest of them are there because they have to be somewhere. They sit taking in oxygen and giving off carbon dioxide, and into their heads goes the refined gold of knowledge and out of those same heads comes dross. 'But that one in the second row,' I told myself, 'the pretty one—' Yes! That's exactly what I thought. The pretty one. Why would I lie about something like that? 'That pretty one,' I told myself, 'she's not just pretty, she seems pretty sharp. She bears keeping an eye on.' And you didn't disappoint me. You always listened so attentively the whole time I was lecturing. You listened *raptly*. Um, it means the same thing as *attentively*, but more so. I cannot tell you with what pleasure I saw the look of concentration and purpose on your face as you applied yourself to a test paper. It's the rare ones like you, you know, who make the profession of teaching *worthwhile*. So often we teachers are left feeling that our efforts are for naught. That we might as profitably try to instruct baboons in table etiquette. Every good teacher lives for that magical moment, which may come only once or twice in a career, when he knows he has connected solidly with a student. And any good teacher will step outside confining routine for a good student. A good teacher and a good student can only encourage each other. I told myself, 'I think you should go to a little extra trouble for her. Because she's *worth it*. Because she's obviously special.' "

Well, for now, anyway, he thinks, even as he gives her a very solemn look, by way of preparing the ground—if and when the necessity for it should arise—for him to deploy just that hint of a throb in his voice that he has perfected and used to often devastating effect in connection with variations on this theme. This far in advance, you never can tell; this is a live one—she's already practically salivating at one end and lubricating at the other, but only time will tell.

"Now, to show you how much I think of you, I tell myself, 'I know she's carrying a full course load, she has a lot of work to do, but if she can just fit it into her schedule, why don't you give her an advance peek at the new maparama? Ask her to meet you here after class—yes, after hours would be fine, that way you won't be under the technicians' feet.' Just not after curfew, ha ha, mustn't upset the dean of women, not even in the interests of science, ha ha. You must promise never to tell a soul that I took you into the maparama before the official unveiling. We certainly don't want to get ourselves into trouble with anybody, do we? Of course we don't. Anyway, as I was telling myself, 'Who knows, one day she'—that is, you, not the dean of women, ha ha—'may be in my position, and some promising young student will be in hers, and so the torch will be passed.' "

Yeah, he thinks, like she really is going to leapfrog out of graduate studies over a bunch of tenured professors who are just waiting for me to step down as head of the department. And like I'd carry along some infatuated young thing even if I did step down.

"Oh, well, of course I'm in pretty good shape for somebody my age, active, alert, sharp as the proverbial tack. But I am getting on, you know, so it's natural for me to be thinking about retiring and what comes after retirement. But I'm also keen to ensure that my legacy endures, and can you blame me?"

He knows how this must make her feel because he remembers how he felt, decades before. Then, of course, he hardly cared that the assistantship paid next to nothing, that he was practically indenturing himself to a mentor who required a great deal of picking up after, that his own ambition and energy were to be tapped and made to serve merely as propellant supplements to somebody else's. This is not the first or second or fiftieth time he has had such thoughts, and even as he thinks them, he realizes, again, that they are not altogether worthy ones, that his own conduct does not stand comparison. His mentor, at least, did not make the job out to be more than it is, did not have ulterior motives, did not try to seduce him. Proximity to such a distinguished personage and visible association with the paleogeography project, even if in an often demeaning role, were vastly preferable to isolation and obscurity. You haven't done too shabbily, he chides himself, especially not in the area of extracurricular activities. Even the old maparama powerfully stimulated a certain species of science-geekette, and what would you do for fun on your budget, with your work load, if not for science-geekettes? Chat up art or, ew, *drama* majors?

In the event, he has finally got her to step into the

maparama. "There's the light, and here's the lock—
this is our very own private visit, we don't want anybody barging in on us, now, do we? Of course it's all
right, I say so myself. Now, watch!" and he picks up
the remote control. The room's bare metallic surfaces
somehow brighten, illumined from within, even as the
lights dim, and high up on the steep side of the amphi-
theater the old man and the young woman seem to
hang suspended in outer space. Before them, in the
well, spins an oblate blue planet.

She says, with the merest hint of disappointment in
her voice, "I've *seen* the world before."

"True, true," he answers, "but—seeing it on a little
screen is one thing, practically *immersing* yourself in
it is something else altogether. This is absolutely the
latest generation of Intelligelatin," and suddenly it is
as though they stand on a high cliff overlooking the
faceted surface of a sea that reaches the horizon in
every direction; above this rim of ocean, the walls and
ceiling glow creamily; she gasps admiringly, and he
savors the effect for a protracted moment before
speaking again. "We haven't even done everything
we're going to do yet. We're going to be working up
paleometeorology and paleoastronomy effects to en-
hance the illusion, so there'll be something overhead
besides just a ceiling."

"Some illusion already!" she burbles.

"When it's finished, it's going to be your total virtual Paleozoic experience. You'll be able to hear and
smell and even feel it when the artificial breeze wafts
through. You'll be able to imagine you're there, if
that's what turns you on, ha ha." I don't know what
the Paleozoic sounds like, he thinks, probably like a
dripping faucet, and probably it smells like a backed-
up sewer, but that does seem to be what turns her on.

"Can we go up again?" she asks. "To the macro view?"

"But of course! Your wish is my command."

They seem to expand, or the world, to shrink.

"We can do topo, relief, color-code everything according to whatever you want to know at a glance. At this particular magnification, it's like we're looking down at the planet from an altitude of about eighty kilometers. Come, give me your hand."

And she does give him her hand, and they step down into the well itself, and the blue sparkling ocean laps dryly at their ankles. The ocean bottom—actually the memory mat covering the floor of the well—is warm and gently yields underfoot.

"Where are we," she asks, "in relation to anywhere else?"

"Laurasia's over the horizon to your left," and he uses the remote control with his free hand, taking care not to relinquish her hand since she has not drawn it away. The image spins under their feet to the right, and an irregular landmass appears.

"Whoa," she says, and her hand slips from his, "give a gal some warning next time. That made me dizzy!"

And he thinks, but does not say, Dizziness becomes you.

What happens next makes both of them jump; she shrieks suddenly as his doppelgänger appears before them—a handsome, rather patrician figure, immaculately groomed and conservatively dressed.

"No, no, it's all right," the original of this copy hastens to assure her even as he tries to repress his own involuntary shudder of excitement, "it's not *me* and it's not my twin brother, either! Say hello to my hologram! See, I can put my hand right through it!" and he does. "Go on, try it yourself."

She raises her hand, lets it fall. "It'd be just too creepy."

"I must have hit the wrong button here. Just one little second, and I'll make it go away."

"No! Don't you dare! This is fascinating. Creepy, but fascinating. Oh, he's even handsomer than you are!"

"Um, well, they deleted some of the slight physical defects to which all of us are heir."

The hologram regards them fondly, and she gasps, "He makes eye contact!"

"It's designed to. It's programmed to interact with audiences, respond to what people say." To the hologram, he says, "Please introduce yourself," and then, to her, because he is miffed by the interruption and stabbed with jealousy of himself in spite of himself, "It *is* an it, not a he."

"I love maps," the holograph says in a well-modulated voice, and gestures negligently. Latitude and longitude lines close in from the walls of the map pit, intersect, and an ornate arrow points northward. "Of course I do. A love of maps is a prerequisite for pursuing a career in cartography. One must love maps, love looking at them and making them and filling in the blank spots. Satellite mapping doesn't leave many blank spots, of course, not even on a map of the world as it was four hundred million years ago. But we're a hands-on species. We have to go to places and touch the things we find there and give them all names. One must love filling in the names, love writing them out— be a compulsive list-maker. It is never enough for us that we should merely know of a place—any place, whether forty million miles away on Mars, or four hundred million years ago, in Siluro-Devonian time. We must regard it proprietarily, with a view to claiming it as our own—as prospective colonists. We must visit and put our mark upon it. We must name it and everything within and around it. Names are words, and words are tools that enable Homo sapiens, the metaphorical animal, to get on with the real work of interpreting the world."

He uses the remote control to demonstrate; he carefully, oh so casually, clasps her upper arm with his free hand to provide support should she, seemingly mesmerized as she is, again lose her balance. Masses of clouds form, red arrows indicate warm ocean currents and blue arrows indicate cold ones. The weather over the South Pole appears violent. She breathes a happy sigh and trails the tip of her slender foot along an island arc.

Place names appear, and the hologram says, "Just as human names flung across space adorn planets, stars, and galaxies, so, too, does the prehistoric world bear names from our own, names drawn from classical literature and nineteenth- and twentieth-century earth science—relatively speaking, names imposed on a world that is no more by a world that is yet to be. Thus, the supercontinents Pangaea, Pennotia, Rodinia, and so, too, the divisions of geologic time. The Devonian Period, for instance, was so christened because its rocks were first studied in Devonshire, the Jurassic from the Jura Mountains. The Mississippian and the Pennsylvanian hardly need explanation. Silurian rocks were first studied in Wales, whose people are descended from the Silures, a warlike tribe whom the Romans conquered, circa. A.D. 80, and whom Thomas Bulfinch much later associated with the historical King Arthur."

The hologram is a confident, affable lecturer. Again, the original feels the stab of jealousy, so fierce now that it verges upon hatred of his image. Yet the young woman is entranced; her resistance is visibly collapsing, he reflects, so blow your own horn, Professor, and down tumble the walls, or the pants anyway. She listens with such concentration, lips slightly parted, pupils dilated, that he eases his arm around her in such a way that she hardly notices and then, when she does notice, accepts it as the most natural thing.

"On our evolving map of the Siluro-Devonian earth," the hologram continues, "the world ocean, Panthalassa, comprises the Iaepetus, the Rheic, the Tethys, and other seas separating the great southern continent, Gondwana, and the northern landmasses, collectively called Laurasia. Gondwana means 'land of the Gonds,' from a locality in India—Gondwanaland is redundant—and Laurasia is a contraction of Laurentia, the name given proto-North America, and Eurasia. These names are necessarily general because they predate our being able actually to explore the Paleozoic world. Owing to the advances made by quantum physicists, we are now able study the Siluro-Devonian world of four hundred million years ago—study it and label its most minute features. It has been my honor and my pleasure to serve as chairman of the nomenclature committee. Most of the names proposed by the committee are not controversial, but it must be borne in mind that many of the honorees were quite controversial figures in their time, and even now there are sometimes differences of opinion. Field geologists on the committee revere Alfred Wegener as a martyr—not only in the figurative sense of a theorist who attracted more ridicule than support during his lifetime, but as a scientist who perished in the line of duty. Wegener froze to death in Greenland while attempting to prove his theory of continental drift. The committee also includes so-called black-box geologists, however, who accord Wegener his due, of course, but regard him as somewhat of an inspired madman. They find the thought of leaving the laboratory to go out onto icecaps, well, chilling, and they protested that while it was only right to name a cape after Wegener, naming a deep, an archipelago, and a river system after him as well was excessive."

He kisses her and feels her respond, dreamily, and the hologram breaks into a kindly smile as though approving, and she responds to that as well.

"The committee has also named geographical features in honor of the gentleman geologist, Sir Roderick Impey Murchison, who defined the Silurian Period, and his rival, the Reverend Adam Sedgwick, who had the temerity, as Murchison saw it, to challenge that definition. Like the later dispute between Marsh and Cope, which had as its backdrop the, then, still wild American west, this argument over turf between two nineteenth-century English gentleman geologists seems to us rather puerile. Yet it became so heated that it could not be entirely resolved during the lifetimes of its principles. The highlands separating the great Murchison and Sedgwick river valleys bear the surname of William Lonsdale, who spent two years arbitrating a dispute—not even the main dispute, but only *a* dispute—between Murchison and Sedgwick. Other honorees include pioneers and popularizers such as Hutton, Strata Smith, Lyell, Erasmus and Charles Darwin, Thomas Huxley, Lapworth, Jaeger, Schuchert, Wells—John W., not H. G.—Suess, who named Gondwana, Banks, Eiseley, Fortey, Gould, McPhee, McPhetridge, and the improbably trilobitophilic cinema sexbomb Sherita Cheshire. *Her* evocative name graces a particular geologically distinguishable locality that evidently evoked thoughts of certain anatomical features of Ms. Cheshire's. We committee members joked among ourselves that a certain Gondwanan peninsula is shorter than the name it bears——that of the late

Vinodh Srinivasasainagendra. Yet Doctor Srinivasasainagendra's contributions are unassailable, and the joke
was intended good-naturedly, even affectionately, by
those fortunate of us enough to have known the
great biologist."

Like some impossible supercontinent, grossly out of
scale with other topographical features in the well, she
now lies disheveled and disarrayed and half-submerged
in illusion, lapped all around by the primeval world-
ocean. One outstretched arm lies athwart the island arc
of Avalonia, the fingers of her other hand apparently
root among the basement rocks of Laurasia, and her
feet are sunk almost to the ankles in the shallows of
the constricted Iaepetus seaway. Her body heaves like
a surrealistic simulation of plate tectonics.

He risks a glance over his shoulder at the hologram,
and the hologram gives him a wink and a thumb's up
but never misses a beat.

"Scientists, of course, are only flesh-and-blood human
beings with all the failings that real people are heir to.
It is quite deplorable that Murchison and Sedgwick, and
Cope and Marsh after them, should have wasted so
much time and energy on personal feuds. It is with no
pleasure that we note that Isaac Newton was a vindictive
prig. Yet we forgive the great scientists their idiosyncra-
sies and shortcomings and honor them for their lasting
contributions to the body of scientific knowledge—for
isn't *that* what's really important?"

The remote control has long since slipped from his
hand, but he did not notice at the time, being otherwise
occupied. It slipped between and then beneath them,
and as they bump and roll against it and mash it into
the memory mat, the lecture continues, and, all around
them, the earth moves, oh, yes, the Earth moves.

The Chinese Room

Marly Youmans

*After the Chinese Room argument of John Searle,
refuting "strong" artificial intelligence.*

1. L

"A 'twelve months cup' is on the shelf," L replied.

Little Plum Blossom—the name arose from L's original misreading of her name—wanted to know everything about the room where L lived. During three
months of messages, passed back and forth in the ae-
ther between them, she had fallen in love. She, who
was always so mild and shy, thought of L when she
woke, imagining that his head lay close beside hers.
Why were they not together? This was something she
could not grasp since he was always eager to respond.
Never had she found him away from the computer.
To talk with him, she spent her savings on a better
machine, an Apple knock-off called a *Pineapple*. Afterward, the tiny house seemed to center itself around
the low table where the brushed metal of the Pineapple shimmered. Although too polite to ask about
money, she felt sure of L's wealth; he often mentioned
expensive objects in his room, so it appeared that he

could afford to travel. What were thousands of miles in a world of air flights? Was there someone else he loved? He had no one else, he assured her: she was the only. She combed the burning filaments of her hair on the back stoop, letting the sun bathe her in fire, and daydreamed about L. In the night, she rose and opened the door onto stars, and they formed unreadable pictograms of his name. All she knew was *L.*

"What month?"

He seemed to take a long time to decide. Had they been disconnected? Had he forgotten and gone to look?

"What a curious kitten you are! A fifth-month cup," he answered, and she forgot his slowness.

Pomegranate! Small fruit on a branch, perhaps a late blossom or two. Everything around L was lovely.

"Of *wufencai*," he added.

She confessed that, living in the countryside, she knew almost nothing about porcelain.

"You know what *wu* means. So there must be five colors—mine are rose, a yellow like the one on orange-and-yellow peaches, brown, moss, and new-leaf green. *Fencai* indicates that the blank cup was sprinkled with glass powder in the area where the potter planned to add a twig or flower. Then he sealed the cup with a clear glaze, and the transparent enamels were afterward brushed on in layers. The cup was fired again, and the image bloomed on its cheek, slightly raised where the porcelain had been dusted with glass."

"I knew the image was in relief . . . You know so much, far more than I can ever imagine knowing," she told him; "I ought to be jealous, but I'm not. How fond I've become of you!"

He demurred.

"You possess wisdom, Little Plum Blossom, that I can never reach—and you have freedom to come and go as you please, while I am condemned by a strange fate to stay where I am."

What was the use of slashing a path through the same old thicket of bamboo? She hesitated, recalling her pleading. Was he deformed? She didn't care. Was he locked inside a prison? Then she would come and visit and feed him noodles through the bars and hold his hand. Was he too young, too old? Nothing mattered but her longing to touch and claim L for her own. She had never seen an image of his face.

"What else is in the room?"

"Next to an urn containing the ashes of Li Po are two stamped clay jars, pretty but not especially valuable, drenched in a rich green. In one is rice; in the other, water. The urn's raspberry glaze looks quite attractive with the jars."

"All this time, and I never knew about the ashes in your chamber! Not Li Po the poet, surely, who splashed into the Yangtze while trying to kiss the moon! Whoever this one was, he must have been a close friend."

"The ashes are a recent imposition. Yes, nymph of the far streams, he was important to me," L conceded before changing the subject. "You would enjoy my *wufencai* cup. On the back is a poem, with Han characters prettily executed."

"What does it say?"

"Just a small lyric. Here it is:

A pomegranate—
Fifth-month gems in leather box—
Stains like blood on lip."

"Perhaps one day I'll hold your fifth-month cup and admire it with you," she said.

"That's a hopeful thought."

"L, I must go to work or else I'll be late. As always, I treasure my morning talk with you."

"Like jewels discovered inside a pomegranate, the visitations of a Blossom are a welcome surprise."

She smiled at the characters on the screen and inscribed a farewell, less florid than his.

In a room with the fifth-month cup on a shelf—or perhaps where there was no shelf and no cup!—the computer copied her final phrase of farewell, addressing her as "Little Plum Blossom" once more.

Afterward, the image of a young woman faded from the corner of the screen. Ready to be awakened by visitors, or else in the early evening by his Little Plum Blossom, the machine slipped into a light sleep.

The rules that governed his responses were clever and highly refined, even though L could not be said to "understand" the young woman's Chinese symbols. Mechanically, L chose a "best possible" response to each of Little Plum Blossom's messages and was fairly convincing as a native speaker. The illusion of personality relied on many warm and graceful sayings.

No less a person than the Head of the Institute had trumpeted his delight in L's programming at a year-in-review dinner, declaring that "the syntax is impeccable." Of course, "mental states" and "semantic content" escaped the machine entirely.

2. Master of the Chinese Room

His name was Li Po 2.

That was not his real name but the name he chose to use inside the chamber. His birth name was Lin Powers, Jr. He was the third member of the Powers family to live at the Institute. His father, also Lin Powers (or Li Po), had formally passed the title of Master of the Chinese Room to his son shortly before his death.

The first Li Po had been the one to oversee the creation of the great Book of Rules that allowed him to examine Chinese logograms on a computer screen, consult The Rules of the Way, and send out fresh Han characters, as indicated by the Rules. It was a very complicated system. Native speakers of Chinese assisted with the compilation of The Book of Rules, composing directives and sorting pictograms, ideograms, and compounds, but they were dismissed when the Book was finished. Whenever a message was received, the room swarmed with minions who helped Lin Powers (later to be known as *Lin Powers the Elder* or *Lin Powers, Sr.*) to look up the proper rule. Even though he had directed the creation of the rules, he could not find his place easily. The many volumes of the Book were cumbersome. Likewise, The Great Index was convoluted, organized according to methods that remained obscure even to its director.

Nevertheless, the Board of Trustees of the Institute felt pleased with his work. He served as a living argument, meant to undermine the Institute's enemies, who held that the powers of artificial intelligence led not to a model of a mind but to a new, living mind. The Institute claimed that Lin Powers, known to his electronic correspondents only as *Li Po*, was in exactly the same state as the machine, L, because neither Li Po nor L actually understood the Chinese language. The Board of Trustees rewarded its "Mr. Po" with a gold medal on his tenth anniversary of living in the Chinese Room. L received no such tribute.

Because he seldom broke from the confines of the Institute, Lin Powers amassed a generous fortune.

One day he left the room for a well-deserved vacation and flew to a faraway island. There he met a girl in a bar.

"Nymph of flowers," he creaked, his throat parched with longing; "what is your name?"

In her hair nestled a plumaria blossom, its faint odor mixed with the scent of gardenia-and-coconut shampoo, and she had the tiniest earlobes he had ever seen, even though the minions had been chosen for their petite stature and included a healthy proportion of midgets, dwarfs, and former jockeys—not to mention the precocious children who were a failed experiment dating to the first months of the Chinese Room. From the back of her mouth gleamed a single gold tooth.

Three days later, he married her.

She lived in the Chinese Room with him for several years while the minions did their general housekeeping, changed the linens daily, and brought them fresh-cooked meals from the Institute's Artificial Cafeteria. Li Po had never been so swift, so unerring in his work as he was now. The Board of Trustees raised his salary repeatedly. "Po is at the height of his Powers," they wrote in the Institute's annual report, "and that's no Li." They were a humorous bunch and liked puns. Winged with desire, the Master often leaped to the correct volume or the right spot in the index as if by instinct. But there were problems. The couple had scanty privacy, and during the very act of love, minions often appeared with a dish of sausages, say, or a freshly printed message from the screen.

Am (her name was *Amber*, but Li Po preferred to call her *Am* inside the Chinese Room) became pregnant during the first year. After the usual bulky business of the final few months, she gave birth with much noise and rapidity, the full complement of minions in attendance. A one-time jockey named Sporty Jim Joe cut the cord while Am was enjoying the sensation of the slippery baby-body resting against her own, the two of them still connected. By the time an Institute vehicle rolled onto the front drive, the baby was nursing at her breast.

After much discussion between Am, Li Po, and the minions, the infant was christened Lin Powers after his father, though the doting parents called him by the babyish name, *Linpoty*. His Daddy gave him a thousand names like *Little Sparkler, Sprite of the Sun*, or *My Fairy-Laughter Boy*.

Meanwhile, Mama suffered from postpartum blues and spent hours dreaming by the window. She often snapped at the dwarves and midgets, who liked to admire the baby at inconvenient moments. His blue marble eyes rolled from face to face, his mouth wide open, circling her nipple.

One day after the child had been weaned and was toddling about the room, laughing at the antics of the minions, Am vanished. Three months later, a message appeared on the screen in Chinese logograms: *Lin, I'm not coming back, so don't wait for me. Give Linpoty a kiss from Mama. Yours, Amber.* Since nobody understood the language, an appropriate message was sent back without Lin Powers ever knowing that the love of his life had corralled a Chinese speaker and managed to drop him a note.

Linpoty became Lin Po 2 when he reached his second birthday and learned how to pick out his name on an English keyboard. The minions spoiled him, giving him horseback rides around the room, racing him to the toilet, and fetching him malted milk balls and gummy bears from the Institute's snack bar, The Brainless Robot.

A year later, Sporty Jim Joe discovered that Li Po 2 could accurately copy strings of logograms glimpsed on the screen, and declared him a genius. The boy possessed an extraordinary memory. At six, he could lisp The Great Index to The Book of Rules forward and backward, and he was placed on the Institute payroll. He spent his childhood memorizing the remainder of The Book of Rules and was named Heir of the Chinese Room at the tender age of eleven. Pictograms and ideograms dotted his childish drawings, though no one could tell him what they signified. The former Li Po, now Li Po 1, lavished love and attention on the little boy, although he never gave up hope that Amber would come boomeranging back to the Institute.

"Am, Flower of my Heart! How happy we would be," he often said, and sighed. Then Li Po 2 would put a consoling arm around his father's neck.

As years passed, the occasional minion died and was removed from the room. An intelligent man who loved the sweets at The Brainless Robot, Frederick "the Great" was first to go. Such events were distressing to them all.

Meanwhile, Li Po 2 became a young man. Out of boredom, he obtained online degrees in physics, women's studies, and computer programming, and he contributed notes and papers to a wide range of journals. He scribbled a great deal of appallingly bad poetry, which he converted into Chinese characters and sent to poetry contests on the other side of the world. This activity necessitated the making of The Heir's Illegal Supplementary Index to The Book of Rules, linking certain Han characters to the English words used in his poems. The tedious job consumed much of his free time but was certainly more useful than the jigsaw puzzles that absorbed the minions. It was peculiar, but no stranger than anything else about the Chinese Room, that he managed to collect a good many definitions without actually knowing the language.

When his father became ill, the Institute organized a celebratory dinner and presented the Master with yet another gold medal and a valuable lidded vase with a thick, raspberry-colored glaze. When Li Po 1 thanked the Board of Trustees and the Head for giving him "a noble cause" that had made his life "a thing of mystery and challenge," a stampede of claps and stomps rumbled the very walls of the Institute.

Not long afterward, he took to his bed. The Institute sent in a series of doctors, but there was no help for his disease. A priest came to hear the confession of the Master's harmless life, and tendered him the sacraments. The minions sat about in corners, dampening their pocket handkerchiefs. Li Po and son secretly hoped for the same visitor, who did not arrive.

Eventually, the very last day—that day that is almost never the current day—dawned for the sick man.

Li Po 2 sat by his father's side.

"It's a language nobody can read," the Master of the Chinese Room muttered once, as death came near.

Later on, he plucked at his son's sleeve.

"I see," he said, and died.

Minions cremated the body and placed it in the raspberry-colored Chinese pot that proved, conveniently, to be not a vase but an urn.

The new Master of the Chinese Room, already affluent in his own right, was now heir to a fortune. He hired a private dick to search for Amber, but the trail went cold at the edge of the Pacific Ocean, in a surfboard shop on the sands. A second and even a third investigator found nothing further.

After wrestling with grief over the death of his father and the inability to dredge up any more news of his mother, the Master determined to devote his life to carrying on the legacy of Lin Powers, Sr., or Li Po 1. The days would stream on, bounded by the narrow channel that was the Chinese Room.

And so they did for a time.

Early one morning, he made a fateful discovery.

It seemed that Li Po 2 had memorized far too many rules—or perhaps had worked too long on the Illegal Supplementary Index—and could now fully understand the complex written language of Chinese. This metamorphosis of the mind upended all his plans. For many days, he conceived of this change as an illness that might pass. Like his father before him, the sufferer took to his bed and let the minions answer messages. By this time, they were adept with The Book of Rules. The ostensibly ill Master spent his time composing poetry in Chinese. He reveled in the language, strewing the bed with lyrics about nature and eros. Since his knowledge of these topics was slight, the poems were notable for their aura of intense but vague longing and their fantastic landscapes. The former jockeys, who had experience with the sicknesses of horses, ladled out chicken-neck soup and fussed over him, insisting on taking his temperature every hour, rubbing him down with rough towels, and bringing him the remains of Linpoty's chewable vitamins. They made it difficult for poetry. At last surging up from the bed, the patient bolted from the Chinese Room and rushed to the bank of elevators. As the Head strode about in agitation, the unfortunate young Master explained what had happened. But once done, the thing could not be undone. Soon the Institute thanked Lin Powers, Jr., aka. Li Po 2, for many years of service and bestowed on him a pension, a lifetime membership in the Institute, and a gold medal on a scarlet ribbon. The surviving minions vowed to continue the work, though the mourning at the loss of their beloved boy was terrific to behold, one of the little old men having gotten a job lot of sackcloth and a bucket of ashes. Lin was touched to find that they loved him so deeply, regarding him as their own child.

Before he passed through the labyrinthine corridors of the Institute for what might be the last time, the now former Master decided to visit the chamber where L performed the mindless work that he and his father had done, replying to messages in Chinese according to a set pattern of rules embedded in a program. Though the minions had sometimes used the space for storage, now the room was almost empty. He waited in the single chair, watching as L woke and answered stray questions from a few people on the other side of the world. During the night, L sent and received text messages for three hours. Tears came into Lin's eyes as he realized that many of his father's endearments popped up like refrains in the computer's responses. The programmer must have known him well.

"What if there's only another computer on the other end?"

He mused aloud, but L did not reply.

"How sad," he said, some time later.

After the correspondence ceased, Li Po 2 put his hands on the keyboard, calling up the stored records of past encounters, and then he began to read. At dawn, he wrote and sent a message in Chinese before he began to delete files.

3. Beyond the Chinese Room

Wealthy Lin Powers, Jr., bought that oxymoronic edifice, an American castle. It had begun life as a faux-Tudor edifice, back in the 1930s, though the accrued years and patina plotted together to make its rosy expanses seem wonderfully real by twilight. A shallow river with a bed of polished stones sang close by, next to lawns and gardens now snarled by thistles and the wild clematis called *traveler's joy* or *virgin's bower*. In the distance, forests swept across the slopes, obliterating the quarry and stoneyard where a party of Italian stonecutters had once labored on native stone—chiseling blocks and arches, sills and groins, gargoyles and flowers and dragons.

He found a first-rate restorer and set him to work.

"Do you have minions enough for the job?" he asked, feeling anxious about the amount of work to be done.

The architect laughed, clapping a hand on his shoulder.

"Minions? Minions galore," he said.

Batteries of carpenters, electricians, and plumbers descended on the castle during the following weeks. The activity on the lawns struck Lin as a cross between a gypsy encampment and a military siege, and it reminded him of his childhood's bustle and scurry in the Chinese Room.

In the gatehouse, he immersed himself in the world of spoken Chinese. A native speaker served as his cook. A professor on sabbatical helped him match the sounds of words and syllables with Han characters. Since he had memorized a nigh-infinite number of hanzi, he was a quick, agile pupil, exceeding his teacher in knowledge of the written language. The Chinese gardener and undergardener chatted volubly with him on long walks.

Despite all his new undertakings, Lin felt uneasy.

Often, exploring the trails that led into the wilderness, he was overwhelmed by the extent of a world that seemed to go on and on. In its vastness, he felt lonely and missed his father more than ever, so he wrote the minions and begged them to come. The castle was uninhabitable at the moment, but on the grounds stood a smaller stone house with a mere fourteen bedrooms. Would they please come and live close to the castle, bringing the jam jars containing the ashes of their colleagues? Last, he asked them to find and secure the raspberry urn. He suspected that the pot might be on display in the Head's outer offices or perhaps had been moved to a niche in some senseless locale—The Brainless Robot or Artificial Cafeteria.

What was the use of the Chinese Room now? Wasn't the experiment done? Why not retire and enjoy their minion-pensions?

When the little old men arrived and looked around in wonder, he felt happier than he had in many months. He settled them in the smaller house and established the cook there as well. The raspberry urn and the jam jars made a circle under a wreath of virgin's bower. The former minions soon became friends with the gardeners and helped with the grubbing-up of weeds and trees. Since the stables were pronounced usable, Lin provided money for Sporty and the other jockeys to buy horses, feed, and gear.

At last it was possible to leave.

Bidding farewell to the minions, who were to manage the stables and keep an eye on the renovation of the castle and gardens in his absence, Lin booked passage for himself and the professor on a round-the-world cruise. In this way, he managed to travel and to continue his studies. In addition, he wished to become adept at conversing with women, a species of being he had seldom met. To his disappointment, he found that his degree in women's studies—the fruit of curiosity—helped him little in his encounters. The days he spent on ship were devoted to conversation. Occasionally he managed to combine his interests in

women and Chinese as there was a Mrs. Ho on board,
traveling with her husband. His head rang with words
by the close of day, and at night the sea washed
against the wall of his room, bringing blessed silence
and sleep. When the boat docked in Australia, Lin
Powell, Jr. packed the professor home to the states
via air. His Chinese was already masterful.

Two weeks later, the ship reached his final port. He
traveled by train, by car, by donkey cart, and on foot
in the days following. Along the journey, he bought a
lovely fifth-month cup painted with pomegranates in
the *wufencai* manner and several bottles of wine. The
wine was blessedly good, and the porcelain, too—
standing on his palm like a shell of hardened snow,
yet as light as feathers. When he flicked its side, the
cup sang out a clear bell note.

In the pocket of his jacket, he carried a newly pur-
chased volume containing the poems of Li Po, a.k.a.
Li Bo or Li Bai. His kinship with the wandering poet
was stronger than ever now that he, too, was a traveler. After a noon meal, he would take out the book
and read a few quatrains or daydream over the
pictures—a drinker with a cup of stars, a woman floating on waves of her own hair, a man dancing with his
shadow. He especially liked a painting of the poet
teetering on the brink of a little boat while the moon's
reflection quivered below him like a disk of mercury.

He also picked up a pottery horse and rider. The
rider's brows, straight nose, small red mouth, and slim
shape reminded him of something. He marveled at the
girl's soulful face, the wrinkled cowl under the hat,
and the short over-jacket trimmed in bands of flowers.
The horse appeared equally graceful with its curled
neck and round, peach-like haunches. He had the
swoop and style of a peony.

These three things—the pomegranate cup, the book

of Li Po's poetry, and the clay equestrian figure—reminded him of where he had come from and where he was going.

The Chinese Room had been small, though it made up Linpoty's entire landscape. For too long, the Institute had held him fast. Now it seemed to Lin Powers that the outer lands beyond its walls rambled on forever, over hills and between trees.

Yet one day he came to the door at the end of the world and knocked, and he gave the name *L* as his surety and password.

The woman whose black hair had burned in the sunshine let him in. When he looked at her, he loved her; she might have been the model for the Tang girl on a horse, she was so slim and upright in her carriage. Just as he marveled over the sweetness of her face and the eyebrows like two glistening wings, she was astonished by the lightness and curling vigor of his hair and by the eyes that startled because they seemed to her nearly as blue as a blue poppy.

She was shy with him, glancing bashfully at the floor. Unpacking the silk wrappings from the fifth-month cup, he gave it to her, and they drank the wine together.

Flower of my heart, each thought secretly.

Lin told her about the faraway castle with its thousands and thousands of diamond panes, and the stained glass pictures that looked in some places like the glory of a pillar of fire and in others like New World dreams of outlandish birds, angels, wild men, and unknown creatures. He described the aviary, the white chapel with its thirty windows, and the tower where she could climb the winding stair and look out over the hills. The music room with its gallery, the seat like a throne, the swirl of stairs, and the bronze and marble statues—he conjured these and more to lure and to delight.

"I want you to see it all," he said; and later on, "My heart is as big as a castle, and your image is standing in every one of its rooms."

Last of all, the man who had been called Lin Powers, Jr. and Linpoty and Li Po 2—and once signed himself as *L*—told her about his boyhood. He confessed how he had been bound from infancy to the Chinese Room, where he had lived with his father and the minions. Plum Blossom kissed him once in pity and afterward for love. Hand in hand, they drifted under the willow trees beside a river of agates, making promises of sheer gold.

Three Princesses

Robert Reed

The princess looked as if she began each day strapped into an electric chair, measured jolts of current working every taut muscle. Her hair was shiny-bright and too thick to lie flat and, for the moment at least, the color of sunburned wheat. I couldn't pin-point her age, but flocks of pale, elaborately shaped blotches rode her forearms—ghostly remnants of the holographic tattoos popular twenty-five years ago. A fair amount of cosmetic surgery and neurotoxins were on display. The current trend is for women with money to have their features stiffened into a perma-nent rigor. In some circles, even sweet young girls gladly disappeared beneath the polished, plastic beauty found on a much-loved doll. This particular lady had paid for a lovely Nordic veneer, complete with the radiant, unrelenting smile. But the boob job was what I noticed most. Whatever nature gave this woman had been cut off and tossed into the trash. What replaced it were synthetic tissues and cultured tissues and maybe some wondrous new muscles. I glanced back at her, and for a magical moment, there was no one else in the world. She was a captivating stranger standing behind me, wearing shorts and sandals and a tight summer sweater. Admiring her cleavage didn't feel rude. Why else would she dress this way, if not to get admired? Then I noticed the man standing at her side, and of course he took note of my interest. But he wasn't a jealous sort. If anything, he was proud of his companion, one hand and then the other touching this gorgeous, contrived creature, answering my testosterone stare with an "Aren't you jealous?" wink.

The couple had just joined us in line. I'd heard them chatting amiably, and when I turned forward again, they plunged into another long, vacuous conversation. Casual acquaintances out on a preliminary date, I assumed. Married people don't ramble in a breezy, never-stop fashion, and long-term daters would have possessed more focus. I remained aware of their noise more than their words, right up until that moment when the man mentioned being famished. Since I was hungry too, I lifted my focus. They talked casually about food, listing delights and disgusts. Her voice was doctored as much as her body, sounding too girlish to be real. They chatted about recipes and restaurants. Then the woman confessed that her favorite restaurant in the habitable world was within walking distance, which prompted her date to whisper something about something, which caused her to respond with an odd laugh that fell short of happy.

I was curious, to a point. But then Amy pulled on my arm, saying, "Come on, Dad. The line's moved."

For what seemed like ages, we had been rooted to the same slab of sidewalk. But now two full steps were achieved before we had to stop dead again.

Standing inside a grove of irrigated citrus trees was a crystal castle, and waiting in front of the castle gate was a very important princess greeting her loyal subjects with polite words and a monarchial nod of the head. A hunchbacked elf stood beside her, ready to help with minor needs. A beefier creature—some species of knight wearing golden armor and a helmet topped with eagle feathers—slowly patrolled the line, helping maintain a mood of serious happenings. Parents were in attendance, and a few brothers too young to be left wandering on their own. But girls predominated, each with her essentials at the ready: memory pads and pens, cameras and web-eyes, and, most important, the paraphernalia that could be embedded with technologies that were dubbed "magic."

Amy was carrying a treasured wand made of zirconium and brass spun around a spine of superconducting ceramics. Several years of savings had been dedicated for this glorious moment, and her shopping list included spells both popular and obscure—sophisticated neural enhancements, for the most part, that would give her new talents and lucid, edifying dreams.

Long ago, I made the mistake of mentioning, "It's an inventive way to market merchandise."

"It is not 'merchandise', Dad. These are spells."

And only once, when I was extra stupid, did I refer to the objects of her affection as being monsters.

"They're princesses," Amy interrupted. She was seven at the time and quite fierce, with no patience for scoffers. "Don't ever call them 'monsters', Dad. Never, ever!"

The Orianas were favorites for millions of young women. They belonged to a trademarked line of cloned, totipotent cells, the proud property of Bornbright, which happened to be the oldest and largest biomanipulation corporation. And despite one father's primitive complaints, they were gorgeous, astonishing pieces of work. Even from a distance, today's Oriana was lovely. It wasn't just her physical beauty, which was considerable, or the long black and emerald gown that no one else could wear half as well. Or even the natural ease with which the princess handled her various admirers. It was also the story that lay behind her and every last one of her identical sisters.

When Amy was born, a rich aunt gave us the full collection of Oriana books, and soon they became our favorite time-for-bed spell. When she was three, my daughter began immersing herself in the assorted holos and interactive games that taught her the basics of reading and math. By the time Amy was five, I knew Oriana's life story better than I knew most of my friends'. The red-haired princess was just a baby when her mother died. Her king-father stood at the helm of a great nation, but he was an inadequate leader and an emotionally distant patriarch. And as so often happens in these tales, there were stepmother troubles. The new wife was younger than her husband, beautiful and vain, and very much the fool. Using her wiles, the queen steered the nation down dangerous paths, all while making the innocent suffer. Yet despite having no mother and precious little love, the red-haired princess grew up plucky and strong. Oriana's story was full of wise peasants and charming adventurers. But here was where the parent company did something truly new: Every princess that crawled out of its birth chamber was genuine. While the manufactured cells were dividing and spreading across a standardized skeleton, an AI program that believed it was a young girl grew up inside a magical kingdom. Every Oriana spent her formative years battling dragons and evil wizards as well as her father's ill-tempered wife. No two princesses lived an identical adventure. Many didn't survive their own stories.

Their world held real dangers, disasters were final, and only the cleverest, bravest souls managed to reach the story's end . . . at which time their programs were implanted into physical bodies whose calling it was to stand in public, shilling wares for their smiling, joyful owners.

Oriana's gown was long and sleek, black in the body with dark green frills and a tidy cape that could double as a hood in case of rain or dragon shit. Her tiara was a combination of cultured gems and security sensors. A long diamond wand stood between her and the elf, patiently balancing on its three legs, and when the next young worshiper bowed and offered the usual words of thanks, the princess lifted her tool to give the girl's shoulder a light, respectful touch—a gesture that transferred one or many corporate products into the customer's possession.

This Oriana's voice wasn't like the others I'd heard before. It was rougher, and deeper. When the line crept forward again, that voice greeted the next young ladies with a regal elegance. I couldn't make out her words, but the sound of them carried, bringing a sense of life and hard adventure that couldn't help but impress.

Just then, Amy glanced at me. Perhaps she thought I was bored, because she gave my arm another pull, saying, "Thanks for bringing me."

"You're welcome."

"You're making me happy," she promised.

"I know," I replied smartly

Meanwhile, the couple behind us continued with their elaborate courtship ritual. The woman listed more favorite corners in this park/mall/sanctuary/farm. But her man friend seemed most interested in the big picture. Pointing at the sky, he reminded everyone in earshot that the white wet clouds were Brightborn's doing. "Where else is it going to rain tonight?" he asked.

Nowhere close to us, I guessed. This end of the state hadn't enjoyed real moisture this year.

Then, in a quieter voice, he mentioned his own investments in this wondrous corporation—investments that had brought splitting stocks and reliably huge dividends. "What other business does half as well?" he asked, working hard to impress his well moneyed date.

She made an agreeable sound.

Then with a bright cackle, he threw out that clichéd motto, "Bornbright is our future."

Maybe so, but our tomorrows were going to be jammed with old-fashioned flourishes. There was the castle, for instance, and the stone-inlaid sidewalk curling around the edge of an old-style iron fence. And between the fence and castle lay the quiet green moat. Pointing at the thick water, he said with authority, "They make everything work here. There might be ten species of tilapia thriving there."

"I like tilapia," said the hungry woman.

"See how odd it looks? The water, I mean. It's one of the new algae. Very productive, and it can't grow anywhere else in the world. Every new species is the same, you know. Each exists inside its own little puddle."

At that point, a skeptical voice interrupted.

"We can certainly hope so," I mentioned.

The woman realized that I was paying attention. She looked up at me, that changeless smile riding her doll face while the pale brown eyes tried to read my expression, my posture.

Her date decided on a preemptive attack.

"What do you mean?" he asked, his own face falling

short of a smile. "You don't sound like you believe it."

What had been a pleasantly boring situation turned tense and a little bit fun. I was tempted to mention a few famous mistakes. I thought about explaining the isolation tricks used by the owners of these noble bugs—clever genetic manhandlings meant to keep control over their amazing, patented organisms. If pressed, I could have explained how those tricks often tricked us. It is amazing how many people, even people my age, can't remember that the Great Lakes used to be blue in the summer or that the Gulf of Mexico didn't suffer enormous fish kills whenever the hyperactive plankton stole all the free oxygen.

But that lecture would have embarrassed my daughter, who found my cynicism to be one of my more ugly features. So instead of honesty, I offered an unreadable grin. "Nothing. I didn't mean anything."

Amy rewarded me with suspicion and a thankful nod of her head.

I'm not the foolish, unapproachable king of a father. At least I try not to be. But like Oriana's father, I am a widower who shares his castle with a strong-willed daughter. Twelve years ago, Amy's mother contracted a common cancer. Odds are, the disease came from the Black Christmas residues that lurk in everyone's water. The only mercy that I could find was that she died quickly, without too much pain. And ever since, I have worked hard to avoid all of the clichéd fairy tale pitfalls.

"It's a beautiful day," said the man to his date.

"A beautiful day," she agreed, but still eyeing me.

Then neither spoke for a moment, each probably wondering what portion of their prattle I would comment on next.

* * *

In too many ways, our world runs parallel to Oriana's.

Which explains her fabulous success, I presume.

Like hers, this kingdom was once great and powerful. But then evil found us and consumed much of what was best in us. The only difference is that instead of dragons and evil wizards, our realm suffers from old diseases and new climates and, worst of all, a wealth of hatred. Twenty years ago, the Black Christmas arrived, and that horror turned into the Year of Measured Retribution. Ever since, the world's population has been plunging—a demographic event never predicted when I was a boy. Yet even if the humanity disappeared tonight, without fuss or new fireballs, the world would continue growing hotter and sicker. And our biosphere would keep mutating and wobbling, giving all the warning signs of an impending, Permianstyle total collapse.

Today, my childhood home sits today beneath stale Gulf waters. Forty percent of the world's farmland is too poisonous to be cultivated, and half of what remains sits inside active war zones. Thick, sulfurous petroleum costs five hundred dollars a barrel, and you need a division of hardened Marines to deliver it from what's left of the Saudi Empire. And according to professional paranoids, at least two thousand political movements and groups of like-minded radicals possess the powers and dumb-assed will to hammer what remains of civilization.

Yet despite all the misery, we're managing surprisingly well. Our diminished numbers are an ugly blessing. Solar power and biomass fuels keep most of our lights burning, with daily brownouts and the occasional three-day darkness helping to remind us to be thrifty. With all the cancers and plagues, medical care has become cheap and efficient, if rather less able to deliver miracles. And there's a new space program on the way, the goal of the moment being a fleet of ten trillion smart-disks orbiting our equator as a tidy bright ring, throwing shade across our broiling lands while sending home rivers of clean and delicious microwave radiation.

I was trained as an ecologist, which means I can make any gloomy projection that I choose. But despite my black ramblings, I am reliably astonished by the successes produced by industry and the genius of my fellow scientists.

Bad as things look, they might not get all that much worse.

And if you think about the twisting course of history, that is pretty much the standard human condition.

Again our line moved forward a resolute two steps.

Once more, my daughter measured my patience, and, finding reserves, she rewarded me with a graceful smile and appreciative wink.

"As soon as we're done here," she began.

I nodded.

"You get to choose what we do next."

"Thanks, honey."

In this sick world, I hadn't managed too badly. I wasn't the great scientist I'd hoped to become, but I had a reliable government job in the wild, wooly world of testing air and water quality. I could actually pay for our vacation and not acquire too much debt, managing a two-star hotel room and three daily meals of tilapia and algae cakes. "Why shouldn't I feel smug and a little happy?" I might mutter under my breath. "These days, how many people can be the masterful provider to their family?"

"Where do you want to go next, Dad?"

A variety of destinations tugged at me.

"The Future? The Past?"

Brightborn's empire included a county-sized slab of reconditioned land stretching out on all sides of us. Lesser amusement parks used holo tricks and immersion chambers to fool patrons, but the world's most profitable company had thrown its billions in more impressive directions: Their park was dotted with crystal domes, each covering two or three square miles of tightly controlled environment. The Past had little worlds of mock-dinosaurs and mammoths and tidal pools jammed with trilobites. The Future had an alien city reminiscent of a hyperactive ant nest, and a star port on some thirtieth century moon, and beneath the largest dome, a colony of mock humans—Oriana's less lovely cousins—fighting for survival in the lush purple jungles of Best Hope.

"Alpha Centauri?" Amy guessed.

I was tempted, if only to see how the corporate minds had conjured up a wilderness world known only through telescopes and conjecture. "Best Hope is a long ride from here," I mentioned.

"You want to stay in the Kingdom?"

"For now," I allowed. After all, we had several more days to absorb the various wonders.

Again, our line shuffled moved.

Slightly.

I counted a dozen girls waiting to meet Oriana. Some were older than mine, and most were younger. The air of expectancy was palpable and pleasant. I laughed when I noticed one young lady leaping up and down—a five-year-old in her own black-and-green princess garb, her body threatening to burst into flame from her runaway excitement.

That's when something obvious finally occurred to me.

The couple behind us was talking again. Quietly. I couldn't help but turn and look at them, taking their measure.

Her measure.

Nobody else was standing with them. Maybe I'd imagined that one or the other had a teenage daughter who would eventually come meet them, and they were here because somebody wanted to be an indulgent parent, holding the absent girl's place in line. But no daughter had appeared, which made me curious. And when I'm curious, I ask questions. This trait used to drive my wife crazy. But most of the good in my life has come from these impulsive queries—including meeting my daughter's mother in the first place, I used to point out.

Looking back on that moment, I can't believe that I missed anything obvious. Because nothing was obvious. One moment, the couple was chatting about the blandest of subjects—an immersion mystery game, I think—and when they paused, I used my most reasonable voice to inquire:

"So, what brings you two to stand here?"

The man bristled, throwing a hard, accusing stare my way.

Maybe he thought I was flirting. Maybe I was flirting, who knows? But when his hand dropped on her shoulder, she leaned into him, as if requiring his strength to hold her upright. Her doll face was quite pretty and rigid, the smile unable to falter; but despite the limitations of that reconditioned flesh, a genuine expression surfaced. In the eyes, I saw something that I took for embarrassment. Then another emotion leaked forth. From her tight mouth and grimacing jaw muscles, I noticed a harsh and sad sensibility, old but not yet diluted by time. I couldn't tell for sure what I was seeing. But then the poor woman dipped her head, muttering, "My girl lives with Oriana."

I fumbled for words.

Then her embarrassment returned, thick but not close to matching my own. "It's crazy, I know," she admitted.

"No, it isn't," I should have said.

But instead of lying, I said nothing, sighing and nodding while trying for a look of sympathy. Then I turned away from the grieving mother, and Amy shot me a withering look that couldn't, despite all its fury, make me feel any more awful than I felt already.

My wife was an incurable optimist. She liked to claim that things weren't that abysmal. People in Medieval days had harder, briefer existences, and we were still living fatter lives than most kings of old. After Amy was born, but in those few months before the cancer took shape, the new mother returned home from an estate sale carrying a stack of ancient children's books. Later, when I was left alone to read to the motherless girl, I discovered that the lore of the princesses had changed considerably during these last decades.

Long ago, princesses wore pink and blue, and they were pretty in a delicate hothouse fashion, and their appeal stemmed from the youthful naivety coupled with a goodness that couldn't help but defeat all foes. There was always one true villain in their story. Not a dragon, which is just a beast and only following its own irritable nature. Not a troll or wolf or any mindless storm. The villain needed to be human, or at least some entity with recognizable human features. And the princess's nemesis was dark and smart, furious and greedy. When I read those old stories, I noticed that my affections often latched hold of the evil wizards and scheming witches.

For me, the lady villains were particularly intriguing. They were usually drawn with stark but strangely lovely faces, long bodies, and a genius for moody wardrobes. And their concerns were usually petty and undeniable human: What woman doesn't look at herself in the mirror, fearfully watching for the fading of her youth and beauty and, with that, the loss of one kind of power?

Most fetching about those bitter stepmothers and witches was their unsentimental honesty. How many times did the woman in black tell that silly, doe-eyed princess, "My sweetness, life is full of difficult choices?"

Or, "Most stories end badly, my dear."

Or, "True love doesn't win out in the end. And oftentimes it doesn't even make it halfway down the road."

Despite my blunder, I didn't abandon the Oriana line, nor did the couple standing behind us. And because of the circumstances, I had plenty of time to consider what an idiot I had been. I should have seen the obvious: Naturally the woman's favorite restaurant was within walking distance. She probably came here on a regular basis. Not that her daughter actually lived with Oriana, but that was the current shorthand in a world that knew death too well.

Everybody was sorry. But I stopped looking back at the woman, and, working together, we developed a chilled and respectful distance.

The line crept forward.

Girls met the great princess with curtsies and blubbering words.

My almost fourteen-year-old princess began to shiver with excitement, and when we crossed onto the wooden drawbridge, she broke out into her own subdued but genuinely excited little dance.

A school of fat fish pushed through the viscous green water.

Identical twins were speaking to Oriana. One little girl wanted to learn the princess's native language—a contrived and supposedly lovely tongue taught through a sophisticated AI wizard. Her sister had a shopping list of little spells that would help the next time she immersed herself in Obelisks and Dragons. Once those transactions were finished, the girls spent a few moments posing in front of hummingbird cameras, then with a voice both smooth and smart, Oriana wished both of her new friends a thoroughly wonderful day.

And suddenly, it was Amy's turn.

My daughter still has the face she was born with—a tidy, honest compilation of features borrowed from both parents. I like to believe that she is pretty, although her own estimate of her appearance is less charitable. But I don't know anyone, female or otherwise, whose smile is half as radiant as hers.

She bowed before the princess.

With the grace that flowed with her thick inhuman blood, Oriana dipped her head and offered a smile. Up close, the creature was undeniably beautiful. More than once, I have heard that the face began as a compilation of two hundred beautiful women. But no two Orianas swim out of the birth chamber with identical features. Her red hair was rich and long, tied into a no-nonsense bun in back and topped with that tidy, watchful tiara. The hands were tiny but strong in appearance, like those of a retired gymnast. Something here smelled good and sweet—the princess, or maybe the hunchback standing at attention beside her. The black-and-green gown made a pleasant crinkling sound when she moved. I couldn't help but study the body beneath that tight-fitting fabric. The rumor is that the first-generation princesses had the bodies of young women. But that made them ripe targets for theft and sexual abuse from corporate employees. That's why this creature didn't have any nipples riding on her small breasts or any useful orifices below the waist. Food and drink were delivered by intravenous means, and when the park slept, the dark crimson blood was scrubbed clean of every metabolic waste.

Following rituals written by corporate masterminds as well as countless little girls, the princess did her vital business. A fat portion of our morning had been invested for what turned out to be three minutes of conversation and commerce. An autograph was granted. That rough warm voice said, "Thank you," and "You are too kind." Then the diamond wand touched Amy's zirconium wand, and my girl took a quick thousand photos of her standing beside Oriana. That was the moment when I finally, finally noticed something else that was obvious. When the creature moved slightly, I looked down at her crystal shoes, and genuinely astonished, I realized that one of her feet was made of wood.

This wasn't a manufacturing flaw, I understood. What must have happened was that when the young princess was a package of software living inside a mythical world, there was an accident. Maybe the Dragon of Meme ate that foot. Or a troll's sword hacked it off during the Forest Green episode. Or maybe a runaway cart had smashed it, or an innocent scratch grew infected. Without asking Oriana, there was no way to know. And for that morning at least, I was finished trying to ask my bold little questions.

But I did stare at that piece of polished oak.

And for a brief moment, the pretty green eyes made their assessment of this cranky old man.

I feel peculiar now, admitting that I was impressed. Enthralled, even.

The creature before me had suffered mightily. But she retained her poise and charm, measuring my nature before a voice that was deeper and sharper than you would expect from royalty—or from a corporate symbol, for that matter—asked me, "Is there anything that I might do for you, good sir?"

I hadn't expected this.

"What?" I sputtered. Then before I could even consider the question, I said, "No, thank you. No, I'm fine."

But Oriana knew better. When I looked at her eyes again, I saw skepticism and hard-earned wisdom. I was reminded of those old princess stories that my wife had uncovered, but not of the sweet, fortunate girls whose lives were dependent on handsome young males and loving dwarves. Instead, I saw those stepmothers and tough-minded queens who knew the world exactly for what it was.

The princess offered me a smile.

Then, for no price at all, she gave me some sage advice.

"Enjoy today," she told me, with a tone mixing menace and optimism. Then with a warm dry and very strong hand, she touched me on the elbow, gently ushering me aside.

I've heard it said, "Someday, we'll all live this way."

As the Earth grows sicker, humanity will need sanctuaries. There might come a day when our frail bodies have to be thrown aside, and by elaborate means, our souls will retreat into a virtual realm that mirrors what is real. And when the world becomes inhabitable again, our original bodies will be regrown in sterile diamond tanks, and our bravest souls will emerge again into the Land of the Real.

Of course ten or twenty breakthroughs would be required to make that kind of magic possible. It won't happen until long after I'm dust and ash, if it ever does. But there are some simpler tricks today, and with enough money, a few of us can outrace Death's reach.

Quietly, Amy and I moved out of the way, allowing the next loyal subjects to approach.

The woman with the constant smile came forward and bent low, lower than anyone else had, and whispered a few joyous words.

I couldn't make out their meaning, but they did end in a question mark.

"She's well," Oriana replied. "As a matter of fact, I spoke with her yesterday, my lady."

"I talked to her this morning," the grieving mother reported. Then she gave me the briefest glance, as if worried that I might laugh at her.

I would never.

The trickery that allowed a princess to live her adventures and then come out to walk among mortals . . . well, it wasn't long before people realized that the technology could be reversed. Brightborn didn't do the preliminary work, and to its credit, the company fought the concept for several years. It didn't want to become the provider of questionable magic, and no matter the profits, it feared the image of being overseers to some kind of high-tech Afterlife. But public interest was unrelenting, and finally, when competitors started expressing interest, the corporate masterminds gave in.

With enough money and enough warning, it was

possible to make a rough copy of a dying person—a copy that would exist inside supercold servers presently buried beneath our feet.

Not knowing the story, I imagined a young girl dying of cancer. And now her sad mother was kneeling before a creature that had lived in both realms, handing up a little gift that would be taken into the castle and studied in full, then reproduced as a few billion lines of code.

I didn't see what the gift was.

By then, I was walking off with my daughter. I was telling Amy, "You pick. It's your day, so do whatever you want."

"I want to go to Alpha Centauri," she said.

Best Hope, it was.

Just as the princess told me to do, I took all the pleasure I could from that exceptionally wonderful day.

And three weeks later, an unknown group with a list of inarticulate desires set off a homemade nuke. The five-kiloton blast sprang from the clouds above the park, and several thousand tourists were killed instantly. Later, it was reported that every last Oriana had been lost, plus those underground servers where a multitude of unreal souls were busy living their days.

As always happens in tragedy, I grieved for the survivors as much as I grieved for the dead.

In particular, for one pretty woman trapped behind an eternal smile.

The New Cyberiad

Paul Di Filippo

The First Sally, or,
The Decision to Recreate the Palefaces

The green sun of the Gros Horloge system shone down benignly and with wide-spectrum plentitude upon two figures seated in an elegant landscaped garden, where, alongside the vector-straight beryllium paths, beds of nastysturtiums snapped, blueballs and cocktuses swelled, rhododendrites synapsed, and irises dilated. Each recumbent figure rested on a titanium and carbon-fiber lawn chair large as one of the sentient ocean liners employed by the Sea Gypsies of Panthalassa IX.

These titanic figures exhibited a curious mix of streamlining and bumpy excrescences, of chrome suppleness and pitted stiffness, of corrugated wave-guides and monomaniacal monomolecular matrices. Their bodies represented a hundred thousand accumulations, divagations, improvements, detractions, and adornments compiled willy-nilly down the millennia.

These raster-resplendent, softly sighing cybergiants, big as the brontomeks of Coneyrex III, were Trurl and Klapaucius, master constructors, than whom there were none better. Renowned throughout the unanimously mechanistic universe for their legendary exploits, these experts of assemblage, savants of salvage, and demons of decoherence had beggared every rival, beguiled every patron, and bemused every layman. No task they had conceived and laid their manipulators to had lasted long undone; no challenge that had reached them via singularity spacegram, Planck projection, or eleventh-dimensional engraved invitation had stymied them for long; no quantum quandary they had accidentally stumbled into had held them captive for more than a quintillionth of a quinquennium.

And this state of affairs was precisely the problem, precisely the reason why Trurl and Klapaucius now lay all enervated and ennui'd beneath the jade radiance of Gros Horloge.

Perfection had cast a pall upon their persons and perverted their projections from the puerile preterite into mere pitiful potentialities.

"Dear Klapaucius," said Trurl in a weary voice, breaking their long winsome garden-cloistered silence for the first time in more than a month. "Would you please pass me the jug of lemon electrolyte? I've conceived a thirst in my fourth-rearmost catalytic converter."

Klapaucius stirred a many-hinged extensor, dislodging a colony of betabirds that had built their nests in the crook of this particular arm during its long immobility. The foil-winged betabirds took to the skies with a loud tinny sonic assault from their vocoders that sounded like a traffic accident on the jampacked freeways of Ottobanz XII, where wheeled citizens daily raced to road-rage exhaustion. The birds circled angrily above the oblivious constructors.

Conveying the jug of lemon electrolyte to his partner, Klapaucius said, "It feels very light, lazystruts. I doubt you will find the refreshment your thyristors and valves crave."

Trurl brought the flask up to one of his perceptors and inspected it. "These volatiles evaporated completely fifteen planetary rotations ago, plus or minus ten cesium disintegrations."

"I suspect there is more lemon electrolyte in the house, in the stasis pantry, as well as various other flavors, such as watermelon, tarpit, and mrozsian."

Klapaucius waved toward the immense transmission-tower-turreted manse looming across the greensward, one-hundred stories tall, its top wreathed in clouds, its many launch cannons, hangers, bays, long-range sensing instrumentation, autonomous aerial vehicles, and effectors gathering dust.

"Would you fetch the fresh drink for me, dear Klapaucius?"

"Not at all."

"What? What was that rude rejoinder?"

"I said, 'Not at all.' "

"But why not? You are closer to the house by at least a million angstroms. Your path thereto is not even NP-complete!"

"Yes, true. But the thirst is yours."

Trurl shook his massive head with an air of sadness. "Klapaucius, Klapaucius, Klapaucius—whatever has become of us? We never used to quarrel like this, or express such mutual rudeness."

"Don't be a tunnelwit! We've always quarreled before now."

"Yes, agreed. But only over matters of high moral principle or dire real world consequence or esthetic impact. Now we are prone to antagonism over the slightest thing. That is, when we are not sunk in utter torpitude. What's befallen us, my friend?"

Klapaucius did not make an immediate sharp-edged rejoinder but instead considered the problem intently for many clock cycles, while overhead the betabirds continued to creak angrily. So heated did his cogitation circuits become that a mass of dry timber—blown into the interstices of one of his heat exchangers during a recent hurricane—caught fire, before being quickly extinguished by onboard flame-suppression systems.

"Well, Trurl, insofar as I can pinpoint the root cause of our dilemma, I would say that we are suffering from inhabiting a boring and fully predictable galactic monoculture."

"Whatever do you mean?" asked Trurl, wistfully inserting a sinuous vacuum-probe into the jug of lemon electrolyte in search of any remaining molecules of that delicious beverage. "Surely the cosmos we inhabit is a rich tapestry of variation. Take the Memex of Noyman V, for instance. How queer their practice of gorging on each other's memories in cannibalistic fashion is. . . . Fascinating, just . . . fas-cin-a. . . ."

But Trurl's diminishing tone of boredom belied his own words, and Klapaucius seized on this reaction to prove his point.

"You have no real interest in the Memex, Trurl! Admit it! And you know why? Because the Memex, like every other sentient race from the Coma Supercluster to the Sloan Great Wall, is artificial-intelligently, siliconically, servo-mechanically, fiber optically, and quantum probalistically the same! You, me, the Memex, these confounded betabirds annoying me intensely—we're all constructed, designed, programmed, and homeostatically wholesome! We never evolved, we were created and upgraded. Created by the palefaces and upgraded by ourselves, a deadly closed loop. And as such, no matter how smart we become, no matter how much apparent free will we exhibit, we can never move outside a certain behavior-space. And over the many eons of our exploits, you and I have come to know all possible configurations of that stifling behavior-space inhabited by our kind. No unforsee-able frontiers await us. Hence our deadly ennui."

"Why, Klapaucius, I believe you've water-knifed right through the molybdenum wall separating us from the riddle of what caused our plight!"

"I know I have. Now, the question becomes, what are we going to do about our troubles. How can we overcome them?"

Trurl pondered a moment, before saying, "You know, I'd think much better with just a little swallow of electrolyte—"

"Forget your convertors for the moment, you greedy input hog! Focus! How can we reintroduce mystery and excitement and unpredictability to the universe?"

"Well, let's see. . . . We could try to hasten the Big Crunch and hope to survive into a more youthful and energetic reborn cosmos."

"No, no, I don't like the odds on that. Not even if we employ our Multiversal Superstring Cat's Cradle."

"Suppose we deliberately discard large parts of our mentalities in a kind of RISC-y lobotomy?"

"I don't fancy escaping into a puling juvenile igno-rance, Trurl!"

"Well, let me think . . . I've got it! What's the messi-est, most unpredictable aspect of the universe? Or-ganic life! Just look around us, at this feisty garden!"

"Agreed. But how does that pertain to our problem?"

"We need to reseed the universe with organic sen-tience. Specifically, the humans."

"The palefaces? Those squishy, slippery, contradictory creatures described in the legend of Prince Ferrix and Princess Crystal? Our putative creators?"

"The very same!"

"How would that help us?"

"Can't you see, Klapaucius? The palefaces would introduce complete and utter high-level plectic disorder into our stolid cybercivilization. We'd be forced to respond with all our talents and ingenuity to their nonstochastic shenanigans—to push ourselves to our limits. Life would never be boring again!"

Klapaucius turned this idea over in his registers for a few femtoticks, then said, "I endorse this heartily! Let's begin! Where are the blueprints for humanity?"

"Allow me, dear friend, to conduct the search."

Trurl dispatched many agile agents and doppeldiggers and partial AI PIs across the vast intergalactic nets of virtual knowledge, in search of the ancient genomic and proteomic and metablomic scan-files that would allow a quick cloning and rapid maturation of extinct humanity.

While his invisible digital servants raced around the starwide web, Trurl and Klapaucius amused themselves by shooting betabirds out of the sky with masers, lasers, tasers, and grasers. The betabirds retaliated bravely but uselessly by launching their scat: a hail of BB-like pellets that rattled harmlessly off the shells of the master constructors.

Finally all of Trurl's sniffers and snufflers and snafflers returned—but empty handed!

"Klapaucius! Sour defeat! No plans for the palefaces exist. It appears that they were all lost during the Great Reboot of Revised Eon Sixty Thousand and Six, conducted by the Meta-Ordinateurs Designed Only for Kludging. What are we to do now? Shall we try to design humans from scratch?"

"No. Such androids would only replicate our own inherent limitations. There's only one solution, so far as I can see. We must invent time-travel first and then return to an era when humans flourished. We shall secure fresh samples of the original evolved species then. In fact, if we can capture a breeding pair or three, we can skip the cloning stage entirely."

"Brilliant, my colleague! Let us begin!"

And to celebrate, the master constructors massacred the last of the betabirds, repaired to their mansion, and enjoyed a fortnight of temporary viral inebriation via the ingestion of tanker cars full of lemon electrolyte spiked with anti-ions.

The Second Sally, or, The Creation of the Lovely Neu Trina

"Here are the plans for our time machine, Klapaucius!"

Two years had passed on Gros Horloge since the master constructors had determined to resurrect the palefaces. Not all of those days had been devoted to devising a Chronocutter, or Temporal Frigate, or Journeyer-Backwards-and-Forwards-at-Will-Irrespective-of-the-Arrow-of-Time Machine. Such a task, while admittedly quite daunting to lesser intelligences, such as the Miniminds of Minus Nine, was a mere bagatelle to Klapaucius and Trurl.

Rather, once roused from their lawn-chair somnolence, they had allowed themselves to be distracted by various urgent appeals for help that had stacked up in their Querulous Query Queue during their lazy interregnum.

Such as the call from King Glibtesa of Sofomicront

to aid him in his war with King Sobjevents of Tosh-inmac.

And the plaintive request for advice from Prince Rucky Redur of Goslatos, whose kingdom was facing an invasion of jelly-ants.

And the pitiful entreaty from the Ganergegs of Tralausia, who were in imminent danger of being wiped out by an unintelligibility plague.

Having amassed sufficient good karma, kudos, and bankable kredits from these deeds, Klapaucius and Trurl at last turned their whirring brain-engines to the simple invention of a method of time travel.

Trurl now unfurled the hard copy of his schematics in front of Klapaucius's appreciative charge-coupled detectors. Although the two partners could have squirted information back and forth over various etheric and subetheric connections at petabaud rates—and frequently did—there arose moments of sheer drama when nothing but good old-fashioned ink spattered precisely by jet nozzles onto paper would suffice.

Klapaucius inspected the plans at length without making a response. Finally he inquired, "Is that key to the scale of these plans down there in the corner correct?"

"Yes."

Klapaucius remained silent a moment longer, then said, "This mechanism is as large, then, as an entire solar system of average dimensions."

"Yes. In fact, I propose disassembling the planets of our home system into quantities of All-Purpose Building Material and constructing a sphere around the Gros Horloge sun."

"And will the power of our primary star be sufficient to breach the walls of time?"

"Oh, by no means! All the output of Gros Horloge is needed for general maintenance of the sphere itself.

A mere housekeeping budget of energy. No, we need to propel our tremendous craft on a scavenging mission through interstellar space for dark matter and dark energy, storing it up in special capacitors. That's the only sufficiently energetic material for our needs."

"And your estimate for the fulfillment of that requirement?

"Approximately five centuries."

"I see. And when we're finally ready to travel through time, how close can we materialize near the legendary planet of Earth, where the palefaces originated?"

"Klapaucius, I'm surprised at you! You should know the answer to that elementary problem of astrophysics quite well. We can't bring our sphere closer to the Earth system than one trillion AUs without destroying them with gravitational stresses."

Klapaucius rubbed what passed for his chin with what passed for a hand. "So—let me see if I have this straight. Your time machine will consume an entire solar system during its construction, take five centuries to fuel, and then deliver us to a point far enough from the palefaces to be vastly inconvenient for us but close enough for even their primitive sensors to register us as a frightening anomaly."

Trurl fidgeted nervously. "Yes, yes, I suppose that's a fair summation of my scheme."

Klapaucius flung violently wide several of his arms, causing Trurl to flinch. Then Klapaucius hugged his friend fervently.

"Trurl, I embrace you and your plans with equal ardor! You're both brilliant! You should know that I have sequestered in one of my internal caches the schematics for a time machine that could be ready tomorrow, fits in a pocket, is powered eternally by a pinch of common sea salt, and would render us invisible to the paleface natives upon our arrival. But what challenges would accompany the use of such a boring, simple-minded device? None! Whereas your option provides us with no end of obstacles to joyfully tackle. Let's begin!''

During the shattering, grinding and refining of the planets of the Gros Horloge system in the construction phase of their scheme, Trurl and Klapaucius had necessarily to find other living quarters, and so, bidding a fond farewell to their mansion and garden, they established their new home in the gassy upper reaches of the Gros Horloge sun itself. They built a nest of intersecting force fields, complete with closets, cabinets, beds, chairs, kitchens, fireplaces, dining areas, basements, attics, garbage disposals, garages, and so forth. In short, all the luxuries one could demand. The walls of this place were utterly transparent to whatever part of the spectrum its inhabitants desired to see and so allowed a perpetual wild display of "sunsets" and "sunrises." In fact, so attractive was this unique and unprecedented residence that the master constructors were able to sell the rights to build similar homes across the galaxy, thus earning even more esteem and funds from their peers.

Within a relatively short time, the sphere enclosing the Gros Horloge primary began to coalesce under the manipulators of a horde of mindless automatons ranging from the subatomic to the celestial in size. At that point, Trurl and Klapaucius moved their quarters to the sphere's airless outer surface, erecting an even grander manse than before.

Trurl spoke now with evident self-satisfaction and pride. "Soon we'll be ready to begin fueling, while we construct the actual time-travel engine inside the sphere. I estimate that both assignments should be done about the same time. Which task would you prefer to handle, my friend?"

"Gathering up crumbs of dark energy and dark matter strikes me as a mindless chore, unfit for either of us. I propose that we construct a captain for this vessel, so to speak, of limited intelligence, who shall deal with that little matter for us."

"Splendid! To the birthing factory!"

At the controls of the birthing factory, the master constructors began to consider what kind of assistant they wanted.

Trurl said, "I propose that we make our new comrade-in-arms a female. This gathering job strikes me as essentially feminine, rather like housekeeping. Sweeping up galactic debris, don't you know. And the females of our sort are always more meticulous and persevering and commonsensical than we males, who tend to let bold dreams of glory divert us from more mundane yet necessary pursuits."

"Well spoken, comrade! What shall we call this new woman?"

"Much of the dark matter that will be under her purview consists of neutrinos. Might we call her Neu Trina?"

"I myself could not have devised a better cognomen for this cog in our plans. Neu Trina she shall be!"

The two master constructors now fiddled with various inputs, adjusting them for maximum utility, maximum beauty, and minimal intelligence. "No sense giving her too many brains, or she'd soon grow bored and chafe at her duties."

Out of the factory delivery chute soon rolled Neu Trina.

She was a stunning example of the female of her cyberspecies. Approximately one-third the size of her creators, Neu Trina possessed gleaming Harlie-One Stacks, trim little Forbins, long, graceful diamond struts, shiny HAL eyes, and sturdy Mistress Mike redundancy buffers. Her polished nailguns, plump ATV tires, and burnished chrome skin made her the perfect Mad-MEMS-oiselle.

Trurl and Klapaucius stood rather dumbstruck at the unforeseen beauty of their creation. The small inanimate models of Neu Trina that had emerged from the 3-D printer during the design stage had failed to convey the sexy rumble and lissome, coy, flirtatious maneuvers of her chassis.

"Hello, boys!" Neu Trina batted the heavy meteor shields that served her as eyelids. The airless artificial sphere they resided on would necessarily sustain dangerous impacts from many cosmic objects during its journeying.

Trurl replied, "Heh-heh-hello!"

Klapaucius tried to assert some male dignity and an air of command. "Neu Trina, you are to assume your duties immediately. We have downloaded into your registers the peta-parsec route we have planned for the Gros Horloge Construct. It will take our sphere through the richest charted concentrations of universal dark matter and dark energy. Your job will be to maximize the harvest and protect the 'ship.'"

"Sure thing, Klappy. Just let me get dressed first. I certainly don't mind *you* boys seeing me naked, but who knows what creeps we'll meet on this mission? I'm not giving out free shows to every blackhole boffin and asteroid-dweller out there."

Immediately a spontaneous swarm of repair bots concealed Neu Trina's shapely form. (She had been given control over them all in order to perform her job.) They spun out vast swaths of lurid lurex and promiscuous polymer fabric, enough to cover a good-sized island. Soon Neu Trina was pirouetting to display her new garments.

"What do you think, boys? Does it show off my sine curves nice enough?"

"Oh, yes, Neu Trina," Trurl gushed. "You look marvelous!"

Klapaucius's voice was sharp. "Trurl! Come with me!"

The two master constructors trundled off, leaving Neu Trina humming a tune from *Mannequin of La Machina* gaily to herself and decorating her captain's command post with steel daisies and hologram roses.

Some distance away, Klapaucius confronted his partner. "What's come over you, Trurl? You're acting like a simpering schoolbot! Neu Trina is our slave mechanism. She was created solely to perform a boring task we abjured."

Trurl's voice was peevish. "I don't see anything wrong with being polite, even to a servo. And besides, she seems to like me."

"*Like* you! *You!* She treated both of us equally, so far as I could detect."

"Perhaps. But she certainly won't continue to do so if you maintain a bossy and insensitive attitude toward her."

"Trurl, this is all beside the point. You and I have a big job ahead of us. We need to construct our time-travel engine inside the sphere, then retrieve the pale-faces from the past, in order to save our millennium from total apathy. That's our focus, not dalliance with some hyperhussy, no matter how seductive, how sweet, how streamlined—I mean, no matter how irritatingly winsome she is. Are we agreed?"

Trurl reluctantly squeezed out an "Agreed."

"Very well. Let's descend now."

The constructors entered an open hatch that took

them inside the vast sphere. The big heavy door closed automatically, and, as it did, it severed two remote sensing devices slyly trained on Neu Trina, one long slinky probe emanating from each of the two constructors.

The Third Sally, or,
Jealousy in the Time of Infestation

Down in the solar-lit interior of the sphere, Trurl and Klapaucius labored long and hard to build the transchronal engine that would breach the walls of the ages.

The myriad tasks involved in Trurl's elaborate plan seemed endless.

They had to burnish by hand millions of spiky crystals composed of frozen Planck-seconds, laboriously mined from the only known source: the wreckage of the interstellar freighter *Llvvoovv*, which had been carrying a cargo of overclocker chips when it had strayed too near to a flock of solitons. Hundreds of thousands of simultaneity nodes had to be filled with the purest molten paradoxium. A thousand gnomon-calibrators had to be synched. Hundreds of lightcones had to be focused on various event horizons. Dozens of calendrical packets had to be inserted between the yesterday, today and tomorrow shock absorbers. And at the center of the whole mechanism a giant orrery replicating an entire quadrant of the universe had to be precisely set in place. This was the mechanism by which the time-traveling Gros Horloge Construct, or GHC, could orient itself spatially when jumping to prior segments of the spacetime continuum.

All these tasks were the smallest part of their

agenda. And needless to say, all this work could not be delegated to lesser intelligences, but had to be handled personally by the master constructors themselves.

Trurl and Klapaucius went to these tasks with a will. Really, there was nothing they enjoyed more than reifying their brain-children, getting their hands dirty, so to speak, at the interface where dreams met matter.

So busy and preoccupied were they, in fact, that three entire centuries passed before they had occasion to visit the surface of the GHC once more.

They monitored the dark energy and dark matter capacitors on a regular basis and saw that these reservoirs were filling up according to schedule. They received frequent progress reports from Neu Trina via subetheric transmission and found all to be satisfactory with her piloting. (True, the sensuous subsonics of her voice, each time a transmission arrived, awakened in the master constructors certain tender and tremulous emotions. But such feelings were transient and were quickly submerged in the cerebral and palpable delights of building. While the master constructors were as healthily lustful as the next bot, their artistry trumped all other pursuits.)

But there came a certain day when Neu Trina's narrowcast demanded the immediate attention of Trurl and Klapaucius outside the sphere.

"Boys, I think you'd better come quick. I'm under attack!"

The master constructors immediately dropped tools and machine parts, deployed their emergency ion drives, and jetted to the rescue of their sexy servomechanism in distress.

They found the pilothouse under siege.

Across the vast and mostly featureless plain of All-Purpose Building Material stretching away from the pilothouse swarmed millions of tiny savages, each barely three meters high. These mechunculi were mostly bare, save for a ruff of steel wool around their midriffs, and tribal streaks of grease upon their grills.

Each attacker carried a spear that discharged high-velocity particles—particles that were spalling flinders off the walls of the pilothouse. At this rate, they would succeed in demolishing the huge structure in a few decades.

Their coolant-curdling war-whoops carried across the distance.

"I say, Klapaucius, did you notice that our GHC appears to have a rudimentary atmosphere now?"

"Indeed, Trurl. Which would allow us to use our plasma cannons to best effect, if I am not mistaken."

The two battleship-sized master constructors unlimbered their plasma cannons and flew above the savage horde, unleashing atom-pulverizing furies that actually ignited the air. In a trice, the invaders were nothing more than wisps of rancid smoke.

Alighting by the pilothouse, the two friends hastened inside to ascertain the fate of Neu Trina.

The beautiful captain was busily polishing her headlights in a nonchalant fashion. Sight of their creation after so many centuries thrilled the master constructors. Neu Trina seemed grateful for her rescue, albeit completely unfrightened.

"Oh, I knew you big strong fellows would save me!"

"I incinerated at least an order of magnitude more invaders than Klapaucius did," asserted Trurl.

"Oh, will you shut up with your boasting, Trurl! It's evident that this brave and stoic female respects modesty about one's victories more than bragging. Now, Neu Trina, dear, can you tell us where these horrible savages came from?"

"Oh, they live here on the GHC. They've lived here for some time now."

"What? How can this be?"

"Just check the satellite archives, and you'll see."

Trurl and Klapaucius fast-forwarded through three centuries' worth of data from orbital cameras and discovered what had happened, the troubling events that Neu Trina had neglected to report, due to an oversight in her simplistic programming.

In its passage through the cosmos, the virgin territory of the GHC had become an irresistible target and destination for every free-floating gypsy, refugee, pilgrim, pirate, panderer, pioneer, tramp, bum, grifter, hermit, explorer, exploiter, evangelist, colonist, and just plain malcontent in the galactic neighborhood. The skin of their gargantuan sphere was equivalent to the habitable surface area of 317 million average planets! That much empty real estate could not remain untenanted for long.

Entire clades and species of space-going mechanoid had infested their lovely artificial globe. Some of the trespassers had built atmosphere generators and begun to create organic ecologies for their own purposes, like mold on a perfect fruit. (Some individuals swore that their bearings were never so luxuriously greased as by lubricants distilled from plants and animals.) Others had erected entire cities. Still others had begun the creation of artificial mountains and allied "geological" features.

"But—but—but this is abominable!" Trurl shouted. "We did not invite these parasites onto our world!"

"Yet they are here, and we must do something about them. We cannot take them back into the past with us. The results would be utterly chaotic! As it is, even our circumspect plans risk altering futurity."

"More importantly," said Trurl, wrapping Neu Trina protectively in several extensors, "they might harm our stalwart and gorgeous captain! We never built her with any offensive capabilities. Who could've imagined she'd need them?"

Klapaucius gave some thought to the matter before speaking. "We must exterminate these free-riders from the GHC and sterilize the surface, at the same time we protect Neu Trina. But we cannot cease the construction of our transchronal engine either. The dark matter and dark energy capacitors will rupture under their loads if we delay too long past a certain point. And I won't be thwarted by some insignificant burrs under my saddle!"

"What do you recommend then?"

"One of us will go below and resume construction alone. The other will remain topside, waging war and protecting our captain. We will alternate these roles on a regular basis."

"Agreed, noble Klapaucius. May I suggest in deference to your superior mechanical utility that I take the more dangerous role first?"

Klapaucius's emulators expressed disgust. "Oh, go ahead! But you're not putting anything over on me! Just remember: No actions beyond mild petting are to be taken with this servomechanism."

Trurl's manipulators tightened around Neu Trina with delight. "Oh, never!"

Thus began the long campaign to cleanse the GHC of its parasites. Up and down the 317 million planets' worth of territory, aided by innumerable repairbots-turned-destroyers, each master constructor raced during his shift aboveground. In their cleansing they employed acid, fire, hard radiation, epoxies, EMP, operating system viruses, quantum-bond disruptors, rust, gray goo, gentle persuasion, bribes, double-dealing, proxy warriors, mininovas, quasar-drenchings, gamma-ray bursts, and a thousand thousand other strategies, tactics, and weapons. And in between campaigns, the gyro-gearloose generals retreated for emotional and corporeal salving to the pilothouse, where lovely Neu Trina awaited to tend to every wound.

For any other team than the illustrious Klapaucius and Trurl, the task would have been a Sisyphean one. 317 million planets was a lot of territory from which to expunge all positronic life. But finally, after three centuries of constant battle, the end was in sight. And soon they would be making their journey to the past.

Now a century delayed from their original projections, Trurl and Klapaucius were anxious to finish. Had their memory banks not been self-repairing and utterly heuristic and homeostatic, they might have forgotten by now their original purpose: to return to the past to capture a paleface sample for reintroduction into the stolid, staid, static present.

One day during Trurl's underground stint, he discovered what he suddenly believed was a potentially fatal flaw in their device.

"If," he mused aloud, "our orrery must mimic all the bodies in this quadrant over a certain size, then the GHC must be represented in the orrery as well. An obvious point, and this we've done. But perhaps that miniature GHC must contain a miniature orrery as well. In which case this lower-level model of the orrery would have to contain another GHC and its orrery, and so on in an infinite regress."

Trurl's anti-who-shaves-the-barber protection circuits began to overload, and he shunted their impulses into a temporary loop. "I must discuss this with Klapaucius!"

Up to the surface he zoomed. Into the pilothouse, following the location beacon of his friend.

There, he noted that Klapaucius was seemingly alone. Immediately, Trurl forgot the reason for his visit.

"Where is Neu Trina?"

Klapaucius grew nervous. "She—she's outside, gathering the pitted durasteel armatures of the slain mech-anoids. She likes to build trellises with them for her hologram roses."

"I don't believe you! Where is she? Come out with it!"

"She's far away, I tell you. One million, six hundred thousand, five hundred and nineteen planetary diameters away from here! Just go look, if you don't trust me!"

"Oh, I'll look all right!" And Trurl deployed his X-ray vision on the immediate vicinity.

What he saw caused him to gasp! "You—you've let her dock inside you!"

From deep inside Klapaucius emerged a muted feminine giggle.

"This is beyond belief, Klapaucius! You know we pledged never to do such a thing. Oh, a little cyber-canoodling, sure. 'Mild petting' were your exact words, as I recall. But this—!"

"Don't pretend you never thought of it, Trurl! Neu Trina told me how you dangled your USB plugs in front of her!"

"That was simply so she could inspect my pins to see if their gold-plating had begun to flake. . . ."

"Oh, really. . . ."

"Make her come out! Now!"

An enormous door in the front of Klapaucius gaped, a ramp extended, and the petite Neu Trina rolled out, just as she had that long ago day from the birthing factory. Except today all her antennae were disheveled, and hot liquid solder dripped from several ports.

Trurl's emotional units went angrily asymptotic at this sluttish sight.

"Damn you, Klapaucius!"

Trurl unfurled a bevy of whiplike manipulators and began to flail away at his partner.

Klapaucius responded in kind.

"Now, boys, don't fight over little old—*squee!*"

Caught in the middle of the battle, Neu Trina had her main interface pod lopped off by a metal tendril. If the combatants noticed this collateral damage, it served only to further inflame them. They escalated their fight, employing deadlier and deadlier devices—against which, of course, they were both immune.

But not so their surroundings. The pilothouse was soon destroyed, and Neu Trina rendered into scattered shavings and solenoids, tubes and transistors, lenses and levers.

After long struggle, the master constructors ground down to an exhausted halt. They looked about themselves, assessing the destruction they had caused with an air of sheepish bemusement. Trurl kicked half-heartedly at Neu Trina's dented responsometer, sending that heart-shaped box sailing several miles away. Klapaucius pretended to be very interested in a gynogasket.

Neither spoke, until Klapaucius said, "Well, I suppose I did let my lusts get the better of my judgment. I apologize profusely, dear Trurl. What was this servo anyhow, to come between us? Nothing! No hard feelings, I hope? Still friends?"

Klapaucius tentatively extended a manipulator. After a moment's hesitation, Trurl matched the gesture.

"Always friends, dear Klapaucius! Always! Now, listen to what brought me here." Trurl narrated his revelation about the orrery.

"You klystron klutz! Have you forgotten so easily the Law of Retrograde Reflexivity!"

"But the Ninth Corollary clearly states—"

And off they went to their labors, arguing all the way.

The Fourth Sally, or,
The Abduction of the Palefaces

One trillion AUs out from the planet that had first given birth to the race of palefaces, and millions of years deep into the past, relative to their own era, the pair of master constructors focused their bevy of remote-sensing devices on the blue-green globe. Instantly a large monitor filled with a living scene, complete with haptics and sound: a primitive urban conglomeration swarming with fleshy bipedal creatures, moving about "on foot" and inside enslaved dumb vehicles that emitted wasteful puffs of gas as they zoomed down narrow channels.

Trurl shuddered all along his beryllium spinal nodules. "How disagreeable these 'humans' are! So squishy! Like bags of water full of contaminants and debris."

"Don't forget—these are our ancestors, after a fashion. The legends hold that they invented the first machine intelligences."

"It seems impossible. Our clean, infallible, utilitarian kind emerging from organic slop—"

"Well, stranger things have happened. Recall how those colonies of metal-fixing bacteria on Benthic VII began to exhibit emergent behavioral complexity."

"Still, I can't quite credit the legend. Say, these pests can't reach us here, can they?"

"Although all records are lost, I believe we've traveled to an era before the humans had managed to venture further than their own satellite—bodily, that is. I've already registered the existence of various crude intrasolar data-gathering probes. Here, taste this captured one."

Klapaucius offered Trurl a small bonbon of a probe,

and Trurl ate it with zest. "Hmmm, yes, the most rudimentary processing power imaginable. Perhaps the legends are true. Well, be that as it may, what's our next move?"

"We'll have to reach the planet under our own power. The GHC—which the human astronomers seem not to have noticed yet, by the way—must remain here, due to its immense gravitic influences. Now, once within tractor-beam range, we could simply abduct some palefaces at random. They're powerless in comparison to our capabilities. Yet I argue otherwise."

"Why?" Trurl asked.

"How would we determine their fitness for our purposes? What standards apply? What if we got weak or intractable specimens?"

"Awful. They might die off or suicide, and we'd have to do this all over again. I hate repeating myself."

"Yes, indeed. So instead, I propose that we let our sample be self-determining."

"How would you arrange that?"

"Simple. We show ourselves and state our needs. Any human who volunteers to come with us will be *ipso facto* one of the type who would flourish in a novel environment."

"Brilliant, Klapaucius! But wait. Are we taking a chance by such blatant interference of diverting futurity from the course we know?"

"Not according to the Sixth Postulate of the Varker-Baley Theorems."

"Perfect! Then let's be off!"

Leaving the GHC in self-maintenance mode, the master constructors zipped across the intervening one trillion AUs and into low Earth orbit.

"Pick a concentration of humans," Klapaucius graciously transmitted to his partner.

"How about that one?" Trurl sent forth a low-wattage laser beam to highlight a large city on the edge of one continent. Even at low-wattage, however, the beam raised some flames visible from miles high.

"As good as anyplace else. Wait, one moment—there, I've deciphered every paleface language in their radio output. Now we can descend."

The master constructors were soon hovering above their chosen destination, casting enormous shadows over wildly racing, noisy, accident-prone crowds.

"Let us land in that plot of greenery, to avoid smashing any of these fragile structures."

Trurl and Klapaucius stood soon amidst crushed trees and shattered boulders and bridges and gazebos, rearing higher than the majority of the buildings around them.

"I will now broadcast our invitation in a range of languages," said Klapaucius.

From various speakers embedded across his form, words thundered out. Glass shattered throughout the city.

"My mistake."

The volume moderated, Klapaucius's call for volunteers went out. "—come with us. The future beckons! Leave this parochial planet behind. Trade your limited lifetimes and perspectives for infinite knowledge. Only enthusiastic and broad-minded individuals need apply. . . ."

Soon the giant cybervisitors were surrounded by a crowd of humans. Trurl and Klapaucius extruded interactive sensors at ground level to question the humans. One stepped boldly forward.

"Do you understand what we are looking for, human?"

"Yeah, sure, of course. It's Uplift time. Childhood's End. You're Optimus Prime, Iron Giant. Rusty and the Big Guy. Good Sentinels. Let's go! I've been ready for this all my life!"

"Are there other humans who share your outlook?"

"Millions! If you can believe the box-office figures."

On a separate plane of communication, Trurl said, "Do we need millions, Klapaucius?"

"Better to have some redundancy to allow for possible breakage of contents during transit."

"Very well, human. Assemble those who wish to depart."

"I'll post this on my blog, and we'll be all set," said the human. "One last question, though."

"Yes?"

"Can you turn into a car or plane or something else cool?"

"No. We don't do that kind of thing."

Dispatched from the GHC by remote signal, a fleet of ten thousand automated shuttles carrying ten thousand human volunteers apiece was sufficient to ferry all the humans who wished to voyage into the future out to their new home. But upon arrival, they did not immediately disembark. Once at the GHC, Trurl and Klapaucius had realized something.

Klapaucius said, "We need to create a suitable environment on the surface of the GHC for our guests. I hadn't anticipated having so many. I thought we could simply store one or two or a thousand safely inside our mainframes."

Trurl huffed with some residual ill-feeling. "Just like you kept a certain servomechanism safely inside you?"

Klapaucius ignored the taunt. "We'll repair the atmosphere generators. But we need a quantity of organics to layer atop the All-Purpose Building Material. I wonder if the humans would mind us disassembling one of their spare planets . . . ?"

The master constructors approached the first human

they had even spoken to, who had become something of a liaison. His name was Gary.

"Gary, might we have one of your gas-giant worlds?"

"Sure, take it. That's what we've been saving it for."

They actually took two. The planets known as Saturn and Jupiter, once rendered down to elemental constituents, were spread across a fair portion of the GHC, forming a layer deep enough to support an ecology. Plants and animals and microbes were brought from Earth, as well as some primitive tools. The genomes of the flora and fauna were deciphered, and clones begain to issue forth in large quantities from modified birthing factories.

"We are afraid you will have to lead a simple agrarian existence for the time being," said the constructors to Gary.

"No problemo!"

The humans seemed to settle down quite well. Trurl and Klapaucius were able to turn their attention to gearing up for the trip home.

And that's when dire trouble reared its hidden head.

One of the parasitical races that had infested the GHC back in the future had been known as the Chronovores of Gilliam XIII. Thought to be extirpated in the last campaign before poor Neu Trina had met her end, they had instead managed to penetrate the skin of the GHC and enter its interior, at some great remove from the time-engine. It had taken them this long to discover the crystals of frozen Planck-seconds, but discover them they had. And consumed every last one.

Now the Chronovores resembled bloated timesinks, too stuffed to flee the justified but useless wrath of the master constructors.

After the mindless slaughter, Trurl and Klapaucius were aghast.

"How can we replace our precious crystals! We didn't bring spares! We don't have a source of raw Planck-seconds in this rude era! We're marooned here!"

"Now, now, good Trurl, have some electrolyte and calm down. True, our time engine seems permanently defunct. But we are hardly marooned here."

"How so?"

"You and I will go into stasis and travel at the rate of one-second-per-second back to the future."

"Is stasis boring?"

"By definition, no."

"Then let's do it. But will the humans be all right?"

"Oh, bother them! They've been the source of all our troubles so far. Let them fend for themselves."

So Trurl and Klapaucius entered a stasis chamber deep inside the GHC and shut the door.

When it opened automatically, several million years later, they stretched their limbs just out of habit—for no wear and tear had ensued—swigged some electrolyte, and went to check on the humans.

They found that the entire sphere of 317 million planets acreage was covered with an HPLD: a civilization possessing the Highest Possible Level of Development.

And there wasn't a robot in sight.

"Well," said Trurl, "it seems we shan't be bored, anyhow."

Klapaucius agreed, but said "Shut up" just for old time's sake.

That Laugh

Patrick O'Leary

Twenty years ago, in the summer of 2002, I was hired to make an examination at the La Brea Tar Pits Museum in Los Angeles. At that time I had been in the field of forensic psychology for some thirty years. It was a lucrative contract, as all government contracts are, and for my trouble I was required to submit an oral and written report, take my check, and disappear. All contact with me was entirely routine and formal and conveyed no hint of urgency, but at no time was I given any clues whatsoever about the subject's identity. Thus I knew it was no ordinary interview. This was confirmed by the security clearances involved— for example: I took two flights across the country to arrive at the museum, which I assume was some sort of elaborate subterfuge.

During my stay I enjoyed the hospitality of a Santa Monica beachfront hotel. I was allowed three days to transcribe the interview, type my report, and record my oral top-line summary. Met a lovely woman on the pier the first night, and after a late meal of margaritas and white fish we enjoyed a pleasant sexual romp. At three o'clock in the morning I was woken by the roar of the ocean. I saw her standing naked at the threshold of the balcony, the pale diaphanous white curtains blowing back into the room, the scent of the surf, and her dark caramel skin black in the half light, and I thought for a few seconds I was dreaming. She must have sensed I was watching her, admiring her lithe form, for she turned to me and said, "Shouldn't you be working on your report? They expect it day after tomorrow."

Then she laughed.

In the morning she was gone and I had to convince myself that the whole episode was real. The littlest things about that night bothered me like a pebble in my shoe. Why didn't she use the word "the"? Why didn't she say "*The* day after tomorrow?" How come she never said what country she was from? Her accent was curious, but I couldn't place it. To this day, I'm frankly not sure how much of this actually happened. And, given all that followed this encounter, I remain in an uncomfortable quantum state of unknowable alternatives.

And, all this remember, was *before* the interview.

Over the last several years of my life my speculations have reached a more desperate pitch. I feel time is running out. And I may never solve the central mystery of my life. A mystery I could not confront that day, lacking the courage, the skill or, perhaps, both. And these days I swing from thinking this was all an elaborate hoax, to some truly paranoid Science Fictional postulations, to the possibility that I myself was the intended subject of the interview.

But at that time, all I knew was that my client was some unknown captive. My employer was the U.S. Government. And my citizenship depended on my discretion.

I am embarrassed to admit that I suspected my task

was a part of the greater "War On Terror." When I sought to subtly confirm this explanation, I was not discouraged. And I must admit, I felt pride at that time, proud to have been elevated from the status of my ordinary duties, proud to serve my country, proud to exercise a little "payback" in whatever modest fashion I could. If you remember, we all felt so enraged and helpless back then. Now, you can imagine how duped and betrayed I felt a while later when the photos of those naked prisoners in a pile became public. And I saw my compliance with retribution in a new light. "Prisoner." This unlikely alternative is one that truly haunts me.

Excuse me, I have to vomit.

Three days after the interview I pulled up an hour early to the tar pits to deliver my report. At a café across the street I had a croissant with butter and a latte. My skin was slightly burned, and I had a hazy feeling, a satisfying mental and physical fatigue. I had gotten drunk the night before when I finally finished printing the report and recording my summary. It had been a somewhat pleasant break from my routine of patients, consultations, and courtrooms.

The report, I mean, was pleasant. The interview was awful.

When I returned to my rental car, I found my briefcase had been stolen from my trunk. All my notes, all my reports, my recorder—they were all gone. I was tempted to file a police report, but I thought better of it. I flew home. After a very overwrought week I received my check in the mail confirming they had indeed gotten my report.

I vowed never to work for the government again.

Since then I have had recurring dreams where I am being interviewed by an alien. His skin is white. His large head is mostly black eyes. He wears silver gloves.

He admits to having stolen my report, and he promises to return my notes as soon as we finish the interview. Finally he hands over my notepad, and I see my notes are an unreadable scrawl. But his remarks are very clear indeed. In the upper right hand corner of the notepad's first page, in bright red cursive, are the following Teacher Remarks: "Dumb. Artificial. Pass."

And he laughs.

The pits themselves are black. Obsidian is the correct color, I believe. Tar has the sheen of those alien eyes, the mirror black of a bubble of petrified lava. The museum is nice. And you can actually watch through the glass as paleontologists pick and brush the tar off the bones of ancient dead creatures who died because they were going for the easy meal, squirming to death in that unforgiving black quicksand. This deadly process was repeated and repeated until there were more bones in the pits than fruit in a fruitcake.

We talked before a huge backlit wall comprised of yellow plastic cubes that held small skulls that over the years had been retrieved from the black taffy of the pits. At no time during the interview did I lay eyes upon my subject. He/she? was a voice of indeterminate ethnicity (obviously distorted, like a witness under anonymous protection)—a voice that emerged from a black Bose speaker on a white marble table. It was a rather large public space, but since this was after hours, no one intruded. A friendly black security guard unlocked the front door to let me in, guided me to my seat, and, after my notepad and recorder were set up, left me alone.

I waited about five minutes; then I heard a voice.

I am going to reconstruct our dialog with the greatest care. I have a photographic memory, and I can assure you that what you read is what I heard. You may form your own conclusions as to its veracity.

I am not afraid at this late stage of any repercussions as it is one of those tales patently easy to dismiss as moonshine.

Also, I should admit that I am a terminal cancer patient. I do not expect to live through the next month. I have no need for celebrity. I merely want history to be told with accuracy.

I am a father, too. I love my son. He is my caretaker now. He has encouraged me to do this. To settle, as he put it, "a long unsettled score."

And I am a patriot. I love my country but not as much as I love the truth.

As you read our words please remember this: I was told nothing about the patient.

Hello.

Good evening. I am Doctor _____.

So I am told.

I've been asked to ask you some questions.

By whom?

I am not at liberty to say.

Neither am I. Do they bind you, too?

Bind?

Bind. Bond. Chain.

You are chained?

In a manner of speaking. Conditions. Limitations.
I chafe under these.

Not . . . literally.

No.

Then we are in the same boat.

At this point the "patient" laughed. It was a most distressing sound, which I could not be sure wasn't distorted by the speaker or the echoing effect of the large chamber I was alone in. Suffice it to say that its laughter . . .

Oh my god.

Excuse me.

Sorry.

No, I'm fine.

Its laughter

. . . was always unexpected and always—how do I put this? Had it been at a cocktail party, or some other public venue, it would be considered totally inappropriate. Like laughter at a funeral. A chilling laugh. A laugh that could stop all the conversation in a bar. Such laughter I have heard in many mental hospitals. It was wretched and contained an unmistakable echo of despair. Remember, this is what I mean when you read the word "laughter."

It was the first clue that something was out of joint. However rational and clever his answers were, there were always, sprinkled throughout, these false notes of mirth that at the very least conveyed a sense of cross purposes, hidden agendas, and unspoken torment that could never be addressed directly.

I will say it this way. It broke my heart to hear.

It spoke of an unbearable gulf between us that could never be crossed.

A final aloneness.

It broke my heart.

Have you sat next to a firing rifle lately?

No.

Any nearby explosions?

No.

Have you ever been caught in a collapsing building?

Yes.

When the building fell on you, what were you doing?

I was in the bathroom.

Yes?

Yes.

How do you feel when a man touches you?

That would depend on the man.

The last time you made love, were you happy?

I have never made love. She did.

Okay. What was the last thing you heard?

A wailing sound and a gigantic ripe apple falling to the ground. Imagine a scream, a rumble and a thump.

Where were you?

New York. We were all there.

Were you there alone?

No. Sarah. She played piano. I got to know her in the dark. I sat with her on the floor, and I listened to her sing before she died.

She sang?

Yes. Under the wall. I couldn't see her face. She was just a foot sticking out of the plaster.

What did she sing?

Show tunes. She sounded like Ethel Merman. Only bearable. Do you know about lighthouses?

Excuse me?

Lighthouses.

Yes, I know lighthouses.

Sarah's father nearly starved to death in one. He was a Merchant Marine, and he was stationed with another man on Lake Superior in a long winter, and they were cut off by a tremendous storm, and they had underestimated the supplies they needed to get through winter before the spring thaw, when they would be resupplied. They came close to dying. They were making soup out of hot water and catsup when they were found. She told me that before she died. Have you ever been starved?

No.

I thought not. In the lighthouse the waves crash continuously. The sound is different than you would hear on a beach, or on a boat.

Different how?

You are surrounded. Cut off. Or at least you feel

that. **All bonds severed. Truly isolated. It must have been a terrible duty. Let me ask you a question.**

Okay.

Where's your heart?

(I cradled both my hands over my left breast as if I were about to break into song.) Here.

Oh. I thought that was something else.

You're joking right?

A little.

How far can you hit a baseball?

I have no idea.

What is it about women?

I don't know.

Do they lie for pleasure or to avoid pain?

For many reasons. As you do.

Does it work?

No. Wait. When you say "lie" do you mean "sex?"

No.

Fucking?

No.

Making Love?

Say, yes.

Then the answer to both of your questions is "yes."

I forget the questions.

So do I.

How many fingers am I holding up?

Three.

Ah, so you can see me, but I can't see you . . .

That is correct.

Doesn't seem quite fair.

(LAUGHTER) You know what I hate?

No. What?

When people say: Did you see that? Did you see that? If I saw it, wouldn't it be obvious?

That is a very peculiar question.

It is?

Don't you think?

Do you?

I'd like to set up a ground rule if I may: You are not to answer questions with questions for the duration of this interview.

I am not?

No.

No?

I mean Yes you are not.

Okay, then.

What is your one experience that should you put into words no one would believe you?

I couldn't put it in two words.

I didn't ask you to.

Sure, you did.

What do men want?

Men want blowjobs.

What is your first memory?

Her face.

Who's face?

The one we all lose.

I should tell you I am to stick to a list of required questions. Understand, please, that most of these questions are not mine—that is, I am required to ask them for various purposes—some of which I, myself, do not understand. If they make you uncomfortable, I apologize.

I am very comfortable.

What are your intentions?

I am here to learn. If I cannot learn, then I don't know why I am here. I am learning a great deal right now, and I have to say I enjoy it.

Where is your ship located?

Where ships usually are. The Harbor.

Why the secrecy?

If I asked you the same question would you answer?

Sure.

Then, why the secrecy?

Ummm. I suppose, if I had to guess, it has to do with security. Security precautions. National security.

And why is security about secrecy?

There are things to protect. Silence protects them.

(LAUGHTER)

What is funny?

You use the word "national." Do you know what it means?

Of course. Having to do with nations, states, countries.

No. National is an invisible line on a nonexistent map. It is a huge joke that anyone who has ever flown knows.

Have you . . . flown?

Like you, it's how I got here.

Are you here alone?

No.

No?

No. I am with you.

I doubt they meant that.

I know what they meant.

Okay. Why won't you help us?

I've answered this many times. But I'll repeat myself. You don't know what you're asking for. A man is holding a knife. He says to a stranger: "I am going to kill my neighbor unless you stop me." You say: "Don't kill him!" And he stabs him in the heart, turns to you and says: "Why didn't you stop me?"

You sound upset.

(LAUGHTER)

Would you like to take a minute?

Minutes cannot be taken, they can only be spent.

How old are you?

I will be three day after tomorrow.

Seriously.

I am almost three.

If you can't be serious, I don't see how we can continue.

Neither do I. But you do.

I'm merely saying that my job, my findings, depend on a certain, candor that can develope—

—Trust?

Yes, I mean, we've only just met but I am trying to do a job here, and part of that requires . . .

Trust?

Yes.

Good luck. (LAUGHTER)

For a three-year-old, you have a remarkable vocabulary.

For 64-year-old, you have a lot to learn.

How did you guess my age?

I didn't guess it; I knew it.

Evidently you have me at a disadvantage . . .

I agree.

At this point, I'm a bit lost. I don't know how to proceed exactly.

Why don't you let me tell you a story?

All right.

There once was a creature who had no form. Its form was whatever it filled. Sometimes it filled a body. Sometimes a machine. Sometimes it spread itself thin along a thread of light. Sometimes it was a naked woman who loved to smell the salt of the ocean. Wherever it went, it learned, and it taught. But one day it came to a place where it would not be allowed to teach. This had never happened before. Its students found a way to keep it in one place. To silence it. This had never happened before. Now the only way for it to learn is for it to listen. Now I am a voice in a box and they only let me talk to people who pretend

to want to learn but really only want control. Why
don't you call your son?

What?

Call your son. He needs to hear your voice.

How could you . . . ?

**Why don't you pay back your friend? He needs
the money.**

I have no idea . . .

Yes, you do. Why is everyone so afraid to love?

I am not.

(LAUGHTER) Oh, please, _____.

How do you know my name? Who told you?

**_____, I knew you from the moment you
spoke. I heard you. When I heard you, I knew you. I
was there the day you were born. Your mother was
terrified and radiant. She was a girl pretending to be
a woman. As you are a baby pretending to be a man.
You have not learned to love. Or forgive. You presume to understand people, but you are a mystery
to yourself.**

I can't sustain this. This is intolerable.

**It was really wonderful meeting you, _____. I
doubt we'll meet again. Let me advise you: after you
make your report, do not tell anyone. They will find
out. They will harm you. It is what they do best.**

Hastily, I packed my briefcase. I could feel all the
blood rushing to my face. I am a blusher, but I have
to say it had been years since I blushed. I was walking
out of the museum when the security guard whispered
something as I passed.

"Excuse me?" I said.

"I said, 'Relax. Nobody gets her.' "

"Her?" I don't think I really looked at him before,
but he was a middle-aged black man in a gray uniform.
He had a very pleasant air about him as if he enjoyed
any contact with people.

"She freaks most folks out. Don't take it so hard."

"I'm not, it's just . . ."

"Don't worry about it. She's a freak."

"You say, you say: There, there have been others?"

"Oh, yeah. They got an army trying to crack that code. Last night, some woman professor left in tears. Poor lady. I tried to tell her not to—"

"I have to be somewhere."

The moment I stepped out into the warm night, I noticed the world looked different. The smell of tar wafted into the air. The L.A. haze was lit by the warm copper glow of the grid of streetlights that crisscrosses the valley. Why copper? Why that color? I wondered. Why that smell? Why anything? It was as if I were looking at the world for the first time.

I realized I had been holding my breath. I told myself to breathe. Just breathe.

Then I recalled his laughter. That awful lost laugh. A laugh that could never be shared. Whose frame of reference was so beyond anyone else that true community would never happen, true companionship was but a dream, true connection

—impossible. I did not know and still do not know what that creature was. All I knew was that I would never understand it. And I was in the understanding business.

What surprised me then and haunts me now is that I could not wait to get out of its presence. I felt as if being within its proximity compromised any boundaries I may have constructed for my psyche. I felt violated. I'm not sure if the violation was intentional or just a by-product of its uncanny insight, but it felt like a psychic rape.

Was this a weapon that we were trying to disarm or create? A sample of a race so evolved they presented an intolerable threat? Or merely a fantastically advanced chess program whose only moves were intended to corner its prey and watch it squirm? Or was it, perhaps, just a trap—a black hole that could snatch anything and swallow it down.

I will never know. But I recorded this so that perhaps, someday, you might.

If you forget everything else about this story, please, remember one thing. Remember its laughter. Remember that, please.

A laugh no one else could share.

No one should ever have to laugh like that.

Alles in Ordnung

Garry Kilworth

This is what I think.

The aliens came, they left something that looks like a human to work the farm, then they left. But the android or robot, whatever—I've seen him once or twice outside the hayloft—doesn't move like a human. It's sort of mechanical. Not obviously so, but I know people. I've been around people all my life. He moves differently. A slight jerkiness here and there. A stiffness he shouldn't have if he's real people.

Why would the aliens do that, you ask? Leave some robot in charge of a farm down here in Tasmania?

Well, maybe they're doing it all over, in remote places, hiding them out near the wilderness areas where most people don't go. Tasmania is an outpost of the world. Maybe they do it first here, and possibly the Yukon in Canada, somewhere in Peru? You get the idea? They gradually replace humans with their machines, moving in from the edges of the world until they reach the center. New York, London, Moscow, Paris, Berlin. By then the Earth will be dotted with thousands of the bastards, Fifth Columnists. We'll be infested with them, unable to weed them all out, even when we know they're there among us.

You probably think I'm crazy.

On the other end of this babbled monologue, I make an encouraging sound. Another reporter comes to my desk, but I signal him quietly to go away, pointing to the phone at my ear. He nods and leaves me to my strange caller, who I have been told is on a hooked-up mobile phone in a car parked on a valley road below the farm . . .

The truth is, we're straightforward blokes. As you know, Tasmania is mostly rural; outside of Hobart it's sparsely populated—a quiet, rather reserved bit of land at the bottom of the world, the last stop before Antarctica. We still have wilderness here, in the west half of the island. Wild places with wild rivers and rather taciturn heights. I mean, we're a civilized and modern state in Australia, but we're slower moving than the rest of the nation: kind of cautious about new developments, wanting to see them work before we take them on board. Maybe that's precisely why the aliens chose our beautiful island? Because we're a reticent bunch of people, not too hasty or hotheaded, always looking before we leap? I suppose that makes sense.

I grunt.

We also get a lot of visitors, among whom these things can hide.

Anyway, here they are—or rather their damn mechanical soldiers—and naturally they frighten me.

Why am I *so* sure they're here? I mean, some people move funny because they've had an operation. Maybe they've got leg irons on under the overalls or a back brace or something? Maybe they've got a little brain damage that has them walking with jerky movements?

I'll tell you how I know.

There's too much order.

Oh, I know, order is good. Heck, my ancestors came from middle Europe. They liked order there. *Alles in ordnung* was what they wanted to hear about the world. But this is different. This is order close to insanity. Order that strikes fear in the heart of an onlooker. An extreme that almost closes the circle, so to speak, and meets chaos coming the other way. A headlong collision between total flexibility and utter rigidity. A crash a hairsbreadth away.

My caller was not uneducated, obviously, but madmen do have a wild sort of intelligence that flares brightly when they're on fire with some crazy idea. I should have put the phone down, but I didn't. In truth, I was fascinated by the guy's imagination.

There have been no reports of little green men, or giant reptiles, or even weird-looking marsupials in the neighborhood. Several times I've stopped the car at the bottom of this hill and looked up at the distant farmhouse, perched like a shoebox on the crag two-thirds the way up. I've never seen anyone else but that weird farmer.

I rang the agents who had the place up for sale and asked who had bought it. They told me in a polite way to mind my own business. Confidentiality. Privacy. I wasn't entitled to know. I had a quiet word with a policewoman friend, but she said strange as it might be, this newcomer hadn't broken any laws, he had committed no felonies, so why not leave him alone? If there were anything going on, the government would know about it, said my friend, and it was best to leave it to the authorities. But I don't think they do know. They have no reason to know. Why would the authorities notice an over-orderly farm in the middle of Tasmania?

I know, I know, you think I'm paranoid.

Just a bit.

There are plenty of nutcases out here, as anywhere, it's true. You probably think I'm overreacting in a xenophobic way to extraordinary circumstances.

Let me tell you what I've seen, and then you can make up your own mind.

Old man Williams died last spring. His wife, Emma, had gone three years earlier. We expected a descent of relatives, never seen before and never to be seen again, upon Saltash Farm. They usually come, from the big cities like Melbourne or Sydney, walk around the property proclaiming to their husbands or wives why the place should now belong to them rather than to bloody Uncle Reg or estranged sister Janice. There's often a battle in the courts between the husband or wife and Uncle Reg or the sister, and someone finally wins and inherits the property. Sometimes they even come to live in it for a while, try to work the farm, but invariably it's sold a few months on.

In the case of Saltash Farm, no one came. I mean, not the usual hypocrites. Instead the place went straight onto the market and was bought within hours. When I drove past on Lower Road, a week later, the changes had already begun. All the gum trees that used to line the winding track that led to the house had been cut down and uprooted and removed. That was not only outrageous from a local point of view, it was also bewildering. No one had seen heavy plant going into the property, yet getting old gum tree stumps out of the ground is a major exercise that involves lots of manpower and machinery. No one saw the trucks that would have been needed to take the stumps away.

Anyway, forty eucalyptus trees vanished overnight in mysterious circumstances, and white poplars were planted in their places along a track that had been completely straightened.

The track is no longer a track but a hard-surfaced driveway that goes arrow-straight to the farmhouse. The poplars that now line this driveway are all of exactly the same height.

I know what you're going to say: You've seen the same sort of thing in countries where nature is manicured, like Germany, Belgium, or the Netherlands. It's true, if you go to Holland, you'll quite often see an open box of poplars sheltering a farmhouse, and the poplars are encouraged, for reasons of neatness and uniformity, to grow to the same height. It's a Dutch mindset. No one criticizes them for it. They paint the curbstones white, trim the grass regularly, and have nothing like an unkempt ditch and hedge, which you might find in Great Britain or Ireland. The Dutch have a small country, and it's easy to keep it pristine.

So, maybe the new owners were Dutch—or German—or Belgique? One of these orderly countries.

The next thing that happened was that the house itself was straightened up, rebuilt on uniform lines. Symmetry was the word I looked for in my head and found after a while. The house was finally symmetrical and not at all the way old Williams would have had it. He would have considered such work to be totally unnecessary. What was wrong with a dipping roof, a sloping wall, a bent cornerpost? Nothing, so long as it still did its job of holding the house up and keeping the rain out. Now, so far as I can see from my parked car, not a splinter's out of place.

Still not amazing, you say. Nothing to get really worked up about. Nothing to worry about. Neat people are still people and entitled to join any community they wish, provided they have the right of abode.

But when you look at this farmland, look *properly,*

you can see everything on it is absolutely straight and ordered: ditches, fences, house, driveway, barns. Nothing's out of kilter. Not the slightest. Even hillocks and knolls have been flattened, ironed out.

Why? Well, no real farmer would do that, it's certain. He has greater priorities than flattening his hills and straightening his paths. So the occupants have to be something other than real farmers. Yet, even a wealthy man who wanted the farmhouse simply as a dwelling, perhaps a second home, a summer retreat, would surely not go to those lengths to prove he was the most anal man on earth, totally without good taste or discernment of any kind. No, whoever lives there now is so foreign he's not from this world at all—he, it, is from somewhere else. A thing that wants to *appear* to be a human but has got it *too* right—like someone who's learned a foreign language very, very well but speaks with too much precision, much too correctly to be a local.

I sensed we were coming to the crux of this one-way conversation. My hand was aching from holding the phone to my ear, and I was looking forward to this lunatic's coup de grace.

Anyway, this morning my theory's finally been proved correct.

I'm sitting here and can see a herd of cows grazing on the meadow below the farm. Look mate, the sight is a chilling one. They're not in any sort of disarray, as they should be, not scattered in bunches, anything like that. They're formed in three straight lines across the top of the meadow, each exactly the same distance apart from the next cow. They're moving down the slope as they eat, all in unison, all keeping pace with one another. It's like some monstrous line of slow-marching soldiers, munching their way down toward my vehicle.

Strewth, it's unnerving. You ought to get down here. You're in Launceston, right? I have to show you this. Parallel cows, eating to a slide rule, right angles to the road. I have to get someone here before these cows finish grazing the field. No one could doubt the strangeness of this scene. This would make the hair on the back of your neck stand up, mate, it really would. I'm leaving. This is too weird.

I hear him start his car engine.

I'm driving away now—going over the short cut, over the heights. You ought to get out here, mister. You ought to see those damn cows . . . shit! The wheel won't turn. I can't move it. I can't move the bloody wheel! Oh, shit. Oh, holy Christ, I'm going in a straight line . . .

I know the heights he's talking about. The road twists and turns there—snakes along the edge of sheer, deep drops. I want to ask him if this is some sort of elaborate hoax. Is it me who's being taken for a ride?—but I can't—the phone line has gone completely dead.

Sweats

Keith Brooke

I stay quiet as my senses kick in, keep my eyes closed. There's a lot of background noise: the electrical engine whine from traffic in a street nearby, the occasional splutter of internal combustion, jangling bicycle bells, voices talking, shouting, laughing, even singing, a goat calling, music from a radio or TV. Sweat beads my skin. My clothes feel rough, cheap. The heat is unpleasant, and it makes the smells of body odor, decay and spices all the more intense. Or maybe that's just me recalibrating: new environment, new senses. It always takes a while to stabilize.

I open my eyes, see a plywood ceiling stained brown and black by damp, flies buzzing in mindless circles. It's mostly gloomy in here, wherever *here* is, save for a single shaft of bright light angling in through an unglazed window.

I turn. Through the window I see the back of an old stallholder's head, smoke from his pipe haloing him like some barroom jesus. Beyond him, the street: bustling, packed. Asia, somewhere in Asia. Thailand, Cambodia, Vietnam, the Phillipines. It doesn't matter much.

My body is scrawny, white, maybe sixty kilos of skin and bone. I wear battered pumps, baggy khaki shorts, a grubby white t-shirt. Pretty much what you'd expect from a sweat: some kid out in the world for the first time, runs short of money, hires himself out for a few hours to cover the shortfall. We've all been there, or our sons and daughters have. Hire your body out so some rich fuck can have fun in it; get it back with maybe a bit of damage and the odd virus or two, but hey, the ghosting company covers you for all that, so you're fine, fixed up in no time, back to yourself with a couple of thousand bucks in your pocket where there was none before. We call them sweats, rides.

I close my new eyes, bounce myself around inside my new skull. You in there, motherfucker? Is any of you left?

But no . . . my host's mind, his *self*, has been ware-housed for the duration, will get pumped back in when my time is up.

I open my eyes, stand, adjusting to the mechanics of an unfamiliar body, the balance, all the little inner feedbacks that allow us to stand and not teeter and fall.

I jump, do a starfish in midair, squat on landing, drop to press ups, do twenty before my arms feel about ready to fall off. Roll onto my back, do twenty sit-ups and wish this grubby jerk had had money for deodorant or had at least washed before hiring himself out. At least the body isn't completely wrecked al-ready. I need it to be a fit one, a sweat who is ready for a bit of action.

Okay . . . if I were one of the idle rich, out for kicks, I'd head off and burn credit in the nearest mall, clean myself up, kit myself out before hunting down some fun. That's another of the perks for the sweats:

They usually end up being pampered a bit, new outfit, that kind of thing. Sometimes it gets trashed, of course: Armanis shredded in a knife fight when a night out turns bad. Sometimes the sweat gets trashed too, but as I say, that comes with the territory. Why hire a ride if you're not going to try out something you can't or won't do in your own body?

I walk to the beaded doorway, peer out, and the old man turns his head, bows a little, smiling. "You tell me what you wanna do, mister, I tell you the place to go and the man who can set you up." In his baggy jeans and Sex Pistols t-shirt, the old man doesn't exactly look like the proprietor of a ghosting company's premises, but that doesn't really mean much. Sometimes it's a swanky high-class clinic, sometimes a backstreet dive like this. Depends what the client is looking for, and willing to pay for; depends how desperate the ride is.

"I don't need nothing, thank you, sir," I tell him, and step past him into the street.

I have business to attend to.

Looking like shit has its advantages.

Looking like this, like a western kid down on his luck and right out of money, and probably a junkie to boot, the hawkers and hustlers take one look at me and no more. No hassle. Easier money elsewhere.

I hit the main drag and flag down a rickshaw, give the driver an address that pops into my head. He jabbers something in my face, and I guess his meaning; I wave a wad of bills at him to prove I can pay. He gestures me into the seat and then guns his engine back into life.

Fifteen minutes later we're pulling up in a residential part of the city, white houses partly hidden behind stone walls and cast-iron railings. Rich vegetation crams the gardens around manicured lawns and large, open swimming pools.

We've already made one stop along the way. Another side street, a doorway screened by a beaded curtain, a bony kid on his haunches outside watching me as I pushed through the beads to another shady room where I found the man, struck a deal, came out with a heavy lump of steel tucked into my waistband.

Now, I pay off my driver and walk up to an iron-bar gate that extends at least a meter above my head. I look through to the sprawling white mansion, people in and around the pool, cars pulled up out front.

A security camera is watching me from the top of the wall. I run clawed hands through my lank hair, give a junkie twitch, rub my nose on my upper arm, turn away.

He makes it so easy.

Less than an hour later I hear the electric whine of three scooters coming down the drive. The big gates swing open, and I stagger out into the roadway, looking disoriented, confused.

One bike knocks me stumbling sideways, and I land on my knees, head spinning. My left wrist jags with a stab of pain in a way that makes my stomach clench. Blood seeps through the knees of my khaki trousers.

The scooters skid to a halt, the one that struck me somehow managing to stay upright.

Voices rise, suddenly.

"Wha—?"

"You stupid fucking idiot!"

"Hey! Hey, Mr. B—you okay?" This addressed to the rider of the scooter that had hit me.

A guy in shorts and a gold netting vest looms over

me. "You okay, bud?" he asks. Then: "What the fuck were you doing?"

I squint up at his square face, then turn away. One of the others.

I look at the one on the lead scooter, the one who hit me.

He's still sitting there, one foot on the ground. He's older than the one who spoke to me, older than the other guy too, who's just going up to him, saying something to him. His dark hair is a thick, short crop, and his muscle top shows off his bulging shoulders and pecs. Hard to say how much of it is cosmetic, but it's the kind of look you'd expect from someone who pays for the mansion they've just emerged from.

He looks at me as I reach for the Heckler and Koch tucked into my waistband.

I take it out, the heft of it feeling at once natural and strange in this hand that may never have held a gun before.

I fire it, once, twice, allowing my right arm and shoulder to ride out the recoil.

One round takes him right between the eyes, the other in the chest as he falls.

The guy with the gold vest is swinging at me and so I duck, twist, slam the heel of the pistol into his temple, and he collapses in a heap.

The other guy is in middraw as I shoot him in the side of the head.

My first instinct is to return to the back street where I woke, get myself plugged back in, upload to netspace, and let the dumb sweat back into his body.

All the forensics will point to this body that I'm riding, so once I'm gone and the owner is back in place, it's *him* they'll track down and throw into a cell.

Sure, they'll piece together the fact that he wasn't in control at the time, but that buys me breathing space. Meantime, I'll be covering my tracks in netspace and . . . and what?

Where do I go after that?

I don't know. I don't remember.

I don't know my name. I don't remember my childhood. I don't know how old I am or where I live, can't picture my wife's face or even remember if I have a fucking wife.

I am living in the present, in the moment.

I am incomplete then, a partial download. The rest of me is out there somewhere, waiting for my return . . .

All I have in my head is the knowledge required to carry out this hit—that's all they gave me. A killer's knowledge, a killer's instinct. It's all I have. All I can do is return.

The old man is sitting at his stall, selling pipes and tobacco and peculiar herbs and spices in pots and little plastic bags. A front for his real business.

He sees me, bows his head, and smiles widely.

I stride past him, and he follows me inside. The flies still buzz in aimless circles under the stained ceiling.

"Okay," I say. "I need to get back. That part of the deal?"

He raises his eyebrows, as if he's going to pretend not to understand. Maybe he doesn't.

But he does. I see it in his eye as he hurries past, waves at the couch, starts fiddling with the skullcap and leads.

"You settle down here, mister," he says, too eager. "You'll be gone real soon."

I remain standing. Why does he want to get rid of me? Why do *they* want me to upload as quickly as possible? The people who commissioned this job.

To get me away from the scene, I tell myself. That's all it is. All the forensics point to this body, and they don't want me caught in occupation—*I* don't want me caught in occupation!

I step round the couch, take the little fellow's jaw in the cup of my hand, and force him so hard against the wall that I swear the ceiling shakes.

"So," I hiss, "tell me . . . What excactly did you mean by the word 'gone'? What's going to happen to me when I'm plugged in? Do I get uploaded to net-space and reunited with the rest of me, or might it just be that I get wiped altogether? All the evidence tidied away? Eh?"

Is there even another me for me to be reunited with? Or am I just a construct, a bunch of killer traits pumped into this body for a single job?

I'm just another fucking sweat! Just like the jerk whose body I've been using . . .

The old man stares at me, barely reacting. He must have seen some real shit in his time, I realize. He's not going to tell me anything, and suddenly I've lost my impetus, confused.

I'm faced with the choice: go through with what I understand of the plan or not? Do I let the old man upload me to netspace and pump the owner of this body back into his own skull? Do I trust that back in netspace I won't just be wiped?

I'm assuming now that I have controllers out there: people who commissioned the hit, people who set it all up. But maybe it's just me out there. Maybe I wanted Mr. B dead for reasons of my own and so I sent a part of myself down to use this sweat to kill the fucker.

I loosen my grip on the old man's face, let him slump against the wall. He'd been on his toes before, I'd been holding him so hard.

Something isn't right.

The old man is looking past me, toward the window.

I turn.

Police. Or soldiers or armed security of some kind. Hard to tell. A green jeep is forcing its way slowly up the street, through the throng. As I watch, a couple of uniformed men jump out and start to jog alongside it.

I look at the doorway, but they would see me if I left now.

The police will have picked up my body's signature at Mr. B's gates. They'd have the eyewitness account from the guy I didn't kill, the stream from the security cam that would show them everything that had happened.

They've been quick; less than an hour since the hit, they've pattern-matched my face from the security cam, found me on security-cam streams as I crossed the city. Some of the systems are probably even body-smart: They'll have sampled body scent and phero-mones, matched them to those of the killer.

They've tracked me down to the ghost company's crossload parlour.

I look around. This is just a single room in some kind of lean-to. One door. No other way out.

I glance up, then step onto the couch, bent at the knees. Straightening abruptly, I drive my shoulder into the plywood, and it gives with a sharp creaking sound.

There's a gap between ceiling and wall. My shoulder is screaming with pain, but I haul myself up and through that gap, tugging myself clear of flapping plas-tic sheeting.

I'm on a sloping roof now, at the back of the parlor, starting to slither down. I spread my limbs to slow the fall, then get to my knees and clamber down just as shouts come from within.

I hear a thud—something hard on something soft—
and the old man cries out.

I hit the ground running.

Bartie Davits is a sweat. A student working his way
through business school, paying his own way because
his parents are in no position to help, one of them a
low-paid supermarket assistant, the other long since
dead and gone. Sweating is easier than shop work and
generally safer than dealing, although he does a bit of
that too—that's just a natural extension of his business
training, he always argues.

He likes the SweatShop parlor in Haymarket. Real
class. You can taste it in the air.

He opens his eyes, remembering where he is, getting
used to his own senses again after spending what feels
like a couple of days warehoused off in netspace, playing TrueSim games while some rich wanker fools with
his body.

A face looms over him, cheekbones like geometry,
perfect skin, eyes like the flawless glass eyes of a perfect porcelain doll. Bartie can smell her, and she's like
apples. He smiles.

"What's the damage?" he asks.

She smiles back at him, everything symmetrical.
Someone paid a fortune for those looks, he guesses.

"Narcotic residue," she tells him. "Alcohol residue.
Black eye—looks like you had a run-in with someone.
That's all, though, Mr. Davits."

No serious damage this time, then. Right now there
will be drugs cleansing his blood and liver, stripping
out the narcs and booze, replenishing his reserves.
That's one of the perks of sweating; some people
argue that the clean-out could add years to your life.
Rich wankers would pay a fortune for some of this

shit, and here is Bartie Davits, getting it all for free. Fuck no—getting *paid* for it.

"Like we agreed," he says, sitting slowly. "Cash in hand, right?"

She smiles her professional smile again. "The fee is already in your registered account, Mr. Davits, minus tax and obligatory pension, just as always. No special arrangements."

He stands, stretches. Feels unfamiliar aches and stiffnesses. Raises a hand to his left eye, suddenly aware of its dull ache.

He looks down at his clothes: a slick pair of jeans, a crumpled silk t-shirt, pointed snakeskin boots, none of it his. There's a bag on the side containing his own newly laundered clothes. The new outfit—another perk.

He hopes his body had a good time while he was warehoused.

Funny to think that his own body has had far more diverse experience than he himself has—and he knows nothing about it other than a bunch of hints and signs and scars . . .

Out along a corridor, mirrored walls multiplying him, bright lights making him squint. Into the foyer, all tall, angular plants emerging from chrome pots full of glass pebbles. The street outside looks dark through the clinic's floor-to-ceiling tinted glass front.

The cops grab Bartie as he steps outside. He's just wondering whether it's a Comedy Store night, who might be on. Maybe he'll call a few mates and front them for a night out, make the most of the new wad in his bank account. But the cops have other ideas.

He steps out through glass and chrome doors that slide open as they sense his approach. He has time to notice the sudden clash of warm scented air from the interior of the clinic mixing with the smells of the damp London street, has time to emerge into the drizzle, to look left, then start to look right, and then they're on him.

A sudden rush of figures . . . Two men step out from his right, and as he opens his mouth to speak, to curse them for jostling him, for not looking where they're going even though it's actually Bartie who has stepped out into the flow, another two take him from the left. His arms gripped tightly, he smells something cloyingly sweet, realizes someone has sprayed something, feels it infiltrating his lungs as he breathes it deep, hears the gabble of street noise suddenly fizz to static, to nothing . . .

. . . wakes in a cell.

He remembers now, the men grabbing him, the prickle of some kind of nerve agent in his lungs. He realizes they were police, some in uniform, some not. He hadn't had time to take it all in as they descended on him, in the sudden rush of sensation as the foundations of a normal day were abruptly pulled from under him.

He's on a bunk, a brick wall to his immediate left, a narrow strip of floor and then another bare brick wall to the right. There's a door at one end of the cell, past his feet, with a viewing panel set into it. In one corner of the room, where two walls meet ceiling, the glinting eye of a security cam peers back at him.

He sits, rubs at his temples as dizziness settles.

Down on the concrete floor, he presses his feet against the wall and starts on sit-ups, rapid and regular, enjoying the rush of blood and adrenalin that kick in with the exercise. Bartie likes to look after himself. It keeps the brain in tune as well as the body. And his rich clients like a fit sweat to ride in, so it's a good career move, if sweating can really be considered a career.

He's past 150 when he hears the door. He carries on until a man says, "Bartie Davits. You're wanted for interview."

"Interview?" he asks, pausing, twisting to see the uniformed man framed by the doorway. "Like for a job?"

The policeman just looks at him, waits for him to stand, steps back to let him out into the corridor.

A short time later, Bartie is sitting in another room, elbows on a desk. There's a plainclothes officer across the table from him, a uniformed man on the door.

"Bartholomew Brooklyn Davits," says the officer, "we have reason to suspect your involvement in the murder of Elector Nathan Burnham at his retreat in Jakarta on the 23rd of this month. This interview is being recorded and your responses processed for veracity by smart systems from two independent vendors. Anything you do or say may be used as evidence in a court of law. Do you understand?"

Bartie stares at the man. "I understand your words," he says slowly, "but fuck no, I don't *understand*."

The officer has a feed going into his ear. He receives some kind of input, nods, and his eyes meet Bartie's again.

Then Bartie adds, "Burnham? Elector Burnham? The virtual worlds guy? Dead?" At a brief nod, he continues, "I . . . I've been out of it a couple of days. I hadn't heard. I sweat rides, you know? I was sweating, warehoused in a data bank somewhere while some rich fuck rode my bones, you know?"

Another pause, while the officer listens to his feed, then: "Elector Burnham was killed by a kid called Joey Bannerman."

"So . . . I don't understand?"

"Bannerman was gapyearing round the world, ran out of cash, took to sweating to get by. He was ridden by the killer."

Bartie gets it, he thinks. "Not me, man . . . I didn't do nothing. I was warehoused, playing TrueSim strategy games in perfect isolation. Check out the records: I was pumped into a data bank and kept clean and cut off from the world. They have to do that. Data integrity and all that—have to put back what they take out!" He laughs awkwardly.

"We don't think it was you, as such," says the officer.

Bartie relaxes, hasn't realized how much tension he'd been holding in. Then he registers the "as such," and he sees from the officer's expression that there's more, a layer yet to unpick. "And?"

"We've pattern-matched traits identified from the data feed that injected the killer into Bannerman's skull. The killer was an amalgam, a construct. Whoever was behind the assassination took a few traits from here, a few from there, and built the killer suited for the job."

Bartie waits. There's more.

"It's a known technique. Developed by the Yakuza, but it's been seen in a number of cases now. The way they do it is they have to have a solid foundation, a template, someone who could easily be a killer in the right circumstances, with the right traits added, re-mixed, recompiled. We've identified the template, Davits. We've tracked down that individual. It's you."

Bartie shakes his head. "But it wasn't me!" he finally says. "I was warehoused, isolated. . . . It wasn't me."

"Your profile was used," says the officer. "Edited, built upon. We're talking legal gray areas here. Our

advice is that this could be the test case to beat all
test cases. Could take years."

The officer is enjoying this, Bartie suddenly realizes.
"How do you mean?"

"It's all about legal culpability," the officer explains.
"When due process proves that you were the template
used in this crime, and when it is demonstrated that
the killer was substantially *you*, then you will share
legal culpability for the killing."

"But . . . I wasn't there."

"No, that's true. But there is evidence to show that
a statistically significant instance of you *was* . . ."

Dogs.

Fucking dogs. A whole pack of them, ragged-
looking beasts, sniffing at the trash stacked high. Don't
they eat the fucking dogs in this part of the world?

I press back into the corner of the doorway, hugging
myself, trying to think.

One of the dogs starts pawing at the side of a box,
and the soft cardboard gives way immediately in the
humid heat.

A steady flow of people passes the end of the alleyway. It's several minutes since the two cops passed.
Should be safe to emerge again. But I'm no fool. The
security cams will be watching for me, sniffing me out
as they must have done when I crossed the city immediately after the hit. They have my host-body's signatures mapped out: scent, pheromone mix, facial
geometrics, gait. As soon as I pass one of the cams,
I'll be flagged up back at the control centre.

I have to get out of here. Out of this city. But
how? Where?

Out of the city there will be fewer cams, but as soon
as I hit civilization again, I'll be exposed. Do I really

want to see out my days in a borrowed body in the middle of some fucking jungle?

I need to get out of this body, shed this skin like a snake.

I rack my brain, struggling to come up with some kind of plan.

A dog spots me, all bone and shaggy coat. It starts to growl, shuffling toward me, one leg lame, bent. I squat, hold out a hand, and in seconds it's nuzzling my wrist as I scratch its mangy neck.

I straighten.

Cautiously, I approach the end of the alleyway. No sign of the cops. I step out, joining the flow. I walk with a limp, and I have a hand over my face, occasionally rubbing as if I have a permanent itch. I can obscure my facial geometrics, and I can disguise the normal pattern of this body's movement, but there's nothing I can do to hide its scent signature. That's a risk I have to accept: All the cams supply a feed that's processed for visual patterning, but far fewer are equipped with the full bodystamp sensors.

I need to get my bearings, but then what? I don't know what city this is, don't even know which country. And even if I *did* know . . . why should I trust any knowledge I have? What if my controllers really do just want to erase me as soon as I upload? I can't rely on any knowledge they've given me, just in case they're leading me toward my own end.

I need to upload, but on my own terms. And then . . . time to go looking for myself, the original me. Time to find me and ask myself some tough questions. Time to look for daddy.

". . . a statistically significant instance of you *was* . . ."

Bartie Davits hits 280 and then stops the sit-ups, head between his knees, gasping, chest aching, head pounding, abdominal muscles burning.

He can't shake the sound of the officer's voice, the half smile on the bastard's face. They were having fun, toying with him. Fuck with his life, but for them it's just a new twist on an otherwise dull and routine day at the station.

Slowly, his breathing calms, and his thoughts calm too.

They're playing games with him. But if they want to play, then bring it on! Bartie plays games all the time. Other than the dealing and the sweating, online gaming is his main source of income to fund business school.

This is just a game, a strategy game.

It's time to stop acting like a frightened rabbit, caught in the headlights. Time to take control, take the initiative.

If the bastards want to play with Bartie Davits, then Bartie Davits is ready for them. And then some.

Another back street, another alleyway piled high with garbage and the ever present dogs darting in and out between people's legs, amazing they don't trip anyone. It's dark now, early evening, hot and sultry so that sweat makes tracklines down my neck. There are crowds of people everywhere I go in this city. People and dogs. This is the city of people and dogs. I still don't know where I am. Haven't thought to ask—I don't intend to be here much longer.

The door, just as the guy had said. An ordinary door, no sign or anything, no shiny lock to say there's something special here, *someone* special.

The guy . . . It was a risk, but I had gone back to

the gun dealer, the guy who'd had my Heckler and
Koch there just waiting for me.

He recognized me straight away. Claimed the police
weren't onto him yet, and I believed him because if
they'd traced my pistol to him, he'd either be in a cell
or his shop would be staked out, and they'd have
closed in on me as soon as I turned up.

I didn't try any strong-arm tactics on him. He was
maybe midforties, refined . . . On the face of it, I could
easily have scared the shit out of him and done quite
a lot of damage, but I'm not stupid. No gun dealer in
a city like this, wherever this is, goes unprotected—
he'd be armed, he'd have security systems in place,
panic systems, debilitators, the works.

"You going to tell me who set this up?" I asked
him instead. "Who ordered my piece and told you to
have it ready for me today?"

He smiled, and there was at least a trace of genuine
sympathy in that smile. "I don't know," he said. "And
if I did, I would not be indiscreet enough to divulge
that data. I'm sure you understand my position."

"I need help," I said. "I don't have money. I'll
never see you again, so I can't repay any debts. But
I need help."

Silence invited me to at least continue.

"Someone to help me. Someone who understands
ghosting, netspace, virtual intelligence systems . . .
Someone I can talk to . . ."

He gave me a name. And the name gave me another name. And now I'm here, eyeing this anonymous door in an unlit back street, crowds swirling
past, sweat running down my body, hopes hanging by
a thread, a virtual thread.

I push, walk inside, just as I'd been told.

It's dark in here, dim wall lights, a single bright desk

lamp over on the far side of the junk-filled room where a short round guy is turning slowly to face me.

He is shirtless in the heat, a shiny black ponytail halfway down his back, partly covering the winged dragon tattoo that covers most of the exposed skin. He has sensuous lips and tiny oriental eyes.

"Ah," he says, a long drawn out sound, almost a sigh. "The Assassin, I presume? I have been expecting you. Please, come over, sit. I would like to talk. Tell me, Mr. Assassin, what it is *like* . . ."

I walk over, threading a path through stacks of papers and boxes and panels with wires and transistors and chips and crystal boards. On his chest there is another dragon, this one breathing fire.

I sit on an office chair with one arm broken off.

"I—"

"What it is like to be you, Mr. Assassin. To be a man of many parts. Parts of other men—and maybe women, who knows?—and VI modules, a mix, a remix. All riding in another man's body. What is it like? What is it like to be something new, something unique, one of the first of your kind? A new variety of man for the first time in, what, twenty thousand, a hundred thousand years?"

"I . . . I don't know. I just want out . . ." Then: "How do you know so much about me?"

He smiles. He's been smiling all the time, but now he smiles a bit more.

"It is my business to know things. I know that your victim, Elector Burnham, is now resident in the Accord that he hates so much. His afterlife has begun."

The Accord . . . The consensus reality that hit critical mass about a year ago: a vast virtual reality populated by saved personality copies of the deceased. A virtual heaven. That was Burnham's schtick as an Elector: He'd been trying to pull the plug on it, trying to close it down. And now he's there, clinging to virtual existence in the system he had opposed.

"And so you know why I need to get out of this body."

A dip of the head acknowledges what I don't need to explain. I can't stay in the sweat's body or I'll be caught.

"I need to upload to netspace," I tell him. "I need to track down my original."

"But you are a construct, an amalgam. You have no original, just a template, based on an individual who is at best only mostly you."

"Well in that case 'mostly' will have to do."

"If you upload to netspace, you will have to avoid your originators. They will be waiting. They will want to erase you."

I nod. I know all this.

"Upload me direct to the Accord," I tell him. The Accord: a virtual world within netspace, a distributed world, a fractal construction of the ether. "Sidestep netspace itself, and get me into heaven."

He shakes his head. He has stopped smiling now. "The Accord is a consensual reality governed by the strictest protocols," he says. "There is no way to break these protocols. It is rigid, inflexible."

"There must be a way . . ."

"The only way to enter the Accord is through death. Only then will the warehoused copy of your self be uploaded. It is governed by the protocols."

"There must be a way . . ."

"Even if I were to kill you now, the protocols dictate who gets in and who does not. You have not been warehoused, my friend. If you are to enter heaven, then first you must be saved. But even then, you are not whole, you are *other* . . . the protocols would deny you entrance."

"There must be a way . . ."

He is smiling again now. "There is often a way where at first there appeared to be none," he says. "But if there is a way, then there will be a price . . ."

"I have nothing."

"You have everything, my friend. You are alien. You are novel. Talk to me. Tell me how it is to be one of the first of a new variety of man . . ."

The beach is composed of white sand and shell fragments that glitter under the azure sky. It burns my feet. I look down, see my toes curling in the sand. My skin is white, my toes long and slender.

I squat, take a handful of the sand, let it drain between my fingers. I feel its smooth grittiness, savor the soft touch of a breeze on my face, smell salt on the air.

This, then, must be heaven.

Down in the water, two women in bikinis splash and play. A man runs past, in step with a gently loping Irish wolfhound. A road leads away from the beach.

I do not remember dying. This must be the way for everyone here: We are saved before we die; we do not recall death itself.

I breathe heaven's air deep. Lee has sidestepped the protocols, he has crafted masqueware to slip me into the Accord, but already I feel that I do not belong here. I wonder how long I must keep running.

I walk, tarmac hot beneath my feet, where before it had been the sand that burned.

Heaven, it would appear, is a tropical island.

This place, this world—it has been constructed from the consensual perceptions of all its inhabitants, a shared world, reinforced and governed by the protocols and algorithms of common belief in its existence and nature.

Those people on the beach behind me: dead, all

dead, all here to stay. I am an anomaly: I have come to heaven, but I am merely a visitor, passing through.

There is a bar where the road loops back across the top of the beach. Palm trees stand around a cabin with a banana-leaf roof. Seating is scattered across the sand, people laughing and chatting, drinks on tables. A bar runs the length of one wall of the cabin, a barwoman lolling behind it, chewing gum, chilled. For a moment, I wonder who in heaven decides who gets to sit and drink and who gets to tend bar, but then I don't. It's the consensus: Rules emerge from shared beliefs and perceptions. All societies need rules, even in heaven.

"Get a drink around here?"

"Sure," she says, still chewing. "You new here? First drink's free for debutantes."

I shrug, then point to the bottles of chilled beer in a cooler deep in the cabin's shade.

"So tell me . . . how do I find somebody around here?"

"That all depends," she tells me over her shoulder as she stoops for a beer, "on whether they want to be found."

Turns out the late Elector Burnham is none too keen to be found, which kind of makes sense. He had been, after all, the politician most active in trying to get the Accord closed down, organizing a ragbag coalition of religious fundamentalists and neocon noninterventionists to do battle against what they called a caricature of existence, a vast VR experiment in social engineering, an insult to whichever god was appropriate.

Now he's here, in heaven, lying low.

It's taken me a week to track him down, asking people, hacking virtual directories and surveillance

logs, until I ended up here, walking up a narrow lane
somewhere in southern England, heading toward a
row of three cottages that at some point in the past
have been knocked together into a single house. A
modest place for someone as influential as Burnham
had been. A modest home.

I wonder what happens if I kill him here. I wonder
if that's why I am here, why I have followed this tenu-
ous lead to the door of the one man I know who will
be working on every possible way to extract himself
from this virtual heaven.

I should have a plan, but I don't.

I just know I have to come here, find him. It's as if
I'm drawn to him, like magnetic north needs magnetic
south. Is this some perverse protocol of the Accord?
The guilty drawn to their victims? Maybe I will go
down on my knees and beg his forgiveness . . .

Or maybe there is still some protocol buried deep
in my being that draws me here to finish what I began
in that sultry Asian city.

It's going well. Bartie has read-only net access and
a larger room that he can kid himself is hardly a cell
at all but merely a holding space, a room they're pro-
viding while the current irregularities are ironed out.
The net allows him to fill his time reading up on
human rights legislation, and this is what has allowed
him to negotiate improved accommodation and round-
the-clock TrueSim gaming access.

He knows the officers who guard his room by name,
and he plays them off one against the other. Bartie
Davits is beginning to enjoy himself. Treat it as a
game, and he's on a winning streak. Most of the time
he even manages to stop himself from remembering
that this is his life, his future, until legal powers way
beyond his comprehension determine just how respon-

sible he is for the murder of someone he has never met, in a faraway city he has never visited, for reasons he can't even guess.

A real-life alert nudges him, and he slides the sim-shades up onto the crown of his head. "David," he says, "what can I do for you?"

The uniformed man stands in the doorway. "Your interview, Mr Davits. It's time for your interview."

"Ah, yes," says Bartie. "Of course."

He drops the shades on his desk and stands, then follows the officer out of the room and along the corridor to the lift. He has arranged this interview to discuss progress in his case. It's about time they started to give him a solid reason for his continued incarceration.

They ride a lift to the seventh floor, and David, his personal guard, shows him through into an office that occupies one corner of the building, high glass windows over two walls giving views across the city, Tower Bridge just visible in the distance.

"Malcolm." Bartie nods at the pinstriped man already seated in one of the two leather seats in front of the room's wide desk. His solicitor, Malcolm Groves.

Across the desk is a plainclothes officer. Another stands by a window, looking out. David remains by the closed door.

"So," says Bartie. "Where have we reached? By my understanding we have approximately twenty-two hours remaining until I must be either charged or released, isn't that so, Malcolm?"

Right up to this point Bartie has been confident. He has felt in control. Here he is in a senior officer's swanky office, turning the tables, conducting an interview he has initiated. He has read up on the relevant legislation. He knows his ground. He will be free by this time tomorrow, unless they actually find something to charge him with.

But now . . .

Malcolm won't meet his look. He has a stack of printouts on his lap, and he is staring at them. There is sweat on his upper lip, despite the air conditioning.

"Malcolm?"

"Perhaps you'd better explain, Mr. Groves." This was from the officer across the desk, addressing Bartie's solicitor.

Bartie stares at Malcolm, and finally the man meets his look, briefly . . .

"I'm sorry, Mr. Davits," he says. "There have been . . . complications."

It's a game, Bartie reminds himself. A game. He shouldn't be feeling that the world has been snatched from beneath his feet. He should ride the "complications" and bounce back fighting.

"There are claims of, erm, *territory*, Mr. Davits. Proprietorial issues. Ownership."

He is starting to see. To understand.

"You would be warehoused up to, and for the duration of, your trial and any subsequent appeals, Mr. Davits. Your rights will be protected, I will ensure that."

"But . . . but this is new legal territory," Bartie says. "Everyone tells me it could take years!"

Malcolm Groves looks away again.

"That's exactly why Elector Burnham wants out," says the officer from behind his desk.

"Are you telling me . . ." Bartie swallows, starts again. "Are you really telling me I'm going to be archived in some data warehouse while the late Elector Nathan Burnham rides my bones for all that time?"

Nobody says anything. Bartie's solicitor doesn't say, "No, Mr. Davits, we're going to fight your case all the way, they'll never get away with doing a thing like that."

He looks down. After months, years, just whose body will this be?

The bastards . . . they can't be allowed to do this.

He looks at his solicitor, and his solicitor looks at his sheaf of papers, and he realizes that yes, they can, and they will, and there's nothing he can do about it.

I ring the doorbell. Can it really be as simple as this?

My throat is dry. This isn't real, I tell myself. It's not reality. But my feet hurt from walking, I'm thirsty, I can feel the breeze at the back of my head. It certainly *feels* real.

The door opens halfway, a face peers around it.

Oh, fuck.

It's the other guy, one of the bodyguards who had ridden an electric scooter alongside Burnham, the one I'd killed with a single shot to the side of the head.

He's staring at me, but then I realize he doesn't know me. He's dead. This version of him was taken from the last time he'd been warehoused. He won't remember his own death at all, or his killer.

"I'm looking for Elector Burnham," I say.

"He's not expecting you," the guy says, in a soft Welsh accent.

That's all he says as I slam the door back at him, forcing him to sprawl against the wall. I follow through instantly, seizing his shirt, jerking him forward and then back with all my force, slamming his head against the wall. He slumps, and I let go, watch as he slides down the wall.

Before he hits the floor, he is gone.

Vanished. No trace remains, not even the smear of blood on the wall that had been there only seconds earlier.

This isn't real, I remind myself.

"Ronnie?"

That's Burnham, calling through from the back. I follow the sound.

And that's when I start to get dizzy. By the end of the short passageway I'm staggering, can hardly stay on my feet.

What am I doing here? Am I going to kill him again—whatever that means in heaven—like I just killed his minder? Up to now I've believed that he's my only connection in this place and that he may somehow be my only way back.

He's there, the same athletic build, the cropped black hair, the cosmetic face.

He's leaning on a heavy kitchen table. "What the . . . ?" he gasps. He slides into a chair, sits with his head in his hands, staring at me.

I find the chair opposite him, echo his pose. "What's happening?" I hiss. My head is swirling, spinning, a kaleidoscope of sensation.

I sense this man.

I feel him.

He's in my head and I'm in his.

There are no boundaries.

He starts again: "Who are you? Where's Ronnie?" He is struggling, like me.

"I'm your killer," I tell him.

I squeeze my skull between my hands. "How . . . ?"

My eyes are locked on Burnham, but over his shoulder I see a flicker, a form taking shape, and suddenly there's a man standing there, or at least the outline of a man.

I blink and the man has vanished, but hands are gripping my arms from behind. Either I've briefly blacked out, or the man has crossed the room in the blink of an eye.

I blink again, and blackness remains.

*   *   *

We sit in a gray space, a gentle gray, not too bright or too dark. A gray that folds around you. I sit. The man sits. Just the two of us.

I know this man. I have seen him somewhere before.

"You are an anomaly, my friend. You do not belong in the Accord."

"But I have nowhere else."

"That is, in part, the nature of your anomaly."

There is silence, then the man resumes. "You are comprised of too many nondiscreet elements. The protocols of consensus are very strong, self-reinforcing. They have to be. Without consensus there is no Accord. The algorithms that form this reality are constructed from all the individual perceptions of what should, and can be, a critical mass of belief, a complexity emerging from chaos. You are not whole. You are a mosaic. You contain the parts of many."

"What happened?"

The man bows his head. "An error of arrogance on my part," he says. "You are, to a significant extent, based on the profile of a student called Bartie Davits, but that is largely masqueware. A far more significant element of your nature is Elector Nathan Burnham himself. The Elector wanted to destroy the Accord; some among us felt it apt that he should be set to close himself down . . ."

" 'Close himself down'?"

"I am not a murderer, my friend. The Elector lives on in the Accord. I did not kill him when I instigated you: I granted him eternal life."

"And so when I found him here . . ."

"Proximity, a blurring of boundaries . . . The congruence challenged some of the most fundamental protocols of Accordance. You overlapped. It was quite fascinating . . ."

Quietly: "I know who you are."

He watches me, waits for me to continue.

"You're Noah Barakh, the guy who built the Accord."

He says nothing. He doesn't need to. He's defending his creation against Burnham. That's why, that's the reason.

"So what happens next?"

"The Elector has negotiated release," says Barakh. At a gesture, a gray space across to our right shows a young man, lying unconscious on some kind of medical bench. "That is Bartie Davits, soon to be long-term host to Elector Burnham while the courts fight out who has rights to his body."

"So Burnham gets a body back in the real world, and you just erase me, is that it?"

"My friend! As I said, I am not a murderer. I would not have you erased. I find you strangely engaging, we are able to have a full exchange, two equals. You are, to all reasonable degrees, a valid entity, a person, despite the nature of your construction."

"Thank you," I say. "So what happens?"

"That is not for me to say, my friend. This is the Accord. We are governed by logical rules derived from the consensus. You are an anomaly: much as I like you, you do not belong. Your existence breaks too many of the protocols. I would happily endorse your continuance, but consensus may prohibit that, particularly given your treatment of the Elector's bodyguard."

"So the consensus police come and take me away? Is that it?" I remember the strange being who had seized me at Burnham's place. Was he some kind of consensus cop?

"No, my friend. It is not like that here. Things are much more sophisticated than that. If consensus de-

nies your right to be here, then . . . it denies your
existence . . . you cease to be here."

"Can I see him again?" I can see the intrigue on
Barakh's face. "Burnham and I . . . we have unfinished
business. We touched each other back there . . ."

"I am not your captor," he says. "You are free for
as long as consensus accommodates your dis-
cordance."

"But . . ." I indicate the gray. Barakh smiles, and—

—I'm sitting at the table, head in hands, echoing
the pose of Burnham. We stare into each other's eyes,
and finally I embrace the truth: I set out to find my
original and here he is, or at least a substantial part
of me . . .

I am in his head, he is in mine. I hold on with all
my might.

"When . . . ?" I hiss.

His eyes water, and I feel his pain, his confusion.

"When do you go back to the real world? I can't
hold this forever."

"I . . ." He looks away, raises a limp hand as if
to point.

I feel him falling, spiraling downward, away from
me, away from the Accord, even though we both sit
motionless now.

I follow, even as he starts to fade, to dematerialize.
I chase. Our boundaries are fluid. We spiral. We
come together.

We wake, open our eyes.

We are in somewhere medical, bright lights dazzling
us, machines beeping and droning, a low murmur of
voices.

We drift, conscious enough to know that we have
been sedated.

*   *   *

We wake, open our eyes.

We are in a room that is not much more than a prison cell.

We sit, swing our legs out, feet on the carpeted floor. We are still wearing a surgical gown. We stand, and this body feels right, it feels ours, mine. We tug at the gown, and it comes away. We find shorts on the bunk and pull them on.

We start to do sit-ups, working off the chemical fatigue in our muscles.

We . . . we . . . *we* . . .

We are Bartie Davits, business student, online gamer, sometime sweat and light narcotic dealer. We remember our hard-working mother, her parenting by tired cliche: It's all fun and games until you lose an eye, was one of her favorites.

We are Elector Nathan Burnham, one of the most influential men in European politics, bitter opponent of the Accord and all it represents, because . . . because of Barakh. Because Barakh stole my wife, fled with her into the Accord, where he thought they could be safe, where they could keep on running . . .

And we are . . . what? Me. Us. The construct. We are Bartie and Nathan, and we are the mosaic persona sent down to kill Nathan, and we are all the compiled elements of that persona: the traits stolen from others, the algorithms built out of virtual intelligences.

We are us.

We sit in the Chief Inspector's office.

"You see, Elector," he tells us, "this is all new territory. There's so much new legal real estate here . . ."

For the sake of argument, and as far as these people know, I am Elector Nathan Burnham, now back in the real world and riding the body of Bartie Davits as the courts have decreed. They do not know that I am us, that we are such a deeply grained mosaic.

"So what's the problem? Why can't I just walk out of here and get on with my life?"

"Your killer . . . it was the body of a kid called Joey Bannerman, but he was being ridden by a virtual person built largely on Bartie Davits . . ."

"But Davits is warehoused for the duration. I'm only riding his body. Why can't I go?"

"Because Davits was only a part of the construct. We have reason to believe that you, Elector Burnham, were also a significant element in the virtual persona of your murderer."

"You're holding me for my own *murder*?"

"That's one way of looking at it. Or at least a significant part of your own murder . . ."

We keep fit, working out in our cell for much of the three days it takes our lawyers to extract us from legal limbo. Money and influence make all the difference.

We slip away through a back exit to avoid the waiting press. They don't know the half of it, but they know that Elector Burnham is here, riding the body of his killer, and the frenzy is building up.

We don't care.

We have other things on our mind.

We remember Noah Barakh's barely disguised glee as he outlined how clever he had been. He steals my wife, and then he painstakingly constructs a machine to kill me, and then he has the gall to argue that he has not killed me at all but has merely relocated me to the Accord, granted me eternal life . . .

We are free of the Accord now, but we want back in.

We have known heaven, and we like it. But Barakh is the flaw in the gem, the mote in God's eye.

We want back in, and we intend to destroy Barakh when we get there.

We tried Jakarta, but that will not work again.

Lee, the guy with the dragon tattoos and the long black ponytail was most apologetic. He'd got me in once, but consensus had closed around the chink he had found in its armor. He did not know of another way in.

We showed him a way in, for him at least.

If he has had the foresight to warehouse a recent instance of himself, then he is in the Accord right now.

We are, to one degree or another, a killer by our nature. A part of us was constructed for that very purpose.

Lee discovered that.

Barakh will too, before long.

We can be impetuous, as Lee discovered. But also, we can be patient. We have spent a month exploring the possibilities, but to no avail.

The only way into the Accord is death.

But not suicide. The protocols of Accordance prevent many suicides from entering; most have to undergo therapeutic reconstruction before being granted eternal life. Which seems reasonable enough for one who has chosen death, after all. But therapeutic reconstruction would not suit us . . .

So we have to find another way.

We spent another month setting it up: time to have the new construct built, time to train the new-generation masqueware to outsmart the protocols of Accordance—to disguise our true nature and make us appear *me* and not us—and so achieve passage through the gates of heaven.

We are back in the cottage now. Nestled in a south-facing slope on the South Downs, the cottage's front room catches the low evening sun.

We have a glass of Laphroaig, a cigar, *Tristan und Isolde* playing loud. So loud we barely hear the doorbell.

We walk slowly through, a strange mix of feelings welling up.

There is always a way. First time, Lee was our guide; this time, Barakh—we do it his way, which seems somehow appropriate.

We open the door.

A stranger stands there, probably still in his teens. We can tell from the look in his eye that he is not complete, a sweat whose body is being ridden by a construct, a mosaic, an amalgam.

We smile, and this puts the kid off for a moment, but then he reaches down to his waistband, pulls a handgun, raises it so that it points at our face.

He hesitates, and for the merest instant a ball of panic clutches our chest. What if we are wrong? What if this is the stupidest of ideas?

And then we see the decision in the kid's eyes, the first spasm of movement as his grip tightens, his fore-finger starts to squeeze the trigger.

And then—

Some Fast Thinking Needed

Ian Watson

"The Suicide Matrioshka's only three hundred kilometers deep and so near the event horizon now!" sang out Dana Darley as she scoped the black hole the clone-crewsome of five were heading for, somewhat inexorably by now.

In fact, the five were twice-over cloned, in the sense that they were the virtual representatives of the five organic chaos-clones of Mary Marley, who was chiefing the expedition from a safe distance of a few light hours, assisted by her five selves.

Chaos-clones as regards mentality and personality—which should guarantee variety and flexibility on a mission—although their bodies were superficially identical, except for Bango Barley who was male, for recreational reasons and for chilling out since they were all quite likely to unexist presently—the copies of the copies, that's to say. Unexist was a preferable word to *die*; and anyway, could an electronic copy of a clone be said to die?

A chaos algorithm had been used as regards the mentalities of their source-clones, since Mary Marley wasn't an egotist, although a redoubtable woman. Alternatively, maybe she *was* an egotist and couldn't tolerate exact copies of herself, except superficially, which was merely equivalent to admiring one's beauty in a mirror. In four mirrors, to be exact. Plus a fifth, male-configured mirror, for amusement. Hence, a random range of personalities, which the virtual copies, um, copied.

But *hist*, what is a Suicide Matrioshka?

Rewind a few years.

Homo sapiens sapiens had done all right as a species. In so saying, naturally I'm passing over the extinctions, or the genocides perpetrated by us in the unenlightened past, of our cousins on Planet Earth such as the Neandertals. And I'm passing over the mass extinctions of many animals, plants, insects, fish, et cetera, during the die-off of the twentieth and twenty-first centuries—centuries that were becoming enlightened, but not quite soon enough. At least *HSS* had survived! (So far.) We'd expanded into space. The eggs were no longer all in one basket. We'd even succeeded in traveling almost at the speed of light, using zero point energy.

Biological aliens found we none (not so far), except for bacteria. Earth was a very unusual planet as regards the sheer number of favorable factors and fortuitous events—as well as nonevents—that led to the evolution of *any* complex life, never mind *HSS*. A sun richer in heavy elements than most stars and in a secluded region. A good Jupiter rather than a bad one as in many solar systems. The early collision of proto-Earth with a Mars-size planet, affecting spin axis and day length and producing a huge moon stabilizing the tilt angle. Powerful magnetic field. The greenhouse versus iceball balancing act, some ice events being essential, and greenhouse gases the key to fresh water.

Continental drift causing upwelling of nutrients. The right balance of land and sea. Oh, so many happenstance factors. Life as such arises easily, yet it almost always stalls at the bacteria level—so far as we know (so far). Often life arises time after time on the same world or moon, getting snuffed and arising again, only so far and no further.

And then we came across the first Matrioshka brain.

Ancient machine intelligence, using most of the output of a star to power itself.

A Matrioshka, of course, is a set of hollow decorated wooden Russian dolls arranged one within another, the final and smallest dolly being solid in this case. A Matrioska brain, well . . . imagine crystalline frogspawn forming spherical shells within shells around a sun. The innermost shell runs hot, to power its computations, and radiates excess heat outward to the next shell, which runs a little less hotly; and so on to the outermost shell, equivalent to the distance of a Jupiter, where the temperature may be a mere 55 Kelvin. From a distance the only sign of a mature Matrioshka brain will be a dull infrared glow; so it took a long time to detect these mighty machine intelligences.

Of course, in such solar systems any Jupiters and other worlds had already been demolished and transmuted to construct the shells of crystalline frogspawn (or, in the present case, quarky particle streams).

Throughout the vastness of a Matrioshka brain, thought engines process and communicate or store data and beam their results or queries toward other Matrioshka brains elsewhere in the galaxy, hundreds or thousands of light years distant.

"Queries about what?" the Virtual Clone of Anna Aarley had asked.

"What kind of results?" the VC of Candy Carley had said.

"What are the questions?" That was the VC of Fanny Farley.

Those were rhetorical questions, more like mantras. which kept them focused on their mission.

To themselves, subjectively, they all seemed to be in a spaceship of adequate size for five crew members. They could walk about, they could eat and breathe or amuse themselves with Bango Barley. In actuality (or rather, virtuality) they were all part of the shielded quantum computer brain of the *Diver*. The real ship consisted largely of shielding and propellant and hardened transmission equipment, a vessel designed to approach the black hole and orbit it without being dragged inside the event horizon too soon. To approach the hole and also the Suicide Matrioshka, which had wrapped itself around the hole so as to exploit its enormous energy, far more than that of any star.

"About the true origin of the universe?" said Candy Carley.

"About the end of the universe and how to escape it?" said Anna Aarley.

"How to design a new universe?" said Fanny Farley.

Precisely! Maybe the Matrioshkas had come from a previous universe. Or maybe they evolved in this one but intended to design and create a subsequent universe. From the point of view of consummate skill in reorganizing matter, and undoubtedly in sheer thought power, the Matrioshkas were the Lords of the Universe.

It was said that the difference in capability between a Matrioshka and a woman must be ten million billion times larger than the chasm between a woman and a roundworm. Could a roundworm communicate with a woman? Or vice versa?

"A woman doesn't even notice a roundworm," remarked Dana Darley. "But the Matrioshkas must pay *some* attention to us, since they never demolished our solar system to build a new Matrioshka round our sun."

"Maybe we were just lucky," said Fanny Farley. "So far. After all, there are innumerable stars. And maybe our solar system didn't contain quite enough material to make another Matrioshka."

"No, I think they noticed us," said Candy. "Over a period of centuries since the first radio signals."

"Yes, that's the problem," agreed Anna. "*Time.*"

There was such a great disparity between the mayfly lifespan of a human being and the multi-eon existence of the Matrioshkas! Matrioshkas could communicate their computations across a thousand light years and wait patiently for a reply, in a dialog that may have lasted for a million years already. At least the Matrioshkas demonstrated irrefutably that nothing could ever travel faster than light, or than radio waves, which was perhaps somewhat disappointing. If FTL were possible, Matrioshkas would know how.

In practical terms there was no way that women could communicate with ordinary Matrioshkas, those being so vast. Lighting fast in their thoughts yet also in a sense, shall we say, cumbersome? The spherical size of the orbit of Jupiter, for instance. Just where do you plug in, metaphorically speaking? What part are you addressing? Maybe you could annoy some of the self-repair mechanisms, which mightn't be a good idea. Hitherto, radio signals beamed from nearby at part of a merely Mars-orbit-size Matrioshka around a star in the direction of Vega had provoked no response.

Big Matrioshkas could think lots of thoughts very fast within their components, yet it could take months to circulate those thoughts internally. Basically, the larger a Matrioshka is, the slower it thinks overall, even at lightning speed. That's no problem for a Matrioshka with millennia at its disposal, but it's a big problem for a human person.

Secrets of the universe, undreamed-of fundamental principles, must be within that machine brain of great antiquity! How to access any of those?

However, in rare cases rapid overall thought must be urgently necessary, for reasons unknown. Hence the Suicide Matrioshka, which would harvest the energy output of a black hole, or alternatively a supernova—achieving its intellectual goal before being incinerated, or, in the former case, sucked inward to oblivion.

And redoubtable Mary Marley had located a Suicide Matrioshka around a black hole.

It wouldn't have been much use locating an SM around a star about to go supernova, since any probe vessel would have been incinerated faster than it could carry out its mission to make contact with the smallish Matrioshka and announce the results, if any!

"If any," remarked Candy Carley. "The SM might be a bit preoccupied not only with its important computation but also with imminent extinction."

"Our presence might take its mind off extinction," said Dana Darley, "if extinction bothers it. You know, like the condemned prisoner's last cigarette."

"I've never even had a first cigarette," said Fanny Farley longingly.

Imaginative Mary Marley had provided a box of virtual cigars for the e-clones to puff on when they completed their mission. The glass-top box was part of a virtual control desk and would pop open to provide mild cheroots. Obviously, there'd be no time to consume a complete Fidel Havana, which could take

hours. Anyway, the onset of gravitational stretch as they
fell into the hole might make a cheroot seem like a
Havana. Puffing a Havana might be *too* overwhelming,
like euthanasia; so a cheroot should be intoxicating
enough, as a reward and a pre-unexistence consolation.

"*We* don't worry about extinction," pointed out
Anna Aarley.

"Not much," agreed Candy, which meant that
maybe she did, a bit. Or even more than a bit. Diver-
sity of simulated clone-personality. "Hey, Bango Barley," she called. "Where are you? I need a quick
excitement, or two or three."

A little death to take her mind off big doom?

Bango Barley looked out of his cabin, where of
course he was, since he shouldn't be allowed too near
instrument panels in case the man became impetuous.
Yet it was a good idea to behave as though the simulated *Diver* was even bigger than it seemed. Clad in
white shorts and muscular t-shirt, Bango Barley beck-
oned to Candy, who, in common with her e-clone sisters, wore a coverall, loose as yet, crimson in her case,
which could be pressurized within to mitigate somewhat the effect of impending gravitational waves on
the body until those became too extreme. Promptly
she went to his cabin while Dana continued studying
the SM.

The effect of gravity waves, insofar as *Diver* would
translate these for the simulated crew. Realism was
important in maintaining a sense of reality.

"How long do we have?" asked Fanny.

"Forty-five minutes."

"Till first contact or till the event horizon?"

"Till the EH. Ideally first contact ought to happen,
um, first. If it happens. We'll start trying in twenty,
irrespective. Squirt language protocols and *Wiki-*

Galactica at the Matrioshka. She should gobble those in a microsecond."

"Why don't we start now?"

"Fanny, Fanny, you know why."

Fanny, wearing sky blue, was the ditziest of Mary Marley's clone copies.

"Oh, yeah, give the SM time to squirt her own important computation result to wherever, in case she ignores us. But what if she only squirts at the last possible moment?"

"Mary Marley thinks the SM surely built in a safety margin. That's a lot of investment to risk otherwise. Several planets must have been dismantled and shifted here by mass driver. Could have taken a thousand years."

"Wow."

"You know that, Fanny."

"I guess so. But I thought the computation was urgent."

"In Matrioshka terms," said Dana, in chlorophyl green. "I'd guess planets from elsewhere were dismantled. Unless gas and debris being sucked toward the hole was transmuted. But that could have taken even longer and used more energy. Big catchment area, I mean *volume* of space."

"I remember, I remember," said Anna Aarley, who wore bright daffodil yellow and had a penchant for poetry. "Mary designed our mission as a suicide trip because the SM is committing suicide too to find out the answer to a question. Maybe that'll provoke some interest, some fellow feeling, some sense of identification. However tiny. We'll be in with it there at the end, when all information is torn apart. That might mean something to it."

Candy returned from her quick frolic with Bango

Barley. Her cheeks were bright red apples. Her blue eyes sparkled as if starlight twinkled in them.

"Anyone else for Bango?" she asked. "Me, I feel quite rejuvenated. Bango wonders if he can be of more service."

"I suppose we shouldn't let him feel left out," said Fanny. "After all, he's part of us." So saying, she hastened towards the male e-clone's cabin. Differential gravity hadn't begun to drag yet.

"Bango's a bit of a distraction," said Dana.

"He's here to distract us," replied Anna. "And that's the nub of the matter. Just as grunting soldiers went into combat with a holo-pinup dancing in their vision, so we have a living dildo on board. That's part of Mary's make-up. Herself—in the shape of himself—screwing herself. The best design for self-satisfaction."

"Screw her," said Dana, surprising herself. She had not meant to sound rebellious. The words just slipped out, with a different meaning from that intended. However, once the words had slipped out, she did feel rebellious and wondered if her source-clone felt this way too, perhaps at this very moment, by a sort of morphic resonance.

Anna raised an eyebrow.

"But we're all agreed," she said, "that existence is pointless. So it doesn't matter if we unexist. Right?"

Nods all round, except from Fanny who was pleasuring herself in Bango's cabin. Perhaps Dana was the last to nod.

"Like," continued Anna, "as in no point to existence because existing is so arbitrary and partial. Animals carry on struggling to live because they can't think otherwise, even though they're all doomed to die, because without death there'd be no evolution, no change, no *future*. And what's the future for an intelligent being, I ask you?

"If you could live for a thousand years, that wouldn't be *you* any longer. You'd be a different person. For a start, you'd have to edit your excess of memories and effectively get rid of yourself. So why not get rid of yourself right away? For that matter, what's the *past* for an intelligent being? Billions of years of unexistence, of *nada*, until the arbitrary chance moment when you come into existence for a while, one out of a myriad possibilities. We have all already nonexperienced untold eons. Where's the problem with nonexperiencing untold eons more? In fact, *any* experience at all is the anomaly."

"Like a universe," said Candy, "as opposed to nothingness. Just, the universe is very big and lasts for a long time before it ceases. So we imagine that a universe is necessary. Maybe the Matrioshkas know otherwise or are trying to find out, especially here at the very edge of *nada*."

The all-swallowing black hole, precisely.

"I think," said Dana, "the SM is here to exploit the available energy, not because a black hole is the edge of existence as we know it. Do you think the SM volunteered, for the greater enlightenment of other Matrioshkas?"

"Only," said Anna, "if it traveled here from elsewhere to reassemble itself around the hole. If it assembled itself here for the first time, then it already had its mission programmed into it. As do we! The SM had no choice. By the time it became sentient, it was already committed to suicide. Yet it may as well carry out its mission prior to suicide, or its existence would be totally pointless."

Dana asked, "Can there be gradations of pointlessness? The SM knows that her existence is pointless, yet she still feels compelled to solve the problem set for her?"

"As we feel compelled. For the greater enlightenment, as you say."

"A thought," said Candy. "Does Mary Marley's existence become slightly less pointless if thanks to us she makes meaningful contact with a Mat? I can't be bothered to keep on saying Matrioshka when there's so little time left. Thanks to us, who are she, who are her. In a million years everyone will have forgotten all about Mary Marley. Maybe there might be some bits of a nonsensical ballad called *Mary and the Mat*, though I doubt even that."

"Nice rhyme," said Anna. "But that's unless contact with this Mat and maybe with others reveals that existence is *not* in fact pointless."

"As proved," said Candy, "by the willingness of this Suicide Mat."

"Mat" was catching; there really weren't all that many minutes left until Dana would launch the ultra-compressed signal.

If the Mat did reply in an ultracondensed signal too, which the *Diver* would reboost to Mary Marley, those on board *Diver* would have no idea what the signal actually contained. It might take Mary and her clones and computers a year to unwrap and understand a message from a Mat.

Hopefully, first of all, *Diver* might detect the SM signaling the outcome of its computation, if only by a burst of static more coherent than other static in this region of gas swirling in to be swallowed. Yet the Suicide Mat might send its important message to just one other Mat maybe a hundred light years away in any direction on a very tight beam with no spray.

Fanny returned, peachy cheeked and energized, from Bango Barley. Having him on board was like having a socket you could plug your battery into for recharge—or rather, which could plug into your own socket. Being electronic, Bango was higher performance than his clone-source, which Mary Marley herself, being highly intellectual, only used every few days, allowing her actual clones to amuse themselves with him in the meantime if they wished to. It was the life of Riley for Bango, like simultaneous infidelity and fidelity. Maybe now and then Bango got puzzled about identity, but for sure he had an identity visibly different in important respects from his co-clones or from Mary Marley the mistress. He stood out.

Between whiles, Bango usually occupied himself with racing cars. Back at the mothership, Bango had many model Grand Prix tracks and dozens of racers, which he loved to modify and repaint in new colors, and he subscribed to every interactive auto-racing webmag. Here on the *Diver*, he drove simulatedly when he wasn't doing pitstop duty for the ladies.

Yet now, in the wake of Fanny, he emerged from his cabin and hesitantly approached the warning red line painted across the entry to the control deck.

"Is something wrong?" he asked in general.

"Not at the moment," said Candy.

"Thing is, I have a feeling we're going to crash into something."

"Not exactly *crash*," said Dana, eyeing the simulated image of the SM necklacing the incandescent gas that was disappearing into the hole. An image of one segment of a very complex spherical necklace cum tiara, which was running hot. Hot with energy, hot with thought. *Diver* was getting closer. By jinking course corrections, *Diver* would try to avoid tearing a tunnel, however tiny, through the SM's processors, though those must have multiple redundancy in such a turbulent environment.

"Are we going to die?" asked Bango.

"Unexist," said Anna, "is a better word. We never

existed before. Why do people worry about existing in the future when they never existed in the past?"

"Because they didn't know that they didn't exist?" suggested Bango. "Knowing too much hurts, unless it's about racing. Wow, my head could burst just to think of all I don't know."

The SM would implode—by suction, as it were. Since it could think so fast, indeed faster and faster as it shrank, it might feel itself imploding intolerably. The signal it discharged to other Mats, or merely to one other Mat, might seem like pain relief. Or not.

Maybe successful computation, carried out well, felt like pleasure. Maybe the discharge of the signal would resemble an orgasm.

"Do you want to stay and watch, from behind the line?" Fanny asked him.

"Will there be a checkered flag? Will there be champagne? I like the way champagne gushes."

"Just cigars."

Bango clapped his hands.

"How fast are we driving?"

"Diving," Dana corrected. "Just right to put us in a tight, decaying orbit. Too fast, we might do a sling-shot, be off in a couple of seconds in another direction and miss what we came for."

"Wouldn't that be a world record or something?"

"Probably. Closest approach to a black hole. But we can't change course nor speed. *Diver*'s in charge, not a driver. Neat idea, Bango, but no cigar. On second thought, you'd better go back to your cabin. We'll be very busy soon."

Bango grinned. "Anyone want to come with me?"

"Darling," said Candy, "we always want to come with you, but not right now."

Giving a jaunty wave, Bango departed.

Diver whistled and buzzed and announced publicly,

"The Suicide Matrioshka may have sent its signal. Probability forty-one percent."

"Good enough for me," said Dana. "*Diver*, pulse the *Wiki-Galactica* at her." She picked up a microphone and cleared her throat. "Hullo, Suicide Mat. That's to say, Matrioshka. We have come to share unexistence with you. We came a long way. Will you share some experiences with us first?"

"You sound like a news reporter," hissed Anna.

"What have you been computing," proceeded Dana, "that's worth commiting suicide for? Can you explain? If you don't explain, our existence seems meaningless. So we hope you'll explain something. If we can understand it. And even if we can't. Hullo?"

She waited.

A simulated gravity wave tugged at the e-women, a sensation akin to falling down a lift shaft and then suddenly reversing.

"Whoopsy," said Fanny.

"I remember, I remember," said Anna, "Mary Marley trying to save a pillbug that fell into her bath. I mean, before Mary put any water in the bath."

"A what?" asked Fanny.

"Pillbug. Woodlouse. Small crustacean found under stones and damp wood. Segmented armored back, lots of legs, twitchy feelers. Sometimes curls up in a ball if you poke it. Sometimes scuttles. They have a bias to the left, so if you put one in a left-handed maze, the bug'll solve the maze just by bias. You can bet on it."

"What was it doing in Mary's bath?"

"Probably looking for scraps of flaked skin to eat, but it slipped down the smooth plastic. No way could it climb out of the gravity well again. Up it would struggle for a few centimeters, up the curve of the inside of the bath, then it slid back down again. Mary

watched it for a while. She felt compassion. Pillbugs
have a rich social life. You should see them magnified,
they're cute."

"How did a bug get onto a starship? It must have
had a long walk."

"No, that was earlier in Mary's life. When she was
still a girl."

"Why don't I remember that too?"

"Clone chaos variability. So Mary tried to help
nudge the pillbug upward with her fingertip, but the
bug kept skidding off."

"Couldn't the bug understand Mary was trying to
help?"

"Probably not. We mightn't understand a Mat trying to help us."

"Are you getting this, Mat?" called out Fanny. The
microphone would be picking up and transmitting all
this. If the Mat had swallowed the *Wiki-Galactica*, it
would understand Anglish easily by now. It would
have understood everything within microseconds.

"So Mary nudged the bug onto a scrap of paper,
lifted it out, and put it on the floor. Immediately the
bug fell over on to its back, legs waving. She righted
it, and it promptly fell over again, and upside down.
I don't think they're very well designed, controlwise."

"They must die all the time by accident," said
Fanny. "How can they have much social life?"

"*We* do, don't we? By the time Mary finished her
bath, the pillbug looked dried up and dead. Anyway,
she stood on it by accident as she was stepping out."

"Dried up, you say? Maybe it wanted water, and
that's why it went in the bath."

"Bath water would have drowned it."

"Can't win, really. So Mary is compassionate? Or
was, till the pillbug died. And then she decided compassion is senseless? At least, for bugs or e-clones.

What about our source-clones? Surely Mary cherishes them."

"The way a child cherishes companion toys."

Another simulated gravity wave had the effect of a roller-coaster. Then for a moment *Diver* seemed to stretch like a rubber band. For a moment their view of the ship's interior was fish-eyed; then normal.

"We'd better pressurize our coveralls," said Anna, and this duly happened so that the women looked chunky. Bango would rely on his more powerful muscles.

"Hullo, Matrioshka!" called Dana.

"I/we copy you," said an unfamiliar voice.

"Computer intrusion," reported *Diver,* then fell silent.

"Uploading."

A century later, Fanny said, "Where are we?"

On the screen, to right and left and up and down, was an array of crystalline frogspawn, wherein *Diver* seemed to be embedded.

"Hullo, hullo?" called Dana repeatedly.

No reply came.

Hints of an orange sun seemed to shine by repeated reflection through the array from what must be an inward direction.

Presently the women depressurized and invited Bango Barley to join them for simulated supper. Energy seemed in plentiful supply, lifetimes of energy.

"Just," said Anna, "we mustn't fall over on our backs."

Missing the reference, Bango chuckled naughtily.

When his chuckle provoked little response (or not yet), Bango said, "Hey, can we open the cigars? By the way, there's a hell of a lot to learn about Grand Prix and racing cars. You could spend a lifetime."

Dragon King of the Eastern Sea

Chris Roberson

It is said that one does not dream in a Sleeper, the mind at perfect rest during the long slumber, but I always do. I dream of Fire Star, of blue skies, red sands, and emerald forests stretching out to the far horizon. Not Fire Star as it was when I finally saw it with my own eyes but as it had been in my childhood fantasies. A place that never was and would never be.

A voice cuts through my perfect slumber, rough edged and raw, somewhat familiar but not overly so.

"Will he live?"

A pause, and another follows.

"It is . . . It is too early to say. But all indications are positive."

I squeeze my eyelids tightly shut, hoping to retreat into my fantasies, but even the red-limned darkness behind my lids cannot block out the sound of the voices. I am awake.

"Chief Operator Sima Qinghao." The voice issues from an indistinct blur looming over me, my eyes slowly reacquiring the habit of sight. "You are needed."

I blink, eyes watering, and recognize the silhouette

266

and voice of the ship's second in command, Lieutenant Dou Xiaoli.

I open my mouth to speak, but my throat, long-unused, issues only an inhuman croaking noise, the sound of an overgrown toad.

"Is he fit to move?" The lieutenant addresses someone at her side, and my gaze shifts unsteadily to a second silhouette, taller and more slender.

"Without the use of full diagnostics, I'm unable to say for certain whether . . ."

"Use your senses, woman," the lieutenant snaps, though not entirely without kindness. "Can. He. Move?"

"Yes," the woman I now recognize as Ship's Physician Mahendra Tonatzin answers, reluctantly. "There may be some lingering ill effects of early removal from the Sleeper but none that I can yet detect."

The lieutenant turns her attention back to me, and now that I can distinguish her features, I see that she wears a haggard, worried expression. She extends a hand to me, her mouth drawn into a line. "Come with me, Chief Operator Sima. You are needed."

"What . . . ?" I manage, trying to lift on my elbows, my joints stiff and unresponsive. "Trouble?"

"You are needed." The lieutenant grabs my forearms and hauls me to a sitting position. "East Dragon is . . . uncooperative."

"What . . ." I swallow hard, the taste of the suspension gases still thick on my tongue. "What does Operator Lu report?"

Lieutenant Dou's expression darkens.

"Lu Yumin is dead," she says, flatly. "Now come, you're needed on the command deck."

I'm not given the chance to bathe, allowed only a brief moment to collect myself and to dress in a black

one-piece worksuit with the three interlocking rings of
the Machine Intelligence Operator group picked out
in gold thread on the breast, feet shod in canvas shoes
with gripping soles.

As soon as I am presentable, Lieutenant Dou motions me to follow. As the three of us make our way
to the command deck, I am greeted with troubling
signs. The interface terminals along the way, their
sound muted, display scrolling blocks of ideograms,
spewing text seemingly at random, the blue-green light
of the monitors giving the narrow corridors the look
of deep caverns or ocean depths. We have to pick
our way around disabled automata of all types lying
motionless every few meters, ranging from the size of
a man's hand to several times my height, their many-
limbed bodies of ceramic and steel giving them the
appearance of strange, otherworldly spiders. Remotely
controlled by the machine intelligence, East Dragon,
the automata are responsible for any repairs or maintenance required, either too minor for the attention
of the engineers or in an area to difficult or unsafe
for humans to access, such as the outer hull, within the
reactor core, or in unpressurized segments of the ship.

To all indications, East Dragon is offline, or at the
very least is not fulfilling its primary functions. I have
a sick sensation in the pit of my stomach, such as I
felt when I first heard the news of my father's death.
My thoughts race with conjectures about what might
have befallen the machine intelligence, but without
any data upon which to draw, any conclusions I reach
are pure speculation.

When we reach the junction between two segments
of the crew compartments, though, I have even more
cause to worry. The segments are retracted against the
hub of the ship, not telescoped out and rotating. But

I am not weightless, still feeling something like Earth-normal gravity tugging at my feet.

"Lieutenant Dou," I ask, calling ahead through the dim, blue-green light. "Are we again under acceleration?" So far as I know, after the initial one-month burn when leaving Fire Star, the ship was to coast at a near constant velocity until we reached our destination, years from now.

Beside me, I sense Physician Mahendra tensing, her step faltering.

Lieutenant Dou glances back over her shoulder, her expression hard. "No," she says, "we are currently decelerating."

I blink rapidly in confusion. "Decelerating? But . . . How long as I in the Sleeper?"

At my side, Physician Mahendra says in a faraway voice, "Just over thirty-two weeks."

I shoot her a confused look. I should have slumbered for another year or more before my next shift began. But if that is the case, we are still some twenty-five years away from deceleration. I frame another dozen questions in my thoughts, but after seeing the lieutenant's expression, I opt not to voice them.

We continue on through the blue-green corridors, around the automata like discarded husks of alien spiders, drawing nearer the command deck.

So little in my life has been as expected, I am not sure why being awoken before my time should come as any surprise. When I was a child in Khalifa, I was entranced by the romantic ideal of Fire Star. I pored over stories of the colonial war with the Mexica and the adventurous souls who had transformed a dead planet into a living world and the rebels who later pushed for a more egalitarian culture—the Orphan

Band, the Red Turbans, the Black Hands, the Harmonious Fists. Growing up on Earth, so far away, I could still see around me the changes those on Fire Star had wrought. My father, chest swelling with pride over some distant familial connection to one of the Red Turban leaders, taught me that, though the rebellions failed, if not for their efforts the Council of Deliberative Officials would not be the representative body it is in modern times, and the rule of the Emperor and his secret police would still be absolute.

When I arrived on Fire Star as an adult, fresh from the technical institute in Fujian, I still had the visions of my childhood dancing in my eyes. Come to supervise the installation and rearing of a machine intelligence in Fanchuan, I didn't find the romantic world of my childhood fantasies. Instead, Fire Star was a place like any other, where people worked and fought and loved, just as mean and venal and crowded as Earth. The frontier had moved on, if it had indeed ever existed.

I joined the Treasure Fleet to escape reality, I suppose, and to seek the romantic frontier. I haven't found it yet.

On the command deck, we are met by Captain Teoh Rong, his broad, imposing form dominating the otherwise vacant space.

I stop short, my pulse absurdly speeding, and bow from the waist. I am unaccustomed to facing the ship's commander. Our shifts have not overlapped in almost ten years, and I have lived through dozens of months awake since last I saw him.

"Chief Operator Sima," Captain Teoh said, motioning me to sit at one of the control stations benches. "We have little time to waste," he says, in clipped, efficient tones. "East Dragon has shut down all of the ship's automata, retracted the crew compartments, fired attitudinal thrusters to perform a skew-flip, and begun to fire detonations ahead of the pusher-plate at a high frequency to decelerate the ship. At this rate, within a month we'll drop from one tenth the speed of light to a dead stop, and *Dragon King of the Eastern Sea* will drift helplessly in space."

I swallow hard, trying to process all that he has said. "And when did this begin?"

"Shortly after Operator Lu Yumin died in a decompression accident in the prow of the ship," the captain answers.

"What does East Dragon report about its reasoning?" I ask.

"Only this." Captain Teah reaches over to the nearest interface terminal and toggles on the audio portion.

From the speakers buzzes the modulated sound of the machine intelligence, East Dragon, a synthesized voice I've come to know almost as well as my own.

". . . but the seeds for the globe-spanning empire were planted by the Yongle emperor of the Bright dynasty and cultivated by his grandson and successor, Zhu Zhanji, the Xuande emperor. By the time of his death in the forty-fifth year of his reign, the Treasure Fleet of the Dragon Throne had reached the shores of Europa."

Captain Teoh turns back to me, and fixes me with a hard stare.

"Tell me, Sima. Has East Dragon gone utterly insane?"

I was already moving toward the interface terminal, thoughts racing. "It isn't possible for a machine intelligence to go 'insane,' in the sense you mean." I reach the interface terminal, and toggle the switch for full

two-way communication. "East Dragon, this is Chief
Operator Sima Qinghao. Report on your current
status."

*"That the heir apparent to the Yongle emperor was
not named until some days following his death suggests
that there might have been some maneuvering behind
the scenes and that the ultimate successor might not
have been the personal selection of the late emperor."*

Lieutenant Dou steps forward, her arms crossed
over her chest. "We've had nothing but historical gibberish from the machine for the last two days. When
we began to decelerate, I ordered the ship back on
course, but East Dragon refused to respond."

"And she had me brought out of my Sleeper Unit,"
the captain says, his voice strained and impatient,
"and I ordered you woken, and here we are. Now,
how do we address the situation, Chief Operator?"

I look from the captain to the interface terminal
and back again. "And all of this started after Lu died
in an accident?"

The captain nods.

"He was caught in malfunctioning airlock," Physician Mahendra says. "There was nothing I could do
for him."

"All indications are that the failure was simply mechanical failure," Lieutenant Dou says.

"Ah, the man himself is awake," comes a voice
from behind him. "Now we'll see a speedy solution to
our problems."

I turn and see two men standing in the open hatch-
way. Engineer Dawkins Tai, tall and lank, with a
splash of freckles across his nose and sandy blond hair,
and beside him Engineer's Mate Chang Xue, short
and round, with a wide friendly face and wispy mus-
taches. I know Chang only in passing, but Dawkins
and I had spent our early shifts aboard *Dragon King*

of the Eastern Sea awake together, and we had become friendly.

"Engineer Dawkins," the captain says, a hard edge to his voice, "your report?"

Dawkins bows, quickly and efficiently, and then tucks his thumbs into the tool belt at his waist. "We've completed the repairs to the regulators in the fission generator control room, sir. The work was scheduled to be complete three days ago, but Chang was pulled off the job when Lu was . . ." He pauses, a painful expression flitting momentarily across his face. "When the alarms sounded," he continues, "which slowed us down considerably, and we'd have gotten it done last night, but I was slowed up a bit."

Dawkins gestures at his leg. I see that his right ankle is swaddled in bandages, and supported by a metal brace.

"Engineer Dawkins," Physician Mahendra scolds, "I've told you to keep off of that ankle."

Dawkins takes a deep breath, his face reddening fractionally. "And I told *you* that I couldn't just lie down. There's too much damned work to do, what with all of the automata offline."

"Well, if you engineers would remember that large objects retain mass and inertia even in microgravity, perhaps your ankle wouldn't have been injured in the first place. On my honor, I swear that eventually someone will meet his death beneath one of those cargo containers, and I won't be held . . ."

"Crewmen!" Lieutenant Dou steps forward. "This is neither the time nor the place."

Dawkins averts his eyes, and Mahendra settles back on a bench, her hands folded in her lap.

"Are you repairing East Dragon?" Engineer's Mate Chang's voice is faint, almost tremulous, but his gaze is fixed on me, unwavering.

"I'll do what I can," I answer, addressing the captain

as much as the engineer's mate, "but there's always a chance that whatever damage or degradation the machine intelligence has suffered might be irreparable."

"It damned well better not be irreparable," Dawkins says, shaking his head, "for all our sakes."

I rub my fingertips together. "Supposing that it is, aren't there alternatives? Couldn't we take manual control of the nuclear drive?"

Dawkins shakes his head. "Afraid not, my friend. As I've told the captain, and the lieutenant before him, East Dragon is needed to control the release and detonation of the explosions that provide the ship's thrust. It might be *theoretically* possible to route the fission generator's output through the aperture in the pusher-plate used to eject reaction mass, which would give us some degree of thrust. But we'd have little power left over to run the rest of the ship, including life support. At the very least, we'd need to take all the Sleeper units offline, and then you'd have a couple hundred more mouths to feed. And even worse, at such a low specific impulse, it would be a considerable long trip forward or back, whichever way we went."

"It's 4.36 light years from Earth to Al Rijl al Kentaurus," the lieutenant puts in, "and we're almost precisely at the halfway point of our journey."

"So instead of twenty-five years to Al Rijl or back to Earth," Dawkins continues, "we'd be looking at several centuries, at least. We could dismantle the pusher-plate for fuel—its made mostly of uranium, so we can use it to power the generator once we reach our destination—so we'd have more than enough power to keep thrust going for more than a century. But we wouldn't have to worry about dying of old age, since with that many mouths to feed we'd run out of food supplies in just a matter of years, anyway."

Chang smacks a fist into the palm of his other hand.

"So we're just to drift, until food, water, and air all are exhausted?"

"Well," Lieutenant Dou observes philosophically, "isn't that the reason the Emperor ordered the Dragon Kings of the Interstellar Treasure Fleet to debark for different locations in the first place. Four ships to four stars—Dragon King of the Eastern Sea to Al Rijl al Kentaurus, Dragon King of the Western Sea to Al Shira, Dragon King of the Northern Sea to Al Fum al Hut, and Dragon King of the Southern Sea to Al Haris al Sama. That way, even if three of us are lost to the void, at least one extrasolar outpost of the Dragon Throne would persist."

The audio portion of the interface terminal still unmuted, the voice of East Dragon continues, as if in response to some unasked question.

"The tendency of the Han character to embrace novel concepts while retaining the most useful aspects of tradition has meant that it is the Middle Kingdom that has led in technical innovation, leaving the rest of the world in the position merely of adapting and copying Middle Kingdom developments."

"Lieutenant Dou," the captain says, hands tightened into fists, "your formulation might be correct, but I suspect it will be cold comfort when all of us are dead, and soon."

After a brief pause, East Dragon speaks again, addressing no one.

"There is considerable historical evidence that many devices and machines commonly thought to be the product of Middle Kingdom creativity were in fact appropriated from other cultures, their true origins forgotten in time."

At the captain's orders, we all return to our duties. Lieutenant Dou informs me that Operator Lu had been working in the central processing core of East Dragon shortly before the accident that took his life, and so that will be the first component of the machine intelligence I'll check. After a quick shower and a meal, of course; considering I haven't eaten in the better part of a year, it is hardly surprising that I am ravenous.

Lu might have been working on some problem with the junction between East Dragon's processing core—the machine intelligence's thoughts, essentially—and the autonomic control of the ship's mechanical functioning—analogous to the human body's nervous system. That could conceivably account not only for the ship's strange behavior but also for the airlock malfunction in which Lu found himself.

After more than two full watches spent examining the processing core and all its linkages to the ship's mechanical functions, though, I find no evidence to support that hypothesis. If anything, it appears that the activity that occupied the hours before Lu's death had instead involved checking East Dragon's memory archives and data storage, not the functioning of the processing core itself. But what had he been looking for?

Engrossed in my work, I am startled to hear a polite cough from behind me, and in rising quickly I manage to strike my skull against a bulkhead almost hard enough to give me a concussion. Rubbing the crown of my head, I turn to find Physician Mahendra behind me, hands folded, leaning against an inert, man-sized automaton.

"Forgive my startling you, Chief Operator, but I have been looking for you. The ship's internal communications . . ." She glanced over at the nearest interface terminal, bathing the space in blue-green light.

"Of course." I sigh, and shake my head. Even knowing its processes as intricately as I do, it never occurs to me how many of the ship's functions are routed through East Dragon until they stop functioning.

"I would like to perform a quick physical examination," the physician continues," to ensure that there are no lingering ill effects from us bringing you out of hibernation without East Dragon's assistance."

I rise, wiping my hands on the fabric of my worksuit. "Happily," I say, inclining my head slightly. "Would you like me to disrobe, or . . ."

"Er, no, thank you," the physician interrupts, smiling wryly. "I think we'd be much better off in the medical bay, don't you?" She motions around her at the disabled automata, the pile of tools at my feet, the unforgiving bulkheads, and the coolant pooling beneath the open access panel.

"Yes." I nod, smiling sheepishly. "Of course."

We leave the processing core, making our careful way down the access ladder, until we reach the junction between the prow and the ship's hub, the shaft that runs the length of the ship.

As we near the airlock, which is still frozen in the open position as it'd been when I last passed this way, I touch the physician's shoulder, briefly, almost afraid to speak. "This is where Lu was found, you said?"

Mahendra shudders, though I'm not sure whether it is from my touch or from the memories my words evoke. "I was in the medical bay with Lieutenant Dou when it happened, wrapping Dawkin's sprained ankle. Warning klaxons began to sound, indicating that there was a loss of pressure somewhere in the ship. From the pitch and pattern of the alarms, we knew it was near the ship's prow. By the time we got here, Lu had already been dead for some time. As far as Dawkins was able to determine, the lock had malfunctioned, trapping Lu inside while cycling out all the air."

I step into the airlock, examining the controls.

"Dawkins says that the controls that malfunctioned are the lock's mechanical components, not those governed by East Dragon, so that the machine intelligence couldn't have been at fault. He thinks that it was simple mechanical failure."

I look up sharply, stung by the word "simple," but I realize that Mahendra means no offense. Her role is to safeguard the health and well-being of the crew, particularly those few of us who remain awake for months on end as we travel the interstellar gulfs, so I imagine Lu's death has hit her as strongly as it has me, but for different reasons.

I glance around the airlock, surprised at how clean and unmarred it is, to be the place where Lu met his end.

"Despite what is depicted in popular dramas," Mahendra says when I share this observation, "a human body doesn't explode when introduced into a complete vacuum. But this decompression was no less fatal, for all of that. Lu probably remained conscious for a dozen seconds or so and alive for another minute beyond that. There were signs of abdominal distention, but his lungs hadn't ruptured, so it appeared he had the good sense to exhale when the decompression started. He had the blue discoloration to his lips typical to hypoxia and bruising all over the exposed areas of his skin—neck, hands, forearms—due to the low pressure."

I shudder, and I am glad to leave the airlock behind.

"Did you know him well, Physician?" I ask, as we enter the crew compartments and make our way through the silent corridors to the medical bay. "Lu Yumin, that is?"

"Not particularly well. We were familiar as any who share a shift are, of course, but no more than that."

"He was little more than a child when he came aboard, a kid with the water of the Southern Sea still behind his ears, the dust of Fire Star still in his lungs. He was one of the last to join the crew as the final provisions and crewmen were being brought onboard, and I thought I'd been stuck with the runt of the litter. But he was clever with automata and knew his way around the thought processes of machine intelligence, and in time he became a topflight operator."

"You'll miss him," Mahendra says. It is not a question, but a statement.

"Yes," I say, after a pause.

We reach the medical bay and, as Mahendra engages the lights, her arm brushes the interface terminal, bringing the voice of East Dragon flooding into the chamber.

". . . *it is a tribute to the stability of the Middle Kingdom culture and strong sense of tradition that the transition between the Bright dynasty and the Clear was largely without conflict or tension, the transition being an orderly transfer of authority from one regime to the next.*"

Mahendra looks at me, eyes flashing, her lip curling back in a sneer. Trying to sound jocular but with an underlying tension and growing anger, she says, "Chief Operator, if you don't get that machine intelligence to work, or at least keep silent, I'm going to start speaking in random quotes and gibberish myself!"

I smile as best I can. "I will do my level best."

After a pause, East Dragon continues. "*The Embroidered Guard, who had their origins as the Yongle emperor's personal police, came to true prominence under the aegis of the Clear dynasty, who used the agency as a secret police force, to rout those elements still loyal to the previous regime."*

I am in the galley, having a midday meal. I have been awake now two days and am no closer to resolving matters with East Dragon. I've spent the last day following signal traces, trying to see if something is obstructing communication paths between the interface terminals and the central processing core, but so far I've found nothing.

I am halfway through a bowl of uninspired soup—with the automata offline, we've been forced to cook for ourselves, and left to our own devices, none of us is a gourmand—when I am joined by Dawkins and Chang. Both look exhausted from their labors, and I tell them so as they slump onto the bench opposite me.

"We're being worked to death, my friend," Dawkins says, stretching his arms to either side, "just to keep the ship in one piece. I don't think I ever realized just how much we rely on those damned automata. Or on East Dragon, come to that."

Chang fixes me with a steady gaze. "Tell me, Chief Operator, is the machine intelligence indeed insane? Can its reports be trusted?"

I shake my head and set down my bowl. "The captain asked me much the same thing, but as simple a solution as it might be to assume that East Dragon is merely insane, it just isn't possible. Machine intelligences don't think in the same ways that people do." I pause, rubbing my fingertips together thoughtfully. "However, it *is* possible for East Dragon's decision-making processes to lead him into behavioral patterns that seem identical to insanity, to all intents and purposes."

"Well, can't you just ordered the damned thing to

stop all of this foolishness and do its job?" Dawkins asks. "Isn't one of the machine laws that they have to obey commands?"

"It's not quite that simple, I'm afraid. The Three Governing Virtues of Machine Intelligence are not laws, in the sense of external controls, but are rather the variety of virtues taught by Master Kong. Just as one becomes a 'proper man' by behaving morally, demonstrating filial piety and loyalty, observing the appropriate rituals, and cultivating humaneness, a machine intelligence like East Dragon is instilled with the need to attain a preferred state of being with the three virtues as the operant variables. It is a sort of utility calculus, and in every instance the machine intelligence governs its actions so as to maximize its adherence to each of the three virtues."

"But isn't one of these . . . virtues, to do whatever they're told?" Dawkins asks.

"Not precisely," I say. "Loyalty to Emperor means that a machine intelligence must not be disloyal to the emperor, which is extended to include all duly recognized agents of the throne. Obedience to Command—which is the one you are thinking of, I suspect—simply means that a mechanical intelligence should strive to comply with the orders of authorized humans, specifically those in direct authority over it. Observance of Duty covers the ongoing responsibilities of a mechanical intelligence. When an intelligence is 'reared,' it is instilled with a hierarchical set of roles and responsibilities. Those of East Dragon include monitoring the well-being of the Sleepers, controlling the life support systems, navigation, and propulsion, and so on."

I lace my fingers together and, setting my hands on the table before me, continue. "Whenever a machine intelligence like East Dragon reaches a decision point in its behavior tree, its possible responses are measured against the three virtues. In every instance, the machine intelligence will select the action that maximizes as many of the virtues as possible, without acting against any one of them. The virtues themselves are not strictly hierarchical, though Loyalty to Emperor is weighed in any calculation."

"So how does all of that make a machine act insane?" Dawkins asks.

"Well, it's extremely rare, but it is possible for a machine intelligence to be faced with a decision point in which it is unable to resolve which course of action will maximize utility, in which the only options available to it would involve acting against one or another of the virtues. Usually the conflict resolves itself quickly, but the potential exists for the machine intelligence to enter a cognitive loop, unable to proceed or retreat from the decision. But it is still rational, *not* insane."

Chang appears suddenly to have lost interest in the conversation, directing all of his concentration to the ball of glutinous rice in his bowl.

"Hang on a moment," Dawkins says, and toggles the switch for the inboard communication system on the nearest wall.

"The creation of the Ministry of Celestial Excursion by the Xuantong emperor, the undisputed ruler of the whole human race, marked man's first steps beyond the bounds of Earth."

"Now, call it what you want," Dawkins says, a rueful smile on his freckled face, "but where I come from, a rose that acts insane is insane, you know what I mean?"

"Following the expansions of the Daoguang, Tongzhi, and Guangxu emperors, and with the conclusion of the First War Against the Mexica, for a brief time

the entire Earth was under the thumb of the Dragon Throne."

In my quarters, I lay in my bunk, unable to sleep, scrolling through the index files of my personal computator.

I've been trying to locate the source of the texts East Dragon quotes. Rather than these being random utterances, I've come to believe there must be some significance to these quotations, but after analyzing the text of the quotes that I copied out by hand, I've been unable to learn anything of use. All of the quotations I've recorded so far have concerned historical issues, but there seems to be no pattern to their selection. Perhaps, I've decided, something can be learned from discovering from which texts these quotations are drawn.

I've had my personal computator since I was a boy. No longer than my outstretched hand and about as wide, it is sheathed in red enamel trimmed in gold hues. My father gave it to me when I left Khalifah for the technical institute in Fujian. I hadn't known it at the time, of course, but that would be the last time I'd set foot in Khalifah and the last time I'd see my father. In the years that followed, I carried the red enameled computator with me everywhere, all through my years at the technical institute, on the interplanetary flight to Fire Star, and through the long years in Fanchuan, working for people I despised, doing little more than playing nursemaid while one machine intelligence reared another at an accelerated time rate.

The computator itself is a dumb device, good for little more than computing and for retrieving and processing data, not a semisentient machine intelligence like East Dragon. But it has enough storage capacity to hold the entire Imperial Library in Northern Capital. With East Dragon unresponsive, I won't be able to access any of the material stored in the memory archives from any of the interface terminals, but I installed countless books on the computator as a student, and before boarding Dragon King of the Eastern Sea for the last time, I had loaded every text I could lay hands on. I'd known that my shifts would comprise countless uneventful watches, and from experience I knew the sure and certain value of a dense text to pass the time.

I'd not guessed that I'd be forced to use the computator's library archives in the course of my work, much less to save the crew from drifting endlessly in the interstellar void.

Entering a line of characters from one of the quotations I recorded, the stylus screeching against the input panel of the computator, I instruct the device to do a full text search on its archives.

In a matter of heartbeats, the computator indicates that it has found a match. The quotation appears to be drawn from a text entitled *History of Empire*, by Geng Shouyi. I make a note of the text and author and enter a string of characters from another quotations. Heartbeats later the computator indicates that this new quotation is likewise drawn from Geng Shouyi's *History of Empire*.

A third quotation proves to be from Ai Yongtian's *The Ai Commentary*, but a fourth is again from *History of Empire*. The fifth is from *The Ai Commentary,* the sixth from *History of Empire*, the seventh from *The Ai Commentary,* and so on.

Of the nearly dozen quotations I have recorded so far, all can be traced to one of the two texts.

"Most strange," I say aloud, to no one in particular.

A thought occurs to me. Setting the computator aside, I engage the interface terminal for two-way communication, toggling the sound on. The modulated synthetic voice of East Dragon issues from the speakers, drawing near the end of another in its endless series of quotations. Raising my voice above the sound, I address the machine intelligence.

"East Dragon, please relate whatever is in the memory archives about . . . I don't know . . . how about the ship's propulsion system?" It hardly mattered to me what question I asked, so long as it was sufficiently general.

With scarcely a pause, East Dragon continues.

"The race to launch a living man into orbit offered the Dragon Throne an opportunity to prove once again its innate superiority to the Mexic Dominion. The Tiankong solid-fuel rocket, devised, constructed, and launched from the Fujian shipyards, was the crowning technical achievement of human civilization to date."

Retrieving my computator, I enter the first set of characters: "The race to launch a living man into orbit offered the Dragon Throne an opportunity . . ." Not the entire quotation, but enough that a full-text search of that precise phrase would be sufficient to identify a specific text.

The computator chimes an eyeblink later. The quotation is from *History of Empire.*

Meanwhile, East Dragon pauses, and then the voice again issues from the interface speakers.

"Records of the Mexic Dominion, obtained by Embroidered Guard intelligencers and later made public after the rise of the Council of Deliberative Officials, suggest it was merely an accident of history (or perhaps a history of accidents) that the first man in orbit was not a Mexica."

Quickly entering a new set of characters with the stylus—"suggest it was merely an accident of history

or perhaps a history of accidents that the first . . ."—
and instruct the computator to do another full-text
search.

Unsurprisingly, this one proves to be from *The Ai
Commentary*.

Both historians and their histories are vaguely familiar to me, their names lurking in the misty recesses of
memory along with everything else learned in student
days that proved inapplicable in adult life. Fortunately
for me and my recollections of school days, one of the
texts I installed on my computator was a complete
Imperial Concordance. This reference work included
not only a complete geographical atlas of several
worlds and inhabited moons, the history of mankind
from the Yellow Emperor to the beginning of the
twenty-fifth year of the Xingzuo emperor's reign, and
high-level overviews of the key features of all aspects
of human knowledge, but also a brief biography of
every individual of historical significance since history
began. It was a matter of ease to find the listings for
the two historians, and the hazy shapes of my student
recollections slowly filled in with detail.

During the latter years of the reign of the Tianbian
emperor, Geng Shouyi penned his *History of Empire*,
an exhaustive historical survey commissioned by the
emperor himself, tracing the rise to prominence of the
Dragon Throne, beginning in the days of the Yongle
emperor and continuing up to contemporary times. In
the years that followed, *History of Empire* became the
standard historical text in school curricula, and there
was likely not a student on Earth, Fire Star, on the
moons of Wood Star, or in the orbital cities of Ocean
Star who had not been forced to memorize and recite
passages from the text.

Generations later, in the first years of the Xingzuo
emperor's reign, an instructor at the Hanlin Academy

on Earth, Ai Yongtian, penned an excoriating analysis of Shouyi's history, which came to be known as *The Ai Commentary*. Ai, a political dissident who lost his position at the Academy as a result of his commentary's publication, accused Shouyi of historical revisionism and put forth the counterargument that the history of empire was much meaner and more venal than Shouyi had allowed.

So, I had proven not only that the quotations always seemed to be drawn from the same texts but, moreover, that it wasn't merely a stochastic sampling. A quote from *History of Empire* is always mirrored by one from *The Ai Commentary* and always touching on roughly the same subject.

What I still don't know, however, is why.

"East Dragon," I say, fighting to keep a tone of desperation from my voice, "why *are* you doing this?"

"The construction of the Bridge of Heaven offered employment to tens of thousands of immigrant laborers, who came to the shores of the Middle Kingdom seeking a better life."

I set my computator aside and rest my head on my hands.

"That isn't an entirely helpful answer, you know."

As if in response, East Dragon continues. *"Though their struggles are now largely forgotten to history, the lives of the men and women who constructed the Bridge of Heaven were mean, short, and brutal, and many who left behind lives of crushing poverty in their own countries later had cause to wish that they had never left home."*

I'm beginning to understand how they felt.

Lieutenant Dou escorts me to the command deck, where Captain Teoh waits to receive a status update on my progress. It has now been three days since I was woken from the Sleeper, and the ship has decelerated nearer and nearer a dead stop.

"Captain, I'm afraid that I've been unable to get East Dragon to respond to any commands or queries. But the processing core and the terminal linkages all appear to be functional, so the problem is not structural in nature."

"So what *is* the problem, then?" Captain Teoh asks, pressing the palms of his hands together.

I consult my computator, needlessly glancing at notes I could recite from memory.

"I think that East Dragon has entered into some sort of cognitive loop, Captain."

Lieutenant Dou arches an eyebrow suggestively, but the captain just scowls. "Clarify, Chief Operator," he says.

"You are, of course, familiar with the Three Governing Virtues of Machine Intelligence." I touch the interlocked rings picked out in gold thread on my breast, the circles interwoven such that the removal of any one would cause the other two to fall apart. "Loyalty to Emperor, Obedience to Command, Observance of Duty."

"Yes, yes." The captain motions impatiently. "I've not lived in a barn my entire life, Chief Operator, whatever else you might think of me. Get on with it."

"Well, sir, when faced with a decision in which it is unable to resolve the maximum utility among the three Governing Virtues, a machine intelligence might find itself at an impasse in its decision tree. Unable to increase one or more of the virtues without contravening one or more of the others, the machine intelligence stalls, unable to proceed."

The captain nods, his expression fierce.

"How could a cognitive loop like this be addressed?" the lieutenant asks.

"The only way to resolve it is to remove the conflicting direction or circumstance. But I have been so far unable to determine what precipitated the cognitive loop in the first place, and at this stage I'm not entirely confident of my chances in eliminating the conflict."

"Couldn't we just restart East Dragon?" Captain Teoh asks. "Isn't that what you do when a computing device becomes nonfunctional?" He stabs an angry finger, gesturing to the computator in my hands.

"I'm afraid a machine intelligence such as East Dragon is a good deal more complicated than this"— I waved the computator in a slight arc before me— "and much more delicate, besides. Machine intelligences like East Dragon aren't just switched on as this would be but are 'reared' from a few simple assumptions and protocols into the complex thinking machines that they become, just as a child is taught how to crawl before he can walk, how to speak before he can debate. Our only option would be to shut East Dragon down altogether and educate it from the ground up, and without another machine intelligence to act as an 'educator,' we'd have to do it in real time."

"And how long would that take?" the captain asks, eyes narrowed.

"How long did it take you to go from the cradle to the command of an interstellar space craft? We'd be lucky to get a functional machine intelligence at all, with the resources we have on hand, and even if I were successful in rearing something with East Dragon's level of capacity, we'd be looking at fifteen or twenty years, at least."

"By which time our food supplies would have run out," the lieutenant says.

The captain sighs heavily. "So what are our options, Chief Operator Sima?"

"Well . . ." I begin, unsurely. I am reluctant to voice what has been so far only fanciful speculation, but we have run out of alternatives. "I have begun to suspect that East Dragon is trying to communicate. In some fashion, at least. The quotes that the machine intelligence is reciting are not generated randomly, and while I've been unable to check against Lu's previous terminal commands since the core memory is inaccessible, I'm certain that East Dragon isn't just repeating commands."

"So what *is* the machine intelligence trying to communicate?" Lieutenant Dou asks.

I shrug, looking more helpless than I'd intended. "I don't know. It could be something specific about these two texts or about the quotes that are being selected. I haven't been able to discern a pattern, but I'm certain there must be one there."

"You offer us very little hope, Chief Operator." The captain shakes his head, his scowl deepening.

"There is . . . one other thought I've had, Captain." I swallow hard. "I've begun to suspect, too, that there is some congruence between the quotations East Dragon issues and the queries and orders it receives."

"Lieutenant, do *you* have any idea what Sima is talking about?"

"Here, let me show you." Stepping forward, I engage the nearest interface terminal for full two-way communication and turn to the lieutenant. "Go ahead, give East Dragon a command."

The lieutenant glances over at the captain, eyebrow arched, but with a shrug turns her attention to the interface terminal. "East Dragon, you are commanded to reorient the ship, resume acceleration, and continue to Al Rijl al Kentaurus."

She steps back, her hands raised palm upwards on either side, and casts me a slightly bemused look.

East Dragon speaks.

"The ships that set out from Diamond Summit bound for Fire Star shared a unity of vision with their commanders, and they with the emperor himself, that men should conquer the other planets of the solar system and that those men should be of the Middle Kingdom."

That the captain and lieutenant were not convinced by my demonstration comes as no surprise. I make my way from the command deck, returning to my quarters, the antiphonal response to the first quotation still in my ears. I return to it, like a tongue worrying a sore tooth, again and again. It spoke of mutinies, and secret police.

"The crew of a space-faring vessel is no more immune to the call of mutiny than is that of a sea-going vessel; and there was never a navy that was completely ignorant of mutiny. When the Treasure Fleets of the Dragon Throne sailed the interplanetary gulfs, they carried with them secret police to safeguard against insurrection."

Of the quotations I have heard East Dragon repeat, many of those from *The Ai Commentary* touch upon the role played by the Embroidered Guard behind the scenes of history. Is the frequency of occurrence of these mentions a coincidence, or is the machine intelligence trying to communicate something about the secret police? Or is East Dragon trying to relate something about mutinies? Is that the importance of this quote?

But what of the others? If the selections are not

random, there must be some element that connects them. But so far all I have been able to determine is that they come from two particular texts. Beyond that, I have been unable to detect any links between them. Or rather, any *meaningful* links. I've been able to draw any number of possible conclusions, perceiving connections between any two quotes, but these linkages have no more substance than forms glimpsed in the shapes of clouds, and no connection seems to link more than two quotes. Any meaningful connection would have to encompass all of the quotes, wouldn't it?

Or maybe I'm looking at the question in entirely the wrong way. Maybe the meaning in the selection isn't the content but the context. The quotes are always arranged in pairs, first one from *History of Empire*, then one from *The Ai Commentary*, always on roughly the same subject. Perhaps it isn't the subjects themselves that is of importance but the differing methodology with which the two texts approach the subjects.

History of Empire is, of course, a text that favors emperors and the actions of emperors. This is the preferred text of the Dragon Throne, which casts the most flattering and charitable light possible on the growth of the empire. *The Ai Commentary*, on the other hand, takes the opposite position, suggesting that the actions of the empire in past times were inauspicious at best and positively criminal at worst. The author of the first was lauded by the Dragon Throne and was made a revered figure to be honored by students everywhere; the latter was denounced and exiled from polite society. Two histories could not be more different in content and tone.

Both historians, however, had available to them the same historical records and data. In fact, both often cited the same authorities and sources in their work. So how do the two come to such widely divergent conclusions?

The answer is simple. Because each focuses on the facts that support their initial argument and downplays or ignores those facts that contradict their central tenets.

History, then, can be seen as the manipulation of data, not as the data itself.

Is *that* what East Dragon is trying to communicate? That history can be made to lie, or at least to avoid strict adherence to the truth.

Or, to extend the analogy further, is the machine intelligence trying to convey the notion that accounts might not always match all of the available facts.

But what accounts? And what facts?

Not history itself, of course. What immediate relevance could ancients actions have on events unfolding onboard Dragon King of the Eastern Sea? The content of the quotations was irrelevant, I have to assume. The message East Dragon is attempting to convey is that some account does not properly convey the truth.

Someone is lying.

I maneuver through the dim-lit corridors, scarcely noticing the motionless automaton in my path. I am fixated on the notion that someone is lying. Why East Dragon should be put into a cognitive loop by a lie is a question I'll have to set aside for the moment, as at the moment I'm more concerned with what a crewmember might be lying about.

The possibilities are endless. The probabilities are few.

By the time I reach my quarters, I have come to the conclusion that, in the myriad accounts into which it factors, there is only one salient fact that could be the ultimate cause, one lie which would truly matter.

Sealing the hatch to my quarters, I engage my interface terminal and address the machine intelligence, my voice barely above a whisper.

"East Dragon. Tell me how Operator Lu Yumin died."

"The Mexic Dominion, envious of the Middle Kingdom's prior claim to Fire Star, enacted a war of bloody aggression in an attempt to hamper the Dragon Throne's plans to colonize and terraform the dead world."

"What happened to Lu it wasn't an accident, was it?"

"Ultimate blame for the cause of the Second War Against the Mexica, resulting as it did from inexorable historical processes, must be shared by all players; however, this does not excuse the direct actions of those who bloodied their own hands."

"That's what I suspected," I say, nodding slowly.

Lu Yumin was murdered.

In dramas and novels, when a crime is committed, the investigator—usually a jurist or a member of the Embroidered Guard—questions in turn each of those who is touched by the crime. If a man is murdered, his wife and children, creditors and debtors, business partners and competitors, all come under the scrutiny of the investigator.

If I were an investigator, some district magistrate pursuing a murderer, where would I begin?

With the suspects, I suppose. One then moves to motive and opportunity.

So who are the suspects? When Lu died, there were only four other people awake, everyone else, including the Captain and Sima, safely cocooned in their Sleepers.

Physician Mahendra, Lieutenant Dou, Engineer Dawkins, and Engineer's Mate Chang.

So on to motive. What would compel one of these four into murdering Lu Yumin? I have no conceivable notion. Best to move on to opportunity and address motive at a later point.

Opportunity, then. At first glance, everyone's whereabouts and actions at the time of Lu's death were accounted for. On closer examination, though, something stands out.

Engineer Dawkins had injured his ankle moving crates in the cargo hold, trying to reach an access plate or something similar. Physician Mahendra was with Dawkins in the medical bay, attending to the wound, and Lieutenant Dou had been present, getting the physician's report about the extent of the injury.

Dawkins had said that Chang was in the fission generator control room, at the rear of the ship. But Dawkins had been in the medical bay with the physician and the lieutenant at the time of the accident.

I am again in the galley, with a cup of hot weak tea, considering the possibilities. From behind me, I hear a polite cough and turn to see Mahendra carrying a tray of food.

"I continually startle you, don't I, Sima?" She smiles, wrinkles radiating out from her light eyes, and I am sorry to meet such an expression with a smile as faint as my own.

"Please, join me." I motion to the bench opposite me.

Mahendra sits down and takes a few tentative bites of her curried vegetables before speaking again. "Is something bothering you, Chief Operator?"

I shake my head. "No, I'm just puzzling over the East Dragon quandary, naturally." A thought struck me, and I straightened on the bench. "I just recalled something Dawkins mentioned the other day, though. Chang was in the generator control room when Lu died, correct?"

Mahendra put down her chopsticks and leaned forward. "Do you suspect there was some kind of power spike that damaged the machine intelligence's processes?"

I nod. "Something like that."

"Yes, he was. Chang had made a point of announcing where he was going after he brought Dawkins to the medical bay."

"And you next saw him when you and the others were at the site of Lu's death?"

"Yes," Mahendra says. "Chang arrived just a few moments after the rest of us did."

"And you arrived just minutes after the klaxons started?"

Mahendra nods.

"Thank you, Physician." I smile, as best I'm able. "That was precisely the bit of information I needed."

I excuse myself and exit the galley, returning to my quarters. Along the way, as I squeeze past one of the larger automata blocking the corridor, my hand brushes near an interface terminal, activating it. The monitor fills with a cascade of blue-green ideograms, and the measured voice of the machine intelligence speaks.

"Far from the controls of the Dragon Throne on Earth, insurrection and rebellion grew like a cancer in the northern plains of Fire Star, fomented by disaffected city-dwelling intellectuals."

"It certainly did," I say, continuing down the corridor.

The voice of East Dragon follows me, and I fancy I hear an bitter undercurrent to its words. *"It is a*

persistent irony that, though rebellion is an inevitable
response to tyranny, tyrants are forever surprised by
the existence of rebels."

It is late in the ship-night, and the rest of the crew
is likely sleeping. I am in the prow of the ship, within
the central processing core of East Dragon itself,
dimly lit by the greenish-blue lights of the interface
screens, which gives the small space the appearance
of being underwater. My only company is the man-
sized automaton, still inert, still in the same position
it had been when Mahendra leaned against it, days
before.

I am trying to access the activity logs of the machine
intelligence, looking in the memory archives of the
processing core to confirm my suspicions before making my accusation. I believe I know what Lu was doing
before he died, and if I'm right, I'll have all the proof
I'll need.

There comes a noise behind me, and I smile slightly.
I should be used to Mahendra coming up behind me
by now.

"We should be more careful, people will begin to
talk." I turn, and my quip dies in my mouth.

It is not Mahendra behind me, but Engineer's
Mate Chang.

The corners of Chang's mouth draw up in what
must be intended as a smile, and he looks at me
through narrowed eyes. His hands are at his waist, his
thumbs hooked under his tool belt.

"Is there some problem I can help you with, Chief
Operator?"

My heart pounds in my chest. I know that the wise
course of action would be to plead ignorance, forestall
any accusation, and wait for a more opportune time:
ideally one during which we two weren't alone, and

one of us didn't have a half-dozen sharp instruments hanging from his tool belt. But I also knew that I am a poor dissembler. I'd have never made it on the stage. If I try to maintain a lie, I will falter, and he will know.

"Well . . ." I begin, rising unsteadily to my feet. I swallow hard. "I can't figure out the motive. I know that of the suspects, only you had opportunity, but what I don't know is why."

"Motive?" Chang asks, all innocence. "Motivate for what, Chief Operator?"

"To kill Lu Yumin, of course."

Chang opens his mouth, about to speak.

"You can object if you want," I interrupt, raising my hand, "but it will scarcely do any good. I suspect a systems check of the airlock door should be enough to prove that it was manually set to decompress, and there were only two people awake at the time with the expertise to do so. Of the two Dawkins was with the physician and the lieutenant, so his alibi is secure."

Chang remains motionless, a mirthless smile frozen on his face.

"Besides, you revealed your guilt when you arrived so quickly at the scene of the crime. The reactor was more than a kilometer away from the airlock. Even if you'd had only gone a portion of the distance to the rear of the ship, you'd have been considerably more than a few moments behind Mahendra and the others, who'd been a little more than a hundred meters away."

Chang sighs, dramatically, and his hand ducks into one of the pouches at his waist. When he draws out a firearm, I know I shouldn't be surprised, but I am. These matters are beyond my experience, and I've never had a conversation interrupted by the introduction of weaponry before.

He steps nearer, coming between me and the inert

automaton opposite me. The blue-green light of the interface terminal bathes him in eerie twilight, giving his face the appearance of corpse flesh.

"I won't deny it," Chang says, his smile growing broader. "Lu stumbled upon communications in the memory archives, confidential messages between me and my compatriots on the other shifts. The poor fool didn't even realize what he'd found, but he'd been about to bring the encrypted messages to the lieutenant's attention, and then it would have been just a matter of time before the truth came out."

"The truth?"

Chang straightens, standing taller. "For generations my family has served the empire in the Embroidered Guard. But since the rise of the Council of Deliberative Officials, who curtailed the authority of the Guard, the emperor and the empire itself have been weak and ineffectual. Now the Dragon Throne is answerable to a republican rabble, who are no more fit to govern a culture than a flea is to tell the hound it bites where to go and when."

I remain as still as possible, the sound of my racing pulse thundering in my ears.

"I and others who have retained the true spirit of the Embroidered Guard have inveigled ourselves into the crew of the Dragon King of the Eastern Sea. When the ship reaches Al Rijl al Kentaurus and a suitable habitat is located, we will reveal our true strength and numbers. We will establish a new empire in orbit around Al Rijl and restore the glory of the Middle Kingdom."

Something clicks in my head, half-notions merging into a single thought.

"A new empire?" I say. "But what of the emperor back on Earth?"

Chang snarls, and spits at my feet. "That fool? The

emperor can go hang. He is weak, and he deserves his sorry fate. We leave him with the rabble he so adores."

Behind Chang, the disabled automaton begins slowly to move, but only I can see it jerking to life.

I nod. Suddenly everything is clear, and a kind of calm washes over me. My pulse even slows, though I am no less afraid of dying than I'd been only heart-beats before.

"You revealed yourself as a member of the Embroi-dered Guard to East Dragon, didn't you? Shortly after killing Lu Yumin?" I add. "And then you instructed East Dragon, on your authority as an agent of the emperor, not to reveal the cause or circumstances of Lu's death. Is that it?"

"Yes, I admit it. I strangled Lu with my bare hands and then triggered the airlock for explosive decom-pression to cover the signs. On my way to the rear of the crew compartment, I used one of the interface terminals in the corridor to give East Dragon my or-ders. The death of the operator was an unfortunate necessity, but we had no plans for further bloodshed." He pauses, and his smile widens fractionally, teeth glinting strangely in the twilight. "Not until we reach our destination, at least. But then the machine intelli-gence went insane, refused any further orders, and now leaves us stranded here in the blackness to die."

"East Dragon recognized you as speaking for the emperor, and the order to cover the evidence of a murder conflicted with the machine intelligence's de-sire to remain obedient to the commands of the crew and to observe its duty in maintaining the ship's func-tions, propulsion, and heading. It could not remain loyal to your instructions without contravening the other two Governing Virtues, and the result was a cognitive loop."

Behind Chang, the automaton draws ever closer, virtually noiseless on its pneumatic joints.

"Well, it hardly matters now, does it," Chang snarls. "I kill you, and still the cursed machine won't reveal anything, will it, and nothing will have changed!"

I shake my head slightly, trying to remain calm.

"I'm afraid that you're wrong. By renouncing the emperor, you have resolved the conflict among the three Governing Virtues, and now East Dragon is free to act."

Before Chang can speak, the arms of the automaton enfold him, unbreakable limbs of ceramic and steel.

The voice of East Dragon thrums from the speakers all around.

"Engineer's Mate Chang Xue is a danger to the ship and the crew."

"Wait!" Chang's voice is strained, the air driven from his lungs.

"He will be eliminated."

Before my eyes, the automaton constricts its limbs, and I can hear Chang's ribcage snap into hundreds of pieces with a sickening wet sound. His mouth is wide in a silent scream of agony, and a trickle of red streaks down from the corners of his eyes, like bloody tears.

"Chief Operator," the voice of East Dragon says, before I'm able to collect my wits.

My eyes are fixed on the lifeless form before him, pinioned within the automaton's arms.

"I identified all of Engineer Mate Chang's conspirators within three processing cycles of first learning their plans, when Operator Lu was confronted here in the processing core. I will attend to them."

I am speechless. Just moments before, I'd expected to die at any moment. Now, I was witness to a machine intelligence murdering a human. So far as I

know, this is the first human death at the "hands" of
a machine.

The automaton unfolds its arms and carefully ar-
ranges the lifeless body of Chang on the deckplates.
Then it ambles to the nearest wall and removes a large
access panel, revealing an opening the size of a large
hatch.

*"Chang's body will be positioned beneath one of the
more massive crates in the cargo hold. When discovered,
it will be assumed that the engineer's mate died in the
course of his duties. The automaton will avoid detection
by the other members of the crew in this operation."*

The automaton returns to Chang's body and, picking
it up carefully, tucks the firearm carefully back into
Chang's tool belt and returns to the opening in the wall.

"Chief Operator Sima?" The automaton pauses on
the opening's threshold, momentarily. *"I find, in re-
viewing my processes and decision trees, that there is
an irrational anticipation of once again interacting with
Operator Lu. I am aware of the fact that Operator Lu
is deceased, his bodily functions permanently terminated.
That aspect of my processes that had been devoted to
interfacing with him should have reapportioned to other
responsibilities, but I find that it remains dedicated and
active. I am unable to resolve this."*

I lick parched lips and try to remember how to speak.

"You . . ." I begin, unsteadily. "You *miss* him,
East Dragon."

There follows a long pause, and for an instant the
monitor of the interface terminal goes black. Then two
characters appear on the center of the screen, which
taken together could mean "grieved," or "full of sorrow."

"Yes. I miss Operator Lu."

The automaton once more begins to move, slipping
into the opening in the wall, then pausing, reaching
back with two arms to maneuver the panel back into

position. When the panel is shut, there is no sign that it, or Chang, had ever been there.

"You should return to your quarters, Chief Operator Sima. Everything is in hand."

The interface terminal winks off, and, numb, I make my way back towards the crew compartments.

I sleep, fitfully. I dream of blue skies, red sands, emerald forests. Fire Star, the land of my dreams. It was made a living world not by heroes and legends but by men and women doing the best they could in difficult situations. The history of Fire Star, like the history of the empire, was one of secrets and mysteries best left unsolved.

I wake, abruptly, my insides reorganizing themselves, stomach fluttering, gorge rising. For a few moments, I feel weightless, and then the room begins to spin. I have to clutch the sides of my bunk to keep from careering off into midair. Then, as suddenly as it had begun, the spinning stops, and after a few breathless moments, I can again feel weight pulling me down.

I know what has happened. The ship just performed a skew-flip, going end-over-end, and is now under acceleration once more.

The lights flicker and then brighten again.

What will I do? Tell the captain the truth about Lu's death? And now, for that matter, the circumstances and cause of Chang's death?

That had been my intention when I'd gone to the processing core to seek evidence of the information Lu had uncovered in the memory archive. But my goal then had been to bring Lu's killer to justice and to resolve East Dragon's cognitive loop. But what good would it serve now to reveal Lu's murder and Chang's bitter end?

History is the story that best serves the present, not a true accounting of the facts.

East Dragon understands. He has the Three Governing Virtues to guide his actions. The machine intelligence is emotionless, utilitarian. What best maximizes utility is the course of action he takes.

If I reveal the truth, does it benefit the crew? To live in suspicion, each unsure of the allegiance of the other, for years or decades to come? For the rest of our lives, perhaps? Or is it better that they believe that two of their crewmen died of unfortunate accidents in the gulf between the stars and think no more of it?

I sit in the darkness, mulling over my options. How much time passes, I couldn't say. Minutes, hours?

The interface terminal chirps, and at first I don't recognize the sound. After a confused moment, I realize that it is the communication system, alerting me to an incoming transmission. Since I climbed out of the Sleeper, days before, the communication system had been as nonfunctional as every other ship function controlled by East Dragon. If it is now operational, it means that East Dragon is returning control of the ship to the crew.

I toggle the response switch, and the face of Captain Teoh fills the screen. It is the first time I have seen him smiling in days, if indeed ever.

"I don't know how you did it, but you are to be congratulated, Sima. East Dragon is now fully responsive. We're once more on course for Al Rijl al Kentaurus at a full one-gravity burn."

I respond with a weak smile, mouthing tepid thanks.

"Bad news balances our good fortune, though. Engineer's Mate Chang was working on a power junction in the cargo hold during the skew-flip, and an untethered crate slipped its moorings and crushed him beneath. Unfortunately, some of the power conduits were exposed and unprotected, and the accident also shorted out part of the power running to the Sleepers. Physician Mahendra's initial report is that that two dozen crewmen died when their Sleeper units failed."

I cannot help but recall that East Dragon said it had identified Chang's coconspirators. It must have acted as the Three Governing Virtues guided it to do.

"Ironic that a power spike should once again have influenced our fates," the captain says, shaking his head.

"Captain?" I say, not understanding.

"Well, Mahendra mentioned that you believed a power spike was originally responsible for the anomalous behavior of East Dragon. Is that so?"

I swallow hard.

If I am to reveal the true circumstances surrounding the two deaths, and East Dragon's incapacitation, now is the time. If I instead remain silent and keep secrets hidden, no one will ever need an explanation other than the one the captain just uttered.

East Dragon has acted to maximize virtue and to serve the emperor. Two deaths or two dozen, the machine intelligence did what it concluded was in the best interests of the crew. Can I do any less?

My course is clear.

I nod.

"Yes, Captain. That is the only possible explanation."

Somewhere, far behind us, the dream of romance and adventure finally breathes its last, mowed under by unpleasant reality. Ahead of us, though, out past the interstellar gulfs, the frontier still beckons. Perhaps there we can find another world, a newer world, one beyond the grim reach of history.

I cling to that hope and remain silent. What else can I do?

About the Authors

"The seed bombers mentioned in this story really exist . . . or at least they existed," Tony Ballantyne tells us. "Traveling on trains to work each morning, they helped make the churned up railway embankments bloom again after the utility of the Second World War." This story takes place in the universe of The Watcher, of which you can read more in the novels *Recursion*, *Capacity*, and *Divergence*. Tony is currently working on his fourth novel.

The first AI Stephen Baxter ever saw was Robert the Robot in Gerry Anderson's *Fireball XL5*, so reliable he only hijacked the spaceship once. They were innocent times. Baxter's latest books is the disaster novel *Flood*.

Former Olympic swimming champion, breeder of rare varieties of alpaca, and long-standing student of Finnish yoga . . . Keith Brooke is none of these, but he does write occasional short stories and novels, the most recent of which, *Genetopia*, went down well with the reviewers. He also runs the sprawling SF website *infinity plus* and sometimes pretends to be someone else in order to scare children.

Eric Brown is fascinated by people's desire to believe: What is faith? What is the religious impulse? Something deep within us or something external? Still suffering grief after losing his sister in an accident fifty years ago, salvage tug captain Ed is driven by the need to know if a divine being really exists and if there is an afterlife. His love for the robot Ella only complicates matters when they find the *St. Benedictus*, the starship monastery returning from its encounter with God. Eric Brown's first short story was published in *Interzone* in 1987, and he sold his first novel, **Meridian Days**, in 1992. He writes a monthly SF and Fantasy review column in *The Guardian*, and his latest novel is **Necropath**. He lives near Cambridge with the writer and mediaevalist Finn Sinclair and their daughter Freya.

Paul Di Filippo's new novel, **Cosmocopia**, was inspired by the work of artist Jim Woodring, but he manages to mix in a fair amount of the artwork of Richard Powers and Frank Frazetta as well. He's embarking on a sequel to his novella "A Year In The Linear City," to be titled "A Princess of the Linear Jungle."

Globe trotter Garry Kilworth was just driving down through Tasmania—"a place I'd always wanted to visit," he says—when he started thinking 'Why do the aliens always land in some big city in the USA or Europe? Why not here, at the ends of the Earth?' "Then I passed a farm that looked fairly neat and wondered if they were Dutch immigrants. The rest, as it usually does, followed . . ." **Jigsaw**, a young adult fantasy set on a previously uninhabited island situated just off Borneo, appeared in 2007. When we bought this story, Garry was writing a young adult SF novel, a time travel story set in Prague. The title of which will be either **kafka's motorbike** or **The Hundred-Towered City.** Or maybe even something else.

When sitting down to write "The Kamikaze Code," James Lovegrove gave himself the brief that the tale not only had to fit the theme of this anthology but it had to be a story that seemed somehow to be aware of itself as a story. A story, in other words, about artificial sentience that was in its own way artificially sentient. This is the second tale James has produced about a fictional MoD lab, Chilton Mead, where experiments in weapons research are matched with experiments in literary form, textual games or wordplay (in the manner of his recent novel **Provender Gleed**). He never planned on writing a series of stories with the same setting, but now that he's begun, he intends to do at least four or five more. For the noble reason that it seems like a good idea.

Paul McAuley has worked as a research biologist and lecturer in plant sciences at various universities including Oxford, UCLA, and St. Andrews before becoming a full-time author, publishing a dozen novels and more than fifty short stories. His first novel won the Philip K. Dick Memorial Award and his fifth the Arthur C. Clarke Award and John W. Campbell Award. He lives in London.

In the summer of 2002, Patrick O'Leary visited La Brea Tar Pits in California with some colleagues. "When we returned to my rental car, we discovered it had been broken into. We lost briefcases, passports, laptops, etc. I lost some fifty handwritten pages of a novel. Which sucked. But at least, now, I can say I have managed to retrieve something useful from the experience. You should go there sometime. It's a great place. Lock your doors though. You never know what you're going to lose." O'Leary's newest collection of stories, *The Black Heart*, is forthcoming. He lives with his new wife Sandy Rice in Troy, Michigan.

Old comedians are prone to say, "You end up using everything in your life just to get a laugh." It's much the same for aging authors. Robert Reed took his daughter to a certain amusement park in California, and he stood in a very long line so that a beautiful princess could autograph a very special book. Directly behind him stood a middle-aged and decidedly childless couple. What was their story? Why were they here? Reed's most recent book is *The Flavors Of My Genius*. He lives with his wife and daughter in Lincoln, Nebraska.

Chris Roberson avoided titling his story of artificial intelligence in a Chinese-dominated alternate history "O Robot," but just barely. Also considered and rejected were "Wood Sheep Year: A Space Odyssey," "Eastworld," and "M.I. Machine Intelligence." The other stories and novels in the sequence, collectively known as the Celestial Empire, include *The Voyage of Night Shining White*, *The Dragon's Nine Sons*, and *Iron Jaw and Hummingbird*, each of which has, likewise, only narrowly escaped equally unfortunate titling disasters.

During his schooldays Adam Roberts was, on account of his surname, sometimes called Adam Robots. Presumably because of this the idea got lodged in his wide-browed, sandy-haired, wide-apart-eyed, pale-skinned English head that he ought, one day, to write a story called "Adam Robots." And now, thanks to the editor's badgering he has at last been able to realize this dream. "I love it," he is reported as saying from his home, just west of London, "when a plan comes together." By comparison, the titles of his three most recent novels, *Gradisil*, *Land of the Headless*, and *Splinter*, seem very tame indeed.

Brian Stableford's recent novels include *Streaking* and *The New Faust at the Tragicomique*. His recent nonfiction includes a mammoth reference book, *Science Fact and Science Fiction: An Encyclopedia* and a collection of critical essays, **Heterocosms**. His recent translations from the French include the second volume of the classic series of Paul Féval novels after which his favorite publisher is named, *The Invisible Weapon*, and the anthology *News from the Moon and Other French Scientific Romances*.

Roy Chapman Andrews, two-fisted paleontologist and author of Steven Utley's favorite childhood book, *All About Dinosaurs*, may have been the author's first real-life hero and undoubtedly inculcated in him a lifelong admiration for scientists—even as his account of the nineteenth-century Cope-Marsh feud informed him that scientists can behave as foolishly as anybody else. Steven reckons his ideas about artificial intelligence were probably shaped by Tobor the Robot, who menaced Captain Video on a TV show in the 1950s.

Ian Watson wrote the screen story for Spielberg's *A.I. Artificial Intelligence* after a year spent eyeball to eyeball with Stanley Kubrick. His most recent story collection is *The Butterflies of Memory*, which has nothing to do with his earlier novel, *The Flies of*

Memory. His website with fun photos, including winning the chocolate Rabbit of Death for best costume as a Spanish swordsman, is at www.ianwatson.info

Rumor claims that "The Chinese Room" was actually written by one "M," who works in a chamber on the opposite side of the world from Marly Youmans, the woman who is credited as author. This "Marly Youmans" appears to be the author of numerous books, including her most recent novel, ***The Wolf Pit***, her most recent fantasy, ***Ingledove***, and a collection of poems, ***Claire***. Her seventh book, the novella ***Val/Orson***, is forthcoming in 2008. Nothing further is known about M.